PENGUIN METRO READS
ARRANGED LOVE

Parul A. Mittal is the author of the national bestseller *Heartbreaks & Dreams!: The Girls @ IIT*. Apart from reading and writing fiction, she loves listening to old Hindi music, cannot resist jiving to dance beats, loves to party with friends and has a keen interest in staying fit.

She did her BTech in electrical engineering from IIT Delhi in 1995, followed by master's in computer science from UMich, Ann Arbor. After twelve years in the corporate world (Hughes, IBM Research and Nextag), she is currently running an e-venture called RivoKids (www.rivokids.com). RivoKids offers parents smart ideas to raise bright, happy kids and free online memory books to capture fun parenting moments.

Born in Delhi, she did her schooling at Lady Irwin School, New Delhi and Navrachna School, Baroda. She is married to Alok Mittal and has two daughters—Smiti and Muskaan.

You can read more about her at www.parulmittal.com, join her Facebook fan page at www.facebook.com/parulmittalbook or email her at parulmittal@gmail.com

ARRANGED LOVE

Parul A. Mittal

Penguin
metro reads

PENGUIN METRO READS
Published by the Penguin Group
Penguin Books India Pvt. Ltd, 11 Community Centre, Panchsheel Park,
New Delhi 110 017, India
Penguin Group (USA) Inc., 375 Hudson Street, New York, New York 10014, USA
Penguin Group (Canada), 90 Eglinton Avenue East, Suite 700, Toronto, Ontario,
M4P 2Y3, Canada (a division of Pearson Penguin Canada Inc.)
Penguin Books Ltd, 80 Strand, London WC2R 0RL, England
Penguin Ireland, 25 St Stephen's Green, Dublin 2, Ireland (a division of Penguin
Books Ltd)
Penguin Group (Australia), 707 Collins Street, Melbourne, Victoria 3008, Australia
(a division of Pearson Australia Group Pty Ltd)
Penguin Group (NZ), 67 Apollo Drive, Rosedale, Auckland 0632, New Zealand
(a division of Pearson New Zealand Ltd)
Penguin Group (South Africa) (Pty) Ltd, 24 Sturdee Avenue, Rosebank, Johannesburg
2196, South Africa

Penguin Books Ltd, Registered Offices: 80 Strand, London WC2R 0RL, England

First published in Penguin Metro Reads by Penguin Books India 2012

Copyright © Parul Alok Mittal 2012

All rights reserved

10 9 8 7 6 5 4 3 2 1

This is a work of fiction. Names, characters, places and incidents are either the product of the author's imagination or are used fictitiously, and any resemblance to any actual person, living or dead, events or locales is entirely coincidental.

ISBN 9780143418825

Typeset in Bembo by R. Ajith Kumar, New Delhi
Printed at Manipal Technologies Ltd, Manipal

This book is sold subject to the condition that it shall not, by way of trade or otherwise, be lent, resold, hired out, or otherwise circulated without the publisher's prior written consent in any form of binding or cover other than that in which it is published and without a similar condition including this condition being imposed on the subsequent purchaser and without limiting the rights under copyright reserved above, no part of this publication may be reproduced, stored in or introduced into a retrieval system, or transmitted in any form or by any means (electronic, mechanical, photocopying, recording or otherwise), without the prior written permission of both the copyright owner and the above-mentioned publisher of this book.

ALWAYS LEARNING **PEARSON**

For my Arranged Love, Alok

A PROSPECTIVE GROOM

'Do women have to be naked to get into the Met. Museum?' The Guerrilla Girls poster, showing the naked back of a girl wearing a Gorilla mask, said in bold, black lettering. It was designed by a group of radical feminist artists after conducting a 'weenie count' at New York's Metropolitan Museum of Art. They had found that less than 5 per cent of the artists in the Met's modern art sections were women, yet 85 per cent of the nude artworks were female. Jay had gifted me the poster on our first 'going out together' anniversary, last month. I had loved its outrageous, raunchy humour, and wanting to make my contribution to the world of art, I had made Jay promise that he would model nude for me.

I had been waiting for the right opportunity to start the painting. So when Neetu, my roommate, told me that she was going to spend the whole Sunday out, canoeing with her boyfriend, I had persuaded Jay to forgo his plans of watching the football match on TV and deliver on his promise. Not that Neetu would mind having a naked guy in her neighbouring room. It's just that she and her boyfriend were way too noisy and I needed some quiet time to be able to concentrate.

So there he was, sitting naked on my queen-sized bed, patiently posing for the last two hours. I stared at the contours of his tall, athletic body. The broad and powerful chest, the bronzed sinewy arms, the thin line of golden brown hair running from his chest down to his navel that drew my eye towards his well-toned abs and his lean hips. Having inherited the best of physical features from his Indian mom and American dad, Jayant Guy was as handsome and delectable as it gets. I smiled, as I forced myself not to get aroused by his maleness and focused on the job at hand.

'Don't tell me it's more fun to look at?' he said, catching a glimpse of naughtiness in my smile.

'It certainly looks unused,' I replied, trying to pull his leg.

'Why don't you fix it?' came his quick, playful response.

'Am trying,' I chuckled as I applied a thick dab of paint on the brush and applied it on the canvas with harder strokes. 'One at a time,' I said teasingly, without looking up at him, as I added another layer of skin-tone to fix the *one* in the painting.

'Can we take a break? My back is hurting from staying still in one position for so long!'

'You need some action, huh?' I said, as I stepped back to look at the canvas.

I felt happy with what I saw. We had made good progress today. I raised my hand above the canvas and gave him a thumbs up.

I heard the faint clicking sound of his strained muscles as he got up from my bed and stretched his arms. Next instant, he was grabbing me by my waist.

'One would say I deserve a reward after two hours of modelling nude for you.' I heard him say, his voice slightly muffled, as he kissed my ear lobe.

'I would say I deserve a beer,' I said, wriggling out of his grip and heading straight to the kitchen.

Usually painting has a meditative effect on me, but today I felt tired. This was my first experience with painting a nude model, and you have to believe me when I say that it's an entirely different ball game from painting fruits on a table. In case you are more of a doer than a listener, try looking at your irresistibly attractive naked boyfriend or girlfriend from a 5-feet distance for over an hour. Okay, we all agree it's provoking. Now try focusing on the body's curves and slopes, observe the shadow and the reflection of light on the skin, all the while controlling that excitement. Exhausting, huh? I guess professional artists get used to looking at naked human bodies as just other works of art. But for me, painting was a passion and Jay was rather good-looking.

'To the Guerrilla Girls!' I said, raising a toast with my beer can, in the direction of the poster that hung over my bed.

'As we attempt to increase the count of female artists and naked male artworks,' toasted Jay, tipping his healthy apple against my calorie-filled can.

Jay had got back into his knickers, so I opened the window shades and allowed the sunlight to fill my room with its own colours and hues. Sitting side by side on the floor rug, we stared outside, admiring the onset of fall colours. The array of two-storeyed, white-coloured apartments with wooden sloping roofs, offered a picturesque contrast to the multitude of colours splashed on the trees around. I noticed the ducks swimming in the pond next to the community centre. Come winter and the pond would transform into an ice-skating rink for the neighbourhood kids. The whole place would undergo bleaching, exchanging its colourful youth for white, serene maturity.

Willowtree Apartments, where we lived, was about a ten-minute walk from the College of Engineering. The North Campus of University of Michigan, Ann Arbor, housing the engineering department, was home to a large Indian postgrad student population. I could see a bunch of these students, carrying back groceries and utilities from Walmart in preparation for the week ahead. A few of our friends were out to the gym while most others were busy in their apartments, slicing onions and frying masala for dinner.

I, on the other hand, was busy enjoying the moment,

soaking in the vibrant colours of nature, while Jay gently rubbed the sides of my back with his thumbs. I took a large swig of the cool drink and let my head rest on his bare shoulders. I didn't realize when my eyes closed and I drifted off, with Jay lying by my side. I was woken up by the shrill ringing of the phone by my ears. I quickly picked the handset lying next to me on the side table. Dad's voice from across the Red Sea and the Atlantic Ocean was clear enough to jolt me back to my senses. My mind quickly calculated that it must be early Monday morning in Delhi and suddenly a fear engulfed me. The weekly call from my parents was scheduled for Saturday mornings, their time. A series of random fears crossed my mind in the fraction of a second and it took me some time to register what he was saying.

'Suhaani. You sound asleep *beta*. Did I wake you up? It's only 8 p.m. your time. I thought you would be awake,' I heard him say.

'I am up, but how come you are calling at this hour?' I asked hurriedly, lifting Jay's arm that lay around my waist. Jay tried telling me in sign language that my dad couldn't see him over the phone, but I shrugged him off.

'Did you check your email?' Dad asked eagerly.

My father typically sent me mails before he went to bed, so that I could check them during my daytime. I normally responded immediately as he hated to wait for my answer, but today I had been so absorbed analysing and tracing the male anatomy that I had forgotten to open my laptop. Even as my laptop came back to life, I asked, 'What's so important in the mail, Pa? Why don't you just tell me on phone?'

But all I heard was the disconnect tone. My father had already hung up.

'So much for the get-back-to-me-at-your-own-convenience protocol of emails,' commented Jay wryly.

I could see the humour. It was like sending an SMS to someone and then calling and telling the person to check the SMS! Yet, I didn't like the scorn in Jay's voice. Just because he doesn't get any calls from his parents doesn't give him the right to ridicule others. Besides, his parents were only a few hours away in Chicago and could drop by any time they wanted to. Not that they ever did, at least not in the last year and half that I had known Jay. His interactions with his family were largely restricted to Thanksgiving and Christmas weekends.

Facebook opened up on my browser as my default home page. I briefly stole a glance to see the status updates of my FB friends. There was a picture of Neetu in a swimsuit, squeezed in the canoe with her boyfriend, his arms tightly wound under her breasts. I am sure she had set the privacy settings on this photo such that her parents back in Agra couldn't see it. A couple of funny one-liners caught my attention. The tall, blond guy from my computer architecture class had posted, 'Practice makes a man perfect! Now you know why I do it all the time.' I clicked on 'Like' bumping up the count to 25.

My Gmail had loaded in the next window by now, so I clicked on my dad's mail. I had ruled out robbery, an earthquake or death as the reason for his urgent call and was back to my cheerful self. The mail had no content. There was only the subject line which said, 'Check out the attachment'. Must be some new family picture or yet another cousin's wedding invitation. I quickly opened the attached file, and found a repulsive-looking guy, falling on me, with a wide grin on his face. I impulsively moved my face away from the laptop screen.

'How do you like the guy?' popped the chat message from my dad on the Gmail chat window.

'Horrible!' I said without hesitation. The guy in the picture was still grinning at me. I noticed that he was standing on a rock, at the top of some mountain, his hands outstretched, perhaps to maintain his balance, as the cold, indifferent wind ruffled his neatly trimmed hair. The shot had been taken by someone lying low on the ground, so it looked like he was falling forward.

Jay prodded me from behind asking if I had asked my old man to send pictures of Gorilla-type Indian male models. I asked him to keep shut and stay away, as if my father could hear him over chat. Unable to control his laughter, he wandered off to the kitchen to fix himself some salad.

Dad: Horrible? That's a start! Remember, you took three months before you started liking powdered milk?

Me: Pa! I was six months old then!

Dad: And you still love the milk powder sachets that come with tea-makers in resorts.

Me: Very funny

Dad: I met him at my guitar class. The boy is perfect for you.

Me: You joined guitar class like only two months back!

Dad: Oh! But I started liking the food your mother cooks from the day we were married.

Me: What's your point?

Dad: That I am quick when it comes to liking things while you take your time to develop the taste. But once you like something, you like it forever.

I was completely losing this battle of words and the speed of developing taste, so I decided to get aggressive.

Me: You want me to marry a guy whom you just met at your guitar class?

Dad: C'mon, you know me better. Of course, I did the background check. He is Tanu's junior's junior from IIT.

Me: What the fuck, Dad! An IITian—I typed, erased and then retyped—You know I don't fancy these arrogant, self-important IIT types.

Dad: This guy is different. I am confident he will slowly grow on you.

Me: I am still studying, Pa.

Dad: Of course, we will wait for you to finish your studies. The boy's email address is there in his biodata. Feel free to drop him a mail.

Me: But, Pa . . .

Before I could type any further, I realized my father had logged off. In any case, what was I going to tell him? 'Pa, I have found myself an American dude who is mind-blowing in bed, but doesn't understand a word of Hindi.'

Jay had come back with his salad bowl and was checking out the word exchange on my chat screen, his eyes wide with amazement.

'Jesus fucking Christ! Is your dad trying to find you a lover?' He didn't try to hide the surprise or the sarcasm in his tone.

'He is finding me a husband,' I said, stressing the word with as much disrespect as I could muster. 'A band that ties you to the house, not a lover,' I clarified.

'So honey, I thought you were very close to your dad. Doesn't he know you abhor the very idea of an arranged marriage and are fully capable of finding a handsome *houseband* for yourself?'

I knew he was trying to needle me. Initially, Jay had problems learning to pronounce my name properly but now he only mispronounced it to tease me and the 'So honey' joke continued. Any other time, I would have run behind him, hitting him and biting him for jeering at my dad. Today, I just sat motionless, hands under my chin, too confused and perhaps even a bit angry to defend my relationship with my dad. Realizing that I was not in the mood for bantering, Jay came closer and started massaging my shoulders. He knew how I loved the firmness of his hands around my neck when I was tired and needed to relax. But right now, I needed to be alone. I told him I was not up to any more fun tonight. Bummed though he was at my sudden change of mood, he got dressed and left without making a fuss. One thing that we can surely learn from Americans is their respect for other people's privacy.

Lounging on my soft, cushiony bed, munching my favourite cheese-flavoured corn chips, I gazed at the snapshots of my childhood pasted all over my room. There was Dad holding me when I was just born. Dad giving me a bear hug on my first day of school. Dad lifting me in the air while he still could. Dad and I out-screaming each other on a rollercoaster ride. The two of us making a rangoli by the door on Diwali, cheering Tendulkar as we watched World Cup live and clinking glasses just before I took my first sip of wine. These were all evidence of the special bond I shared with my dad. Sure, there was stuff pertaining to boys and sex that I hadn't told him, especially in the last few years. Like the reason why I had begun to despise IIT guys or my affair with Jay. My mom would inquire once in a while, but my dad had never pried into matters of my heart and I had appreciated that about him. As an only child, I was never denied anything by my parents and I had done my best to live up to their expectations. But everything has its pros and cons, its own free hits and leg byes. Having grown up without any siblings, I had never learned to confront, especially the people who mattered to me. My very presence on this campus, pursuing a master's degree in engineering, was testimony to that. But, it was one thing to do a course of your parents' choice and an entirely different thing to do intercourse with your parents' choice!

I couldn't force myself to fall in love with a guy that my parents picked for me, and I obviously couldn't marry a guy I didn't love. This much was clear. The only problem was, how to eject this IIT suitor without hurting Dad's feelings?

I heard the SMS beep on my mobile. There were two messages from Jay.

Message 1: Save your brains the burden of too many thoughts.
Good piece of advice, I thought.
Message 2: No more than ten pieces of chips.

I immediately shifted my attention from my mind to my mouth, stopped chewing in mid-bite, and peeped inside the packet in my hand. Somebody had stolen my chips while I was lost in reverie. The bag looked more like half-empty. Damn! Now I will have to run an extra mile tomorrow.

Given that I couldn't indulge in any more alcohol or junk food to beat the stress, I flipped open my laptop to play some music. Jeez, that suitor guy was still smirking at me! Not only was he a gross-looking IITian with a typical Indian moustache, his sense of dressing was hideous too. Trust Dad to know how to get on my nerves! I clicked on the close button to give his jaws some rest and put on my favourite playlist. *Pal pal dil ke paas, tum rahti ho . . .* Kishore da's mellow voice filled the room and a wave of nostalgia swept over me. I was back in our little house; the aroma of freshly baked pizzas wafted from our open-air kitchen as my mom cooked and Dad and I huddled underneath a comforter listening to these songs.

I was about to call it a day when I noticed a new mail icon blinking on my screen. It was a 'Hi! I am . . .' message from that smartass suitor. It was Monday morning in India—people didn't have to work in office or what!

I curled up on my bed, my eyes tightly shut to wipe out the day's events, my fingers playing with my belly-button, as I waited for sleep to overtake me. As my dadi would have said, it seemed like planet Saturn had entered my 7th house and even Kishore Kumar was having a tough time driving him away.

EMAIL, YOUTUBE AND A PHONE CALL

Hi, I am a random guy from your dad's guitar class. Your dad visited my house yesterday to meet my parents. He left a printout of your matrimonial profile, with some vital and some not so vital stats. I can see that you have 1 maternal uncle with 7-figure income, 6 paternal uncles who are well-established, 5 aunts who are married to known business families, 1 cousin from IIT-Delhi, 2 from IIT-Roorkee, 2 from IIM Bangalore and 1 from XLRI. I am assuming you have more than 6 cousins from 7 uncles, but they didn't make it to your biodata. There is also a studio photograph of a beautiful, homely, Indian girl in salwar suit. I took the liberty of checking your FB profile, and it shows a more free-spirited girl, in a sexy spaghetti top. Wondering who is the real you? BTW, there is a joke among IIT boys that there are only two types of girls in this world—nice and very nice :)

From what your dad talks about you, and he talks a lot, you are not the kind of girl who would marry a random guy, even if he happens to be an IIT, Stanford graduate. I myself haven't thought about marriage yet, so let's be friends. You can read more about me and my life at www.dgblahblah.com.

Deepak Goyal

P.S. Please don't send me a Facebook Friend Request yet. I only add people I know well, and like, to my friends' list.

Who did he think he was? Ranbir Kapoor? Some guts he has telling me not to send him a friend request like I was desperate to increase my friends count. And what was Dad doing? Giving out my biodata to guys in his guitar class! Eyes still glued to the computer screen, I took a bite of my bagel with a large helping of cream cheese, while pretending to do some research work.

'Any guess on how many calories that bite has?' quizzed Jay, as he walked up to my desk in the computer science lab.

'235 based on a 2000 calorie diet, 10 per cent saturated fat, 5 per cent cholesterol,' I mumbled, recalling the count from our last discussion on the topic.

Realizing that I was reading the suitor guy's email, he flirtingly asked if I was checking out the new guy. His distraction spared me a lecture on Omega-3 and healthy fats. For the time being, at least.

'Just clearing my Inbox,' I clarified. 'I couldn't possibly delete the mail without reading, in case Pa inquired about it.'

'Jesus fucking Christ! I didn't know you have so many aunts and uncles,' exclaimed Jay, as he skimmed through the first few lines of Deepak's mail. 'Don't they sell condoms in India?'

Jay sounded genuinely surprised, but I was least interested in discussing the size of my extended family or birth control measures in India. I felt humiliated at being valued in the marriage market on the basis of my uncles' wealth and my cousins' academic achievements.

'What kind of a guy ridicules a girl's family and comments on her looks in his first mail?'

'He is quite witty, if you ask me.'

'Do you think he is . . .?'

'No, he is definitely not gay.'

'How dare he look at my FB profile pic?'

'Honey! It's public info, and last I checked the dictionary, public meant *belonging to people*.'

Jay didn't realize that the issue was not just that Deepak had looked at my picture. I was also addled by the cheap IIT guy's joke.

'Does he mean I look very nice in the suit and nice in the spaghetti or . . .?'

'Very nice in the spaghetti! I mean, look at that cleavage!'

I was miffed that Deepak had dared to stare at my cleavage in my very nice public profile pic. Even more annoying was his implication that I was trying to cheat him with a *sati-savitri* matrimonial picture.

'How can he assume he doesn't like me? He doesn't even know me,' I rambled, still on my own trip.

'To be fair, he is simply saying he doesn't know you and hence can't like you or add you to his friends' list.'

'Wouldn't make friends with him if he was Wilson, the volleyball, and I was Tom Hanks in *Cast Away*,' I continued to curse.

'Frankly, this Deep-Ache-Go-Hell chap doesn't seem that bad.' Jay was finding it all very amusing and for once, I found Jay's anglicized pronunciation of Indian names funny.

'Wouldn't marry him even if I was single at forty,' I vented.

Unable to see any signs of improvement in my mood, Jay squeezed my hand comfortingly and pushed off. 'See ya for Frisbee at six,' he communicated with lip movements from across the room.

Finishing off the rest of the bagel and cream cheese, I moved the email to Trash. I didn't know whether to like Deepak's sense of humour or hate his spunkiness, but I was not going to give him the satisfaction of knowing how his email had irked me.

I glossed over the day's schedule. The next lecture was in an hour's time. I did a quick scan of the room to see if someone was up for a chat. Four Indians, two Chinese, one Korean and two Americans. All PhD students, all guys, and all were hammering away at their laptops. I got up from my chair, straightened my little-above-the-knee black skirt, and proceeded to the coffee machine in the adjoining room. The overpowering fragrance of hazelnut-flavoured coffee wafting out of the room tantalized my tastebuds. As a master's student, I was lucky to have an office space and access to free coffee. This was thanks to my advisor! I glanced towards his room at the end of the corridor. It creaked open and I saw the tiny frame of Professor Girpade materialize in front of me. Reminded that I ought to be working, I tiptoed back hurriedly to my desk, careful not to make too much noise from my click-clacks.

I examined my to-do list, and rearranged the items one through thirty-five while sipping the coffee. Satisfied with the re-prioritized item list, and unable to concentrate any longer, I saved and closed the file. Feeling restless, I again surveyed the room. Barring some minor shifts in positions, I felt like I was at Madame Tussauds, surrounded by wax figures. Sitting in a lab full of dummies, I could not engage in shopping, socializing, or sex. So I decided to watch the song *Crazy kiya re* on YouTube to jazz up my spirits. The boys slowly began to glide towards my laptop. It can hardly be my fault if the wax statues got aroused by the sexy lady on the floor. Guys, I tell you! I bet Professor Girpade also watched Aishwarya Rai sway her hips and seductively glide her hands over her curves, before making his presence known.

Generally speaking, Professor Girpade, BTech IIT-D, PhD CMU, currently working as the associate professor, EECS department and my advisor, was a good-natured and lenient man, especially compared to professors back home. You could eat, drink, sleep and even walk out in the middle of his lectures. Understandably then, I was scared when he called me to his room and shut the door behind him. In the next five minutes, he made it clear to me that he will not tolerate any behaviour that causes distraction to his other students. He even threatened to cancel my research assistantship if I didn't complete my master's thesis in the next twenty days.

First Deepak and now Professor Girpade! My horoscope for the day must have read, 'Watch out for attacks from IIT-D alumni. You are likely to incur emotional setback and financial loss.'

It's not like I was a good-for-nothing slacker, tarnishing the image of Indian students in a US university. Although people did often mistake my 'Live each day—*Kal ho na ho*' attitude as a sign of my incompetence and lack of dedication. Just like you need a healthy mix of vitamins and minerals for a balanced diet, I preferred a healthy mix of alphabets in my grades to maintain my work–life balance. The balance, however, came with a fair mix of good and bad days, and today was turning from bad to worse. Any chance I could win a settlement suing Aishwarya Rai or YouTube for stripping me off my hard-earned scholarship?

'Guess I better work on my thesis topic then!' I resolved, albeit grudgingly, to take a break from YouTube and focus on work. I needed the moolah to survive the rest of this semester and complete my master's. Although I had a provisional job offer starting next February, I doubted Lehman Brothers would allow a master's-incomplete, funds-withdrawn candidate to join their IT division. Of course, no one could have predicted that twenty days later, I would still have the scholarship but not the job.

All work and no play, freaked my boyfriend Jay, and he put me on a low carbs diet. Other than that, the next three weeks passed without any mishaps. Fortunately, Deepak didn't report my 'no-reply', and Dad continued to believe that Deepak was slowly on his way to becoming my chocolate-cream soldier. Thesis submitted and my self-imposed entertainment ban lifted, I was watching a new episode of *Friends*, when my mobile rang.

'The new guy who joined us last week is so damn cute!' I heard

Tanu di's cheerful voice say. Almost ten years elder to me and still waiting for her soulmate, Tanu di, my *tauji*'s daughter, was my icon for the Woman of Today. However, right now, she was an accomplice of my dad in the husband-hunting crime.

'Fuck him!' I said reproachfully, least interested in casual boy talk. 'Five unanswered emails, ten missed calls and fifteen SMSes. Where have you been absconding for the last three weeks?'

'*Balike,*' she addressed me in a calm, saint-like manner, 'I was away in the hills, looking for the *sanjeevani booti* to save your love life.'

'You could have saved yourself the trouble if you hadn't verified that IIT suitor's credentials to begin with. First you create a bug and then you try to find its solution. I thought only Microsoft is allowed such flimflam.'

'I am innocent My Lord. I was victimized,' said Tanu di in a theatrical courtroom voice now. 'I was led to believe that the suitor inquiry was for one of our many unmarried, wheatish-fair, working but family-oriented cousins Pinki, Chinki or Dinki.'

I couldn't stop myself from laughing out at her melodrama. 'Anyhow, I think the situation is under control. Dad hasn't bothered me . . .'

'Chachu will . . . exactly after a week!' she prophesied confidently.

'You asked Professor Trelawney or what?' I joked.

'Better still, I sneaked on his Muggle phone. He has a reminder set for 15th of every month to check on the Suhaani–Deepak progress.'

'I don't understand. Why has Dad suddenly gone off-track, searching for a groom?'

'Babes, but of course you realize that Chachu simply wants you back home. Once you finish your studies and start working in the States, chances of your coming back are poorer than me having sex with that new, cute trainee.'

'Well, an underwired bra, stilettos and some Viagra can help increase your odds,' I teased.

'I will certainly work on your suggestion, ma'am, but you will need more than sex toys to fight your battle.'

She then explained her comprehensive combat strategy, starting from Deepak's debacle to my subsequent marriage with Jay. For now, I was supposed to just dilly dally on this marriage proposal. She would ensure the discovery of some gross flaw in Deepak, fabricating a pregnant girlfriend or a history of smoking pot if required. Basically, Deepak was go, went, gone as far as I was concerned. I will stay put in the US for another couple of years, unable to take time off for an India trip due to my new job. My parents could visit me instead and also get to see a new place. Over the next two years, I will gradually get my parents to doubt my sexual orientation and fuel their paranoia about my marriage. Occasional, accidental Facebook comments, a kiss here, a hug there, and a few random girlfriend pictures would do the trick. Once convinced that their daughter has homosexual inclinations, my parents would be glad I married a GUY, even if he was Jayant Guy.

Impressed by Di's plan and convinced that trying to mislead parents doesn't amount to lying, I told Tanu di to start a consulting service on 'The Art of Staying Single'. She agreed it was an awesome idea and we both hung up, me with a satisfied grin. Super-excited, I dialled Jay's number. It went unanswered. He must be at the gym, I figured and started dressing up for the evening bash.

GETTING LAID

'Someone is looking ravishing tonight!' said Ashraf, as we exchanged a sideways, cheek-to-cheek kiss.

Ashraf was the host for the evening. Having managed to convince Neetu's parents about their inter-community marriage, he was celebrating his DDLJ moment. Dressed in a crisp, white, lucknawi kurta and churidar, he seemed all set to climb the *ghodi* and take the vows.

'Sorry we are late, AshRough,' apologized Jay. 'I was busy exercising.'

'With a girlfriend like Suhaani,' said Ashraf, raising his eyebrows and giving me an obvious once-over, 'I can understand your temptation to (s)exercise.' He winked at Jay and showed us inside his uncle's house.

The place was teeming with students from all parts of the world. A self-serve bar, stacked with expensive wines and high-class liquor, was set at the corner table. Plates full of cocktail samosas, veg pakoras, tandoori paneer and chicken lined the snack counter. Ashraf was known for his lavish tastes, wide circle of friends and amazing inter-personal skills, all of which had helped him woo his in-laws. While the *desi*s were guzzling liquor like their bodies were composed of 70 per cent alcohol, the *gora*s gorged on the spicy Indian savouries.

I was searching for familiar faces in the crowd when my eyes locked with Denise's, Jay's ex-girlfriend and my sworn enemy. She was one among the many bimbos surrounding Neetu, admiring her bejewelled, backless blouse and designer saree. I wanted to look away but couldn't stop myself from eyeballing her. She was wearing a short, strapless, body-hugging dress that could barely contain her assets from spilling out. The outfit was a fashion disaster if you ask me, but men rarely notice such stuff.

She gave me a contemptuous smile, turned away, and glided effortlessly in her high heels towards her destination. Next moment, I saw her 'accidentally' fall on Jay. I could see a helpless Jay, holding glasses in both hands, unable to stop her body from touching his. Then she flashed her boobs at Jay, while casting a smug glance in my direction. Now, I considered myself reasonably broadminded as far as staying in touch with an ex was concerned. And, I appreciated that Jay shared similar views, but Denise always managed to evoke the worst in me.

Before I could uproot myself and go slap her, she had disappeared among the many people thronging the bar and Jay was standing next to me with two glasses of wine. Feeling furious at her sleazy act, I gulped down my wine in a single shot, and kissed Jay fully on the lips to establish my claim on him. Pleasantly surprised by my public display of affection, Jay shoved me, through the thick of the grooving crowd, to the centre of the dance floor. I wondered what he was doing, for he had two left feet, but a quick look around cleared my confusion. Most couples weren't dancing. They were dirty dancing! Their bodies grinding against each other, they were gyrating to the beats of music. I felt uneasy. I was cool with casual physical contact in public, but my outdoor limits were governed by what I was comfortable with uploading on Facebook. Today, high on wine and fuelled by jealousy, I had already violated my boundaries. Jay's fingertips were lightly tracing circles on the exposed skin above my lehenga. The coolness of his touch sent shivers of excitement down my spine. I tried to pull away but Jay tightened his grip around my waist. Pulling me closer to his body, he started gyrating our hips together in a rhythmic fashion. His other hand was exploring its way up, under the lower hem of my choli. I was struggling to control my own desires and stall Jay's advances, when suddenly the music stopped and the room was filled with bright lights. Sobering up a little, I managed to get off Jay's hand from under my blouse.

Ashraf was standing with a mike, in the centre of the room, thanking everyone for their presence. He made a toast to his and Neetu's togetherness and announced that we would now play a game of 'Truth or Dare' and he would have the prerogative to decide the questions.

'I will start the game and my Dare will be decided by my high-command.' He stood in front of Neetu, and bowed towards her with exaggerated gestures, making us all laugh. Like a queen, she demanded that he sing a Bollywood number for her. Now that, I thought was unfair. Neetu knew Ashraf couldn't sing to save his life, not even in the shower, and how he hated being embarrassed in front of other people. Or maybe, that was the bachelor Ashraf I knew! For this recently engaged Ashraf was anything but hassled by Neetu's demand. He held both her hands in his, looked affectionately into her eyes, and started singing the song, *'Chaudvin ka chand ho, ya aaftaab ho / Jo bhi ho tum khuda ki kasam, lajawab ho . . .'*

Whether this was a temporary 'I will do anything for you' phase or a more permanent 'who cares how I sing, the girl is mine now' take-for-granted attitude, or unabashedness caused by alcohol, the moment was full of love.

The song ended to a huge applause, as Neetu rewarded Ashraf with a passionate kiss. He had sung horribly, even unbearably, but I couldn't help feel envious of Neetu. I looked longingly at them. This is what I wanted. This is what every Indian girl wants. To have a lover who would praise her and sing for her. To marry the guy she loves, with the consent of her parents. I felt a sudden sadness in my heart, like if I married Jay a part of me would stay empty forever. While Tanu di's plan could get me my parents' blessings, I knew Jay would never be able to sing like a Bollywood hero. Damn the wine! I shook myself out of the self-pity. This was my choice.

The next guy decided to tell the 'Truth' and Ashraf asked him to name a person that he could have had sex with, but chose not to and the reason for the same. His answer offended the girl concerned, who counterattacked by broadcasting that her current boyfriend was four inches bigger.

The next person opted to 'Dare' and was made to expose some body part. She willingly lifted her dress to bare the crawling scorpions tattooed on her butts. As the game progressed, it ruffled some more egos, broke a few couples, and revealed a lot more skin.

When the turn came to Denise, she chose a Dare. Ashraf asked her to kiss a person other than her current beau. 'I am willing', 'I can lend my lips', 'Look here baby'—the cries came from many leering mouths. Fluttering her false eyelashes, Denise paraded the room, pretending to be in a fix. She then stopped by my side, gave me a wicked smile, and planted her wet, thick, pink lips on Jay's. She snogged him for what seemed like the longest kiss ever, before she eventually let go of her grip on him. 'I have already tasted him before. I thought this couldn't hurt anyone,' she explained. Smiling triumphantly, she strode back to her seat among roars of cheers and shouts of 'good choice'.

I could feel the pitiful glares from all the girls around the room, while guys regarded Jay with new respect. I tried hard to control my anger and keep from blushing. Taking a sip of the wine, I held the glass in front of my face to hide the anger flashing in my eyes and the humiliation contorting my features. I stole a quick look at what Jay was doing. He seemed absolutely normal, like Denise had cast an imperious curse on him and he was under her control. He even looked back at me and gave me his usual smile.

Unable to withstand any more humiliation, I was about to leave when Jay held my hand and said, 'Take it easy, hon.'

'How could you let her smooch you?' I muttered accusingly, while looking down so that others would not know we were arguing.

'This is just a game. Be a sport.' He continued to smile casually and fake interest in the game that was still going on.

'So a full-blown lip-to-lip kiss by your ex means nothing.'

'She is an ex, honey! She has kissed me before, on my lips and elsewhere.'

'By that logic, according to you, it should be okay to have sex with an ex because you had done it before.'

'You are just overreacting, hon. I didn't do anything.'

'My point exactly! You didn't do anything to stop her.' I was looking him directly in the eye now.

'Okay, I am sorry. I didn't realize it would hurt you.'

What was there to realize? You can't get kissed by your ex, unless you were dying and needed a kiss of life. Wasn't this obvious? Surely this was easier than differentiating between mauve and magenta. Men and their inability to understand the simplest of situations! I didn't know what else to say so I kept quiet. Soon, it was my chance to take part in the hideous entertainment. Having lost my sense of humour and not feeling very bold, I opted for Truth.

'Lehman Brothers has filed for bankruptcy,' Ashraf suddenly said with disbelief.

'Not sure if that is a Truth or a Dare?' I remarked, rather confused.

Just then someone switched on the TV and I knew the party was over!

Soon after that night, everyone around was talking about the market crash, lay-offs and debts. Shops were offering huge discounts to boost the economy and make people spend. My lay-off letter came in within a week. To be precise, it was a withdrawal of the provisional job offer due to unforeseen circumstances. The only people celebrating were my parents. Unless I found another job in the next four months, enrolled for a PhD under Professor Girpade, or settled for delivering pizzas—all of which were unlikely—I was home-bound now. Papa had even started scouting for jobs back in Delhi for me.

In those days, after my job offer was withdrawn, I tried all sorts of permutations and combinations on my savings with possible loans from friends. I did spreadsheet analyses multiple times. It all led to the same result: I could survive a maximum of two months after the scholarship ended before running out of cash.

My FB status read, 'Looking for job with H-1B visa sponsorship. Huge discounts in salary for early bird offers.'

HOMECOMING

'How can you make love to a stranger just because you took seven rounds around the holy fire with him?' I blurted out, my eyes busy scanning the *Sunday Brunch*, and my mind visualizing a jewellery-laden bride, clad in a flaming red saree, sitting on a bed with a naked groom. I was reading an article on how arranged marriages were more successful and led to fewer divorces compared to love marriages in Indian societies. 'Just like you can have sex with a hot guy at the beach, a cool dude in college or a handsome bachelor in a bar,' Ma quipped.

I wasn't expecting any response, least of all from my mom. I had forgotten I was back at home in India, sitting in the living room with my parents. Uncomfortable, the nude groom in my imagination quickly got dressed.

'Only, the outcome here will be illegitimate in case you forgot to use a condom,' she added. She was clearly against the notion of random, experimental sex that our generation was eagerly lapping up.

I raised my eyes to examine my mom's face and read her expressions. Sitting across the room on a sofa, with the laptop creasing her crisp cotton saree, she was busy harvesting crops and milking online cows on Farmville.

I contemplated explaining to her the difference between having sex and making love, but then I decided against it. Why disillusion a simple, pious lady? However, one thing was clear. On the first night in an arranged marriage, people just have sex.

I didn't want to bring up the marriage issue with my parents, at least not yet, but the article was slandering love marriages. It was a clear case of confirmation bias.

'Just because people don't opt for divorce in arranged marriages doesn't mean that they are happy.' I raised my doubts on the article's underlying assumption.

'It means, they are trying to make relationships work,' my mom rationalized, her fingers busy harvesting the ripened crops before they die.

'Like they have a choice! Girls are financially dependent and guys are scared of their emotionally blackmailing mothers.'

'I am not financially dependent,' clarified my mom, who was a maths teacher at a well-reputed school.

'And I am certainly not scared of my mom, who *is* one hell of an emotional blackmailer by the way,' informed my dad, who had been quietly braiding my hair all this while.

'Ditto!' I chuckled, giving a high-five to my dad, and we all laughed, enjoying the family banter.

The morning was perfect. It was early March. The cool breeze made me curl my fingers around the warm cup of herbal tea and relish its fragrant flavours. The last few weeks had gone by in the blink of an eye.

After I landed in India, Dad had surprised me with a ten-day South Africa, vacation. It had cost him a fortune, and Ma had been upset about the extravagance, but that was typical. Soon, I was amidst the African bush tracking the Big Five. I was having breakfast with giraffes necking a few yards away, admiring the silkiness of zebra skin and drinking beer in a makeshift camp while a rhino marked his territory. When the wildlife got too much for us, we switched to sunbathing on the beaches with penguins. There had been so much to do and explore that I hadn't had the time to miss Jay. I had briefly written him emails, updating him on my wild escapades, and promising more details when I got back.

Now suddenly, when back at home with nothing else to occupy my mind, I found myself yearning for Jay. Instinctively, I unlocked the phone lying next to me, and then wistfully locked it back again. The local time in Michigan was 12.30 a.m. The first time I had felt the impact of the earth's rotation, other than the obvious day and night, was when I had tried to chat with Jay during my stopover at Frankfurt. I had been so disappointed to realize that he was still asleep. I had craved to hear his voice, and the fact I couldn't do so had made me miserable. I remembered the last night we had spent together in my apartment. He had held me tight, close to his body, and kissed me voraciously over and over again, but he hadn't asked me even once to stay back. Not that I could if he did. On the whole he had been quiet, casual and composed about my untimed departure. Was he being practical, bold or indifferent? Did he not fear that he could lose me?

I felt Pa's hand on my shoulders and realized that I had been lost in another world.

'Mom won't like it, but you can tell me if you love someone,' Dad whispered in my ears as he bent down to pick a fallen rubber band from the floor.

I hesitated. Had he seen the restlessness in my eyes? Did he already know there was someone?

I was tempted for an instant to tell him about Jay. He hadn't mentioned Deepak even once since I got back. As always, Tanu di had guessed correctly. Dad had just wanted me back home. And therein lay the crux of the problem. He may be open to love marriage, but he wasn't open to my settling abroad. In any case, Jay had at least two years to go before he finished his PhD, and I was mentally unprepared to have a showdown, just yet. Leaving tomorrow's troubles to tomorrow, I shook my head in a vague no. Keeping an impassive expression plastered on my face, I pretended to be absorbed in the magazine. Mom was frantically ploughing land so she could earn some farm-coins and buy more livestock.

'I think I have found my alternate profession, in case I ever get chucked out from my job,' exclaimed Dad, giving his handy work a satisfactory glance. He had braided some thirty, small-diameter cornrows in the last hour in my hair.

'She looks like the Swahili girl from the African game reserve,' commented Ma, examining the tight plaits braided close to my scalp.

'I will take that as a compliment,' said Dad and then looking at Ma's disapproving glare, raised his hands in the air and added, 'Okay. I won't take all the credit. Suhaani's recent perm helped.'

'Those chemicals are harmful for her hair,' stated Ma, who had been shocked to see a frizzy mass of curls on my head in place of my smooth, straight mane. She had wasted no time in expressing her displeasure, right at the airport.

'Sometimes, a little harm can do a lot of good. Haven't you heard of retail therapy?' joshed Dad, tickling me on the waist.

I knew he understood my need for a change. I would often experiment with my looks, especially when I needed a morale boost. I had hit the beauty parlour the very day I got my job withdrawal letter.

'The only harm that can help this generation is self-discipline,' advocated Mom, and soon sighed, 'See, you guys distracted me and now the tomatoes I had planted last night have withered.'

'Ma, your Farmville time is up,' I reminded.

'Someone needs self-discipline here,' remarked Dad gently, who loved picking on Mom.

Knowing well that she can't win an argument against Pa, Mom closed her laptop and asked if we wanted another round of chai and pakoras. Suckers that we were for my mom's cooking, we nodded hungrily, and she retreated to her kitchen kingdom. Pa and I got busy with solving the Sunday crossword. It was good to be back home.

Over the next month however, as the initial excitement of homecoming subsided, I started to see life as it really was. Public toilets were clogged with sanitary napkins and condoms. Bras and panties, hung on clotheslines, proudly adorning the apartment balconies. Aunties left their own gas unattended to see if the neighbour's milk had overflowed. Drivers made sure to honk when breaking a traffic rule to warn the others. The stars appeared in the sky only on events like the Earth Hour.

I had lived in India for twenty-one years, without noticing and perhaps even contributing my bit to the state of affairs. Now, one short stay at a five-star hotel suite and I was complaining about life at the shack. Yet, these were all external, environmental differences. What I was missing the most—apart from the aroma of the hazelnut coffee, my nude artwork collecting dust in Jay's apartment and Jay's check on my daily calorie intake—was company. My college mates and school friends were either studying or working somewhere. Tanu di was again away to the hills, this time searching for the sanjeevani booti to save her own business. Mom had her hands full with home, school and Farmville. Dad had his routine set with office, music classes and IPL matches. That left me alone, most of the time, to do whatever I wanted, and all I did the whole day was eat, eat and eat some more. My clothes were beginning to get tight from my consumption of unrationed calories, and I could feel the extra fat beginning to bulge out of my jeans. I hadn't even bothered to unwrap the canvas and brushes from their bubble wrap. Enough of lazing around like Garfield. I needed to take a break from my break.

Swallowing my pride, I decided to call DeepAche. Yes, the same Deepak Goyal. No, I wasn't calling him to ask if he will be my friend. The call was strictly business. Of course, it was my dad's idea. As soon as I had become jobless, Dad had posted my resume on Naukri.com and started searching for suitable job openings. He had even shortlisted a few companies and a couple of those had expressed interest in hiring me after brief telephonic interviews. I merely needed to make up my mind on which one to join. Apparently, the US realty crash hadn't hit the IT sector in India so far.

I was unsure how Deepak would react to my call. He might snub me because I hadn't replied to his email or he might misinterpret the call to mean that I was *maroing line* on him. Worse still, he might not even recall who I was.

I felt a wave of apprehension build up each time I heard a fresh 'trrrr. . .ing' begin and subside as the call went unanswered. I was about to disconnect, when he answered after the seventh ring.

'Hello!' he said in a rather charismatic voice, a complete mismatch to the geeky, grotesque image I had in my mind.

'Hi!' I said, stupefied.

'Hey, Meeta!' he exclaimed enthusiastically. 'When did you change your number?'

'No . . . er . . . actually I am sorry,' I stammered. 'I mean I am Suhaani,' I replied coming back to my senses. 'I wanted to . . .'

'Can you please hold on for a sec?' he said, speaking in a more formal tone this time.

I heard a girl's voice in the background. I caught scraps of their conversation. She was saying something like 'I am not done yet,' and he was telling her to hang loose. My single-track mind wondered if I had interrupted something intimate, but I couldn't hang up now. I had already told him my name. I heard a door open and shut.

'Hi,' he said, coming back on line. 'The signal strength in our office building is very poor, so I just stepped out.'

Shucks! In my all-day-Sunday mode I had forgotten that it was a weekday and Deepak would be at work.

'But I thought you were with a girl . . .' The words escaped before I could pass them through the faux pas filter.

'You know . . . we happen to have female staff in our office,' he replied in a plain voice, but I thought I heard him snicker.

I chided myself for being careless. It was none of my business if he was hobnobbing with female employees.

'I was wondering if you could help me with my decision. I believe my father has spoken to you about it,' I asked, coming straight to the point.

'Who all have you shortlisted?' he asked offhandedly. This also meant that Dad had spoken to him about it and he was aware of my dilemma.

'One is in the VLSI design and the other is in the Internet domain,' I said, without revealing the specific company names.

'Why don't you tell me what you think about them?' he asked, tossing the ball back to me.

This was going like a typical job interview where the interviewer first asks the candidate to describe his or her background even though he has already gone through the resume.

Clearly he considered this discussion a waste of his time.

'While VLSI is older and more mature, Internet is comparatively young and more fun,' I summarized my opinion rather than bore him with details.

Something in my response must have been funny, for I heard suppressed laughter in his voice as he asked, 'Which one has a better package to offer?'

It was apparent that he paid little significance to such superficial aspects, so I told him that they both were equally attractive and rather alluring in their own ways.

'What is your comfort level with them?' He asked a little more seriously, sounding like this was an important parameter to decide upon.

'Well, I understand VLSI better and hence feel more at home there, but I have always been fascinated by Internet,' I answered.

'Guess there is only way to choose then,' he concluded. 'Which one do you see spending your entire life with?'

Although he was asking straightforward questions, I got a vague feeling that he was somehow mocking me.

'None really, I hope,' I replied candidly. 'I mean, times have changed, you know. People get bored after a while, find a better package and switch. Won't you?'

'I prefer long-term relationships,' he admitted, his husky voice unknowingly teasing my senses.

Hypnotized, I waited for him to say more.

'If it's only a short-term fling that you are looking at, then just go with your gut feel,' he suggested playfully.

As I am not a gut feel person, I told him that I believed in concrete data points.

'Are you sure I am the right person to advise you on this?' he asked with a hint of mischievousness. 'Apart from the ramblings of a doting dad and your matrimonial write-up, I know little else about you.'

'But, Dad told me you went through a similar situation four years ago,' I argued.

'Did I? I don't remember ever having to deliberate about prospective suitors!'

Hang on. What did he think I was asking him about? Prospective suitors!

Before I could bombard him with profanities, I heard him

chuckle, and say, 'Sorry. I couldn't resist myself. You offered such a tempting bait.'

I did a quick mental recap and realized that he had been talking in innuendoes, and I had almost played my part by giving befitting answers. Even though he was pulling my leg, I couldn't help but be amused by the hilarity of his joke. *Mature suitors vs fun suitors. Suitors with attractive packages. Switching suitors when bored.*

I tittered self-consciously, and asked him, measuring every word carefully, if I should join a VLSI company or a dotcom start-up.

This time, he methodically explained to me the positives and the negatives of the two sectors.

I was impressed by his thorough, in-depth analysis of the current market situation, and his opinion on the companies' future prospects.

'Do you have a spreadsheet capturing this data?' I inquired.

'I am more of a people person than a paper person,' he replied. 'I prefer to do what you are doing just now. Call a few close friends and decide based on their inputs.'

What did he say? Close friends! Either he was desperate to get close to me or was too conceited to assume that I was trying to get close to him. Ugh! Just when I thought I could buddy up with this guy, he had gone back to being an IITian. Before I could clear his misconception, he said he needed to rush to a meeting. I politely thanked him and disconnected.

I had nowhere to rush, so I sat down with a paper and pencil, and reflected on our conversation.

'Ultimately, the decision depends on your risk appetite,' Deep had said, summarizing his advice. If being adventurous and experimental counted for anything, then I had a helluva appetite for risk. However, to me, the risk was immaterial. I wasn't here to make a career. I was only looking for a good experience while I was stranded in India. As I had no other claims on my time, the long hours only seemed like a blessing. I also figured that the crowd in the dotcom start-up would be younger and hence more *fun*.

Unlike Deep, I was a numbers person and favoured a systematic, step-by-step approach. I made a table of all the pluses and minuses, and assigned my preference weight to each of them. Next I gave points to each company against each factor, and finally I computed the weighted score. The decision was done.

I logged onto Facebook to check the latest news in my social circle. Jay was rooting 'Go Blue' for the UMich football team. Neha, my all-time best friend, had posted, 'Coffee, Chocolate, Men...Some Things are Just Better Rich'. I commented, saying I prefer mine strong and hard. Neetu had posted some more pictures from her party. There was one of me kissing Jay on the mouth, to which Jay had commented 'Sweet times'. I recalled how I had lost my head over that boobs-on-display Denise, and kissed Jay in public. I immediately messaged Neetu to remove the picture from FB. I then wrote a long mail to Jay telling him how lonely I was and how badly I longed to be in his arms, how I had gained love handles in the absence of any physical activity and how he was to be blamed for that, and how under all circumstances, he was to stay away from Denise.

Before I logged out, I edited the employer section in my Facebook profile to 'iTrot.com'. I had no idea that this seemingly professional and relatively insignificant change was going to decide how, when, where and with whom my children would spend weekends in the future.

DEEP SHIT

I was sitting with my legs crossed, tightening my thigh muscles to prevent my wastewater tank from leaking. Must be all the diet coke that I had guzzled last night to stay awake and chat with Jay. The cab driver relentlessly honked, zigzagged, bumped and cursed through the office hour rush. The couple of kilometres from IFFCO Chowk to the Udyog Vihar exit that usually takes five minutes had taken us more than an hour today. The reason, as always, was a car that had broken down in the middle of the road. Cursing the situation of Indian traffic, and following the directions printed from the company website, I finally saw the sign of iTrot.com gleam from the top of a building at the next crossing. As I paid the driver, I spotted a guy shamelessly taking a leak at the opposite wall grinning to himself, all the while. Lucky him! Applying *moolbandh* to keep the lid on my pee outlet, I somehow scrambled up the stairs, signed my name in the office register, and asked the reception lady if I could use the loo.

She looked at me like I was some ill-bred, uncouth peasant, who had walked in from the nearby village, looking for an air-conditioned place to empty my bladder. For once, I wished I had dressed ostentatiously in showy, Dilli-type clothes rather than sporting the dignified Fab India look. Unwillingly, she swiped her smart card and showed me in, instructing me to be out as soon as I was done.

As I came back, smoothing out the creases in my kurta and visibly relaxed, I approached the receptionist and showed her my entry ticket to the office loo. One look at the appointment letter and she immediately rewarded me with newfound respect and a professional smile. She checked my name in a list, called someone inside, and politely informed me that the new joinee induction programme had already begun, but I would have to wait for the HR manager before I could join the rest of the newbies. I knew I was late, but why waste time now. Dubious about whether I had chosen the right job, I took a seat in the lobby and started flipping through some travel magazines. An hour later, I was still lounging, but now I was an expert on all the beaches in South East Asia, places to shop in Bangkok, best sushi restaurants and the special Thai massage parlours. Two cups of coffee, and one more trip to the loo later, I was finally called in.

Guided by a secretary, I walked through the maze of cubicles, watching young, energetic faces, planning and selling dream vacations. We stopped on reaching the glass door that said 'HR Manager'. I peered through the glass, and sighted a smart-looking female in western formals. She was busy talking to someone on the phone. She motioned me to come in. I pulled open the door, when I read the sign that said 'Push'.

I pushed the door to enter the room and found the HR manager busy on a call.

'Finding a new maid is not easy,' I heard her explain to the person on the phone, as she gestured me to take a seat. 'Yes, I am in HR, but I recruit professionals, not house help,' she said irritably. 'Why don't you call your son? My job is not just chatting with people, it requires thinking as well,' she said, trying to defend herself, but the person on the line seemed persistent.

Listening to her conversation, which I found to be rather entertaining, I detected a sense of familiarity in her voice. I felt like

I had heard it before, although I was certain that this was the first time I was meeting her in person. It was hard to forget someone with that Audrey Hepburnish, mini-bouffant hairstyle. Interesting, but a trifle stiff and old-fashioned for my taste.

'Okay, I will ask the office boy if he knows any full-time maid,' she finally acceded, and hastily cut the line.

'Mothers-in-law! I tell you. They are like these overpowering, hard-to-please bosses. You can never get along with them.'

Coming from a nuclear family, I had little experience in the matter, but I nodded sympathetically.

Having dealt with home relations, she greeted me warmly, introduced herself and inquired how I was 'liking' the training so far. Puzzled, I explained that I had gotten delayed, and had actually been waiting outside rather than attending any training. 'Did you enjoy the wait?' She asked with utmost sincerity.

But for the kindness in her eyes, I would have assumed she was trying to humiliate me for being late. 'Not particularly,' I replied honestly.

'Have you ever wondered how much time in our life is spent just waiting for things to happen?' she grilled me further.

I raised my eyebrows as if to ask what point she was trying to make.

'Roughly sixty-two minutes a day,' she answered. 'Every day we wait in the bus lines, for the elevator, for the doctor's appointment, at the traffic signals, at the supermarket cash counter, to be served at a restaurant, for files to download, friends to call, the other person to make the first move . . . and for the love of our life.'

Only the last in the list seemed worthy of the time to me.

'Never make customers wait. It's the most important part of our customer sensitization module,' she articulated. 'I am sorry you were held up, but I hope it was a lesson well learnt.'

'Wow! So every new employee gets to browse the magazines and while away their time?'

She shook her head, and despite sensing the slight mockery in my tone, she replied with a smile, 'Only the client-facing team.' And then reading the confusion on my face she added, 'I know you will not have direct customer interaction, but your immediate manager insisted you go through this experience.'

Completely baffled by this unique training methodology, I pondered what in my resume could possibly have made my manager decide that I be honoured with this wisdom. My sex? Was he, assuming it was a he, anti-women? I felt a strange unease in my stomach, wondering what I had signed myself up for.

As I followed her out of her office, I remarked that her push door shouldn't have a pull handle. It was a bad user experience. Pleased with my observation, she gave me an all-knowing smile, but said nothing. We kept walking across the cubicles and climbing up the stairs. I observed that there were several customer service posters adorning the staircase walls. When she stopped, I looked around and realized that we had reached the centre cubicle on the second floor. 'This is yours,' she said, pointing to the only empty seat in the cubicle. I put my purse down on the chair. She then called out to a guy, wearing a purple checked shirt, sitting diagonally across from my chair, with his back facing us. 'Deep, here is your new joinee.'

The purple-checked shirt swivelled around his blue, ergonomic chair, stood up and extended his right hand for a shake. Stunned, I stared at the familiar, square face with a big mouth, and the 10 mm lip brow. Unlike the hilltop photo however, his hair carelessly fell on his forehead, sort of like SRK. I was hallucinating. My mind had conjured up DeepAche's image at the sound of the name 'Deep'. Surely the random guy from my dad's guitar class couldn't be my manager.

'Welcome to iTrot.com,' I heard him say, in his deep, husky voice.

Admittedly, I had been tempted to call Deep once or twice in the last couple of weeks. You know, just to have an intelligent conversation, and also to hear his rich, sexy voice. I had even visited his website dgblahblah.com and browsed through his photo gallery to confirm if he indeed looked as repelling as I remembered. This time, he had appeared agreeable for a casual acquaintance, though not cool enough to hang around with, and definitely undesirable as a boss.

'Frankly, I thought you would choose the VLSI firm, but I am glad you chose us,' he said, his eyes twinkling with mischief behind his round glasses.

Choose us! I had just chosen one of the many thousand dotcom companies in Delhi-NCR. Not you! I tried to clarify, but the words died in my throat. Someone had cast a body-binding spell on me.

'You were damn right about selecting her for the special project,' the HR manager commended. 'She sure did comment on the pull handle.'

'Thanks, Kavita. I am rarely wrong about people,' Deep said, accepting the compliment as his birthright.

I heard him tell me the name of a systems person who could help me with my PC, the secretary who would get my ID batch and the rest of the team. Well, to be precise, the special project team comprised of Deepak, me and an MCA final year trainee. I still said nothing. I was immobilized, my mind had temporarily switched off to sleep mode and my heart was pounding hard. If this was another of their novel training techniques on how to deal with unexpected events, I was certainly not doing well.

'Are you all right?' Deep asked, sounding genuinely concerned. I think he had a faint idea of the confusion and bewilderment I was experiencing.

'Yeah, I am fine,' I managed to utter this time. It was more of a reflex response than a thought-through answer.

Assured, that I was going to survive the jolt, he turned his attention to the HR manager, and said, 'Kavita, let's finish where we left off the other day.'

As I watched the duo leave, it dawned on me that Kavita was the same woman whose voice I had heard on the phone when I had called Deep to ask about the companies. At least, now I knew why she had sounded familiar.

Shell-shocked, I let myself sink in the empty chair. What are the odds that I join a 250+ people company and land up in a team of three, with a prospective suitor I hadn't bothered to respond to, as my manager.

'Bade bade shehron mein aisi choti choti baatein hoti rahti hain, Senorita,' mimed the girl sitting adjacent to me, as if reading my mind. She introduced herself as Madhuri Dikshit, a big Bollywood buff, and our third team member. Then she offered me a piece from her dairy milk chocolate which I promptly devoured. I was already beginning to like this girl.

'Hi, I am Suhaani,' I said, amused by her filmy name. I was too dumbfounded to decipher the relevance of the *DDLJ* dialogue yet.

'It's so good to meet you at last,' said Madhuri, bubbling with excitement. 'You look even more beautiful than your biodata picture.'

'Don't tell me,' I said, taken aback that Deep had told her about the marriage proposal.

Thinking that she might have offended me, she quickly apologized, 'I simply meant to say that the perm suits you very well.'

'Sure. Thanks,' I answered. I figured gossiping is a way of life when you are parked in the 'Single, looking to mingle' life slot. I had shared a laugh about Deep's picture with my lab guys too.

'Kammo was so upset to see your photo,' she chirpily informed me.

'Kammo?'

'Kameeni Chopra,' she elaborated, elongating the 'i' sound in the name to 'ee' on purpose.

'She is in the content team and sits on the first floor. Everyone knows she has the hots for Deep sir,' Madhuri divulged.

Whoever this Kammo was, she was clearly not in Madhuri's good books. However, for some reason, it appeared that all the females from Kavita to Kammo were enchanted by Mr DeepAche's seductive voice. I wondered if he had used the nice and very nice girl joke on them.

'Your Deep sir seems to be quite in demand,' I remarked informally.

'Oh! Wait till you hear him sing,' she raved. 'He can even yodel-ay, yodel-ay-ee-oo like Kishore Kumar.'

I knew Deep's voice could cause havoc, but comparing it with Kishore da was a little too much.

The incredulous look must have been plain on my face, for she further added, 'His deep, mesmerizing voice can make any girl's,' and started humming the number, *'My dil goes mmm . . .'* from *Salaam Namaste*.

'Does your dil go mmmmmmm?' I asked teasingly, somewhat regaining my sense of humour.

'No no no no no no no no,' she said in rapid succession, her hands waving at superfast speed with every no. 'I am just happy to be working under him.'

I couldn't stop my wild imagination from visualizing her 'working happily' under him. I bit my lips to stop a naughty smile from creeping on my face, but I think she caught the amusement dancing in my eyes nonetheless. Assuming that I doubted her, and in a bid to convince me of her chaste intentions, she reiterated, 'JEE 2 and a gold medallist from IIT, Deep sir is like GOD to me.'

It was quite clear to me that she was completely awestruck by his IIT stamp. It's ridiculous that people give unnecessary weightage to a chosen few three-letter combinations like IIT, IIM and IAS.

'I personally find IITians to be too full of themselves,' I objected.

'Deep sir is different,' vouched Madhuri. 'He has been awarded the iTrot best innovator award for three consecutive years.' Her voice was filled with deepest admiration and utmost respect.

I gave her a whatever shrug, which she misunderstood to be my defeat.

'Any girl would be lucky to get a guy like him,' she said, smiling enthusiastically and looking eagerly at me. Clearly, she expected me to be thrilled at being the chosen one.

'Deep and I . . . err . . . we are barely friends,' I said hesitantly, to straighten things out.

'Of course,' she said, almost too abruptly, her face breaking into a silly, wide grin.

It was evident that she so did not believe me.

'I had no idea that he works here,' I emphasized, glad to have someone to discuss the absurdity of the entire situation with.

This time, she seemed to believe me. 'Deep sir didn't know either that you were joining iTrot. Kavita ma'am informed him only two days back.'

'Sheer coincidence, don't you think?' I exclaimed.

'Kismat Konnection!' she replied excitedly.

I was about to tell her that I had little faith in fate, when a fat, fair guy walked in, snapping the fingers of both his hands alternately to produce a sort of musical tune.

He squeezed his bulky frame into the chair next to me. I could smell the coconut oil in his hair even from a distance.

'Namaste bhabhiji. Myself Sanjeev Sharma,' he introduced himself, in a typical *dehati* style.

Bhabhiji! Was he living in the black and white era? I gaped at him in disbelief. Sporting a tilak on his forehead and a partially unbuttoned, orange shirt, he looked like an avatar from Govinda's Coolie No. 1.

Seeing the perplexed expression on my face, he reasoned, 'IIT Brotherhood, *bhabhiji*. Deep is my brother from another IIT.' He paused to laugh at his own joke, before adding, '*To, aap bhabhiji huin na?*'

It was obvious that he, too, was aware of my matrimonial goings-on. 'How many people exactly do you think know?' I inquired, shifting uncomfortably in my chair.

I saw Sanjeev carefully survey the people in the neighbouring cubicles, take his hands out from his shiny black pant pockets, and start counting in binary finger notation. (You can count up to 1023 using base 2 notations on 10 fingers). He stopped at 8. With 2 to the power of 8 being 256, this meant that the entire office knew about my arranged marriage proposal to Deep.

'Deep sir is an open book, you know, like Saifu in the movie *Dil Chahta Hai*,' Madhuri offered, trying to salvage the situation.

Immediately the image of a friendly, funny and flirtatious guy popped into my mind. I had quite liked that character, but I just could not see the connection now.

'Suhaani ji, we have all been eagerly waiting to meet you, following every move of yours ever since you stepped out of the taxi,' explained Sanjeev. 'First you paid the taxi, then you signed the register, then you talked to the receptionist, then you went to the ladies' room, then you had a coffee, then you looked at the *Travel Times*, had another coffee . . .'

Flabbergasted, I looked at him blankly, as he narrated a minute-by-minute account of my entire day since I had arrived at iTrot. com. Discernibly, the entire office had been spying on me.

'What kind of rumour-mongering happens in this office?' I blurted out in exasperation. In general, like most people,

I enjoy surprises. They add spice to day-to-day life. But too much spice can be difficult to digest, and today was turning out to be three red chillies' hot spicy.

'It's not what it seems like,' said Sanjeev calmly. 'Deep had just showed us the biodata long time back, but when Kavita got to know that you were joining our company, all of us started teasing him,' he justified.

'Sharma ji,' I replied respectfully, 'I think there is a slight problem.'

'They are just friends,' interjected Madhuri, in an effort to restore peace.

'We are not even friends,' I said, a bit more sternly this time. I noticed the colour drain from Madhuri's lively face, and she immediately returned to her seat. Sanjeev also glared at me accusingly for being unreasonably rude, and glided his chair back to his corner.

I was left alone staring at their backs. I wanted to be angry with Deep for landing me in this soup, but as it was not exactly his fault, I was confused as to whom I should blame. I knew both Madhuri and Sharma ji thought I was stupid to dislike Deep, but I couldn't tell them that I already had a boyfriend or that I didn't feel sexually attracted to Deep. Well, if you leave out his husky voice for a second. Speaking of which, I heard the unsettling voice from the aisle and quickly turned to face my workstation. The last thing I wanted was for Deep to catch me mucking about. I clicked on the folder named 'Special Project', opened the hundred-page requirements document, and started reading. But of course, not a single word reached my mind, which was busy processing the day's bizarre events. Not only was I now reporting to a guy my dad wanted me to marry, the whole office seemed to know about it, and wanted me to say yes to him.

C'mon. Give me a break! Such things are supposed to only

happen in movies, not real life. Baffled and in dire need of some sane advice, I sent an SMS to Tanu di and Neha, 'SOS. In Deep Shit.' Surprisingly, I got an immediate response from Di.

'I am back. Let's meet tonight after work.' There was some silver lining to the dark, cloudy day.

I was sitting in my room with Jay next to me, sipping cool beer, and laughing at Jay's funny pronunciation of Hindi words. He was massaging my shoulders with his powerful hands, his touch causing ripples of excitement to flow through my body. He bent down slightly, and brushing his lips against my ears he whispered, 'Can I have a word with you?'

As usual, I answered flirtingly, 'As long as the word is not SEX.'

'Well, I was thinking along different lines,' he said.

But this time, his voice was not a soft murmur. It had a gruff, husky tenor that startled me out of my daydream. Deep was standing next to my seat, with an amused smile, his eyes playfully mocking me.

'I am sorry. Um. . . I was just thinking about this crossword clue. Aaa ... three letter word for *a fun way to exercise*,' I blabbered incoherently.

'Run?' he suggested, with a quizzical look on his face.

'Yeah . . . quite possible. Both sex and run will fit,' I mumbled sheepishly, checking out Madhuri and Sanjeev one by one, from the corner of my eye. They were seemingly busy working. Not that I could feel any more humiliated, if they had heard me. I was already feeling an amalgamation of confusion, anger and helplessness. Adding embarrassment to the mixture could hardly make it worse.

'Let's go some place else and talk,' he suggested.

Gathering a notebook and a pen, I quietly followed him. On my way, I felt curious glances from the people I passed. I tried to walk cautiously so that no one could hear the clicking of my heels or the thumping of my heart. Finally, we found an unoccupied meeting room at the far end of the floor, next to the stairs. The room had a soothing blue paint and glazed glass windows so no one from outside could see what was happening inside. It was a relief to be hidden from peering eyes, and I felt my formerly frazzled self beginning to calm down amidst the meditative nest of blue walls.

'Is there a problem?' he asked, looking straight into my eyes.

His nonchalant expression was a total contrast to the addled state of my mind.

'Should there be?' I sassed back, forgetting momentarily that he was my manager.

'You are fiddling with the ring in your finger,' he pointed out.

Boy! He was a keen observer and quite perceptive too. Usually I had to tell Jay when I was upset with him or I could sulk for weeks in vain. Yet, I was not ready to tell Deep how awkward I was feeling. 'I thought you wanted to talk about something,' I reminded him.

He looked earnestly into my eyes, and said, 'Your biodata was the first-ever arranged marriage proposal that came my way.'

I noticed that he was blushing.

'I would be lying if I say it didn't give me a high,' he added.

This time I pulled my eyebrows together, forming two vertical wrinkles on my forehead, to show my scepticism. I mean, all the girls at office seemed willing to rub shoulders with him.

'I have an elder brother who is still unmarried, so my marriage is not on my parents' radar yet,' he explained.

I was still not convinced, but I appreciated his forthrightness, and let him continue.

'I did share your biodata with friends around, but I had no way of knowing that six months down the lane you would be joining the same company, leave aside the same group.'

Now he was lying through his teeth. 'The HR manager said you actually selected me for this special project,' I accused him.

'Well yes, but that was only two days ago. I felt that your user interface skills would be an asset to our new initiative. Plus the project has high visibility and scope for immense impact. I thought it would be a good exposure for you.'

I honestly thought he was making a mistake here. 'My resume doesn't mention any UI ability,' I warned.

'Let us say, I can often see what others can't,' he replied conceitedly.

Over-confidence is a widely prevalent virus among the breed that is IITian. I saw no point in arguing with him. If he had indeed misjudged my capabilities, it was entirely his problem.

'If you have any issues working with me, I can talk to Kavita and we can have your group changed,' he offered.

Issues, my foot! Like I had any feelings for him! I already had a handsome hunk for a boyfriend. I shrugged my shoulders and shook my head to convey my indifference.

Was it my imagination or did I actually see relief sweep across his face? Feeling an inexplicable urge to put him down, I demanded why he didn't call me earlier to warn me, for he knew that I would be joining his group two days in advance.

'I didn't want to influence your decision by telling you that I work here,' he paused as if to think, and then added, 'Besides, I assumed you may know.'

Know? How so? Was he now implying that I had joined iTrot because I knew he worked here and I wanted to get close to him? 'Last I knew I didn't have the ability to get into other people's minds,' I retorted. Only Professor Snape could do legilimency even in the magical world.

'Your dad knows where I work,' he stated simply, and left the room, leaving me speechless.

I stared at the framed picture hung on the opposite wall, aptly reflecting my state of mind. There was a picture of a female customer, her hair flying back, eyes wide with disbelief and mouth hanging open in shock. At the bottom was a quote from Michael Stipe that said, 'Sometimes I'm confused by what I think is really obvious. But what I think is really obvious obviously isn't obvious . . .'

DEFERRAL OR DENIAL

'Indian girl, studying abroad, lying naked with her ABCD boyfriend . . .' narrated Tanu di, like she was reading a book's back cover.

'Jay is an "Indian Mom, American Dad, Completely American" and I was not naked. I was painting him nude,' I corrected.

'Indian girl, studying abroad, painting her naked IMADCA boyfriend, receives an arranged marriage proposal from her parents. She returns to India to convince her parents, takes up a job in the meanwhile, but GUESS WHAT?' She gave a dramatic pause for impact and then continued, 'The guy whom her parents want her to marry is her NEW BOSS and he has a nipple-hardening voice.'

'I never said that,' I protested, but Tanu di argued back that stories need exaggeration.

'Is this destiny or her dad's conspiracy?' Another pause. 'What will happen next?' A longer pause. 'Will she marry her sexy-sounding boss or will she go back to her gorgeous-looking guy?' she said, concluding the blurb with romantic suspense to keep her listeners on tenterhooks.

I felt transported to my childhood, when I had once listened to a multi-part story on Vividh Bharti, sitting in front of a cooler with Tanu di on a blazing summer day.

'Not a bad plot for a chicklet,' I admitted, 'but, I thought you were writing a book on "Girls at IIT"?'

'There could always be a side-track like a senior who is studying abroad,' she giggled.

'Oh! Please, Di. Stop making fun now!' I begged.

She immediately put on a straight face, pretended to be serious, and asked, 'So, did you figure out why you were chosen for the customer service training?'

'Holy moly!' I sighed as I exhaled slowly. I had not had the chance to ask Deep about wait-the-talk lesson yet, but there was something else that had just caught my attention. 'Do you really think it could all be Dad's ploy?'

Tanu di narrowed her eyes in speculation and she started tapping her fingers on her lips. She looked like a lawyer focusing on the details of a case. I could tell that she was seriously racking her brains now.

'Chachaji did shortlist the companies for you,' she said, thinking out loud, 'and he also knew where Deep works.'

'Pa also proposed that I call Deep for advice,' I pitched in.

'Yes, but it was your decision to join iTrot,' Tanu di countered.

Unable to nail Dad, and in a desperate attempt to hold someone responsible, I took a shot in the dark. 'Is it plausible that Deep knew the Internet company I was considering and purposely gave me the arguments that would make me choose iTrot?' I surmised.

'He might as well have caused the Lehman Brothers bankruptcy and engineered your homecoming,' said Tanu di, bursting into mad cackles of laughter at the ludicrousness of my proposition.

Not only was I implying that Deep had a thing going for me, but also that he knew me well enough to be able to manipulate me. I saw the farfetchedness of my idea and let it drop.

Looking at my crestfallen face, Di advised that rather than debating on how I got into the soup, we should now focus on swimming out of it.

'Sidelining Deep should be easy. Accept his group change offer,' she recommended.

I acceded that initially I had declined the offer to switch the team because of my ego, but now my reasons were purely social. I had since learned that the special project would give me access to FB which was otherwise banned within office.

'Oh, yeah! Updating one's Facebook status every few hours is a must, for periodic release of tension,' she said seriously. 'I usually go to the loo or take a walk, but that is so twentieth century.'

I could sense the sarcasm in her voice. 'Besides, FB updates are the fastest, easiest, most non-intrusive and completely eco-friendly way of letting the world know that you are alive.' Tanu di joshed at my reasons and broke out into a loud guffaw.

I couldn't help but crack up at her humour. After we were both done indulging in comic relief, and exercising our facial muscles, she suggested an alternate way out of the Deep trouble.

'Tell him you aren't interested in a relationship as yet. This will not be a NO and yet be a NO.'

Trust Di to come up with an euphemist way of rejecting guys. Years of practice had made her perfect in this field. It had always worked, except for her very first time, when it had backfired. She was all of twenty-one then, inexperienced and naive in matters of the heart. She had asked him to wait, give her more time, but interpreting her deferral to be a denial, he had moved on. For a split second, I saw the longing in her eyes for that half of hers that she had lost, before she veiled her sorrow behind her vivacious smile.

'Having swam across the Deep end, let's now deal with the Dad end,' she said. 'If not for *Dostana*, Chachaji, Chachiji would have surely taken the bait on homosexuality, but the current situation demands a change in strategy. I think you now ought to let them know about Jay,' Tanu di advocated.

'Ha, ha, ha . . .' I tittered. I might as well go to the war front in Israel or walk the streets naked. Better still, I could also confess to stealing from my mom's purse in grade four, losing Dad's collection of old songs, cutting my mom's wedding saree to make my doll's lehenga and flushing down Dad's car key so he wouldn't go to the office.

I couldn't imagine confronting my parents or conceding that I had betrayed their trust. The thought of not being their ideal daughter was frighteningly unthinkable.

'Do you think they don't already know? All kids make mistakes and all parents know and forgive.'

'Fine, then what's the need for me to say anything.' I knew I was behaving like a stubborn four-year-old who was being asked to apologize to her friend for hitting her.

'For one, you are not a child any more. Kids hide the truth because they can't draw the fine line between joking and lying. Moreover, parents deserve to know the truth,' Di explained.

I was still unconvinced, although the guilt was weighing heavily on my conscience now. Was I unsure of myself and Jay or was I just being careful not to hurt my parents? 'I will tell them when the time is right.'

'I said that to someone many years ago and lost him forever,' she spoke softly, with a pensive look on her face. 'When you are scared to do something, the right time never comes . . . until it is too late.'

I was well aware of whom she was referring to. Among all my cousins, Tanu di was the one I was closest to. We were both alone. I had no siblings and her siblings had moved on in life. We could talk about anything inside or outside an Oxford dictionary. YouTube and tube8, girl talk and boy talk, ditching and getting ditched, there was nothing we didn't share, but this was the first time she had admitted regretting her decision to choose her ambition over her love.

'Let's look up Champ on Facebook,' I suggested, in an effort to bring back the lovely, dimpled smile on her face. 'Who knows, he might be available? Perhaps his wife divorced him because they were sexually incompatible?'

At the very mention of Champ's name, a faint smile spread on her face. 'I already did. He is not on FB,' she said, twirling her plait in a self-conscious, shy manner.

I was surprised that Tanu di had checked FB. Facebook for Tanu di was like wearing make-up for my mom. You do it because others are doing it, although natural beauty was the best.

'I found him on LinkedIn though. He works as an independent consultant in the bay area, advising start-ups on survival.' One moment her face had the bright, blushing grin of a bride and the next instant she wore a far-off wistful look of a widow.

'Why are you frittering your life away for a guy who couldn't keep his pants up for a couple of more years, and went about knocking boots with your best friend's sister,' I counselled, our roles reversed.

'I do go out on dates with other men,' she defended herself.

'Oh! But you are still a . . . I mean you can't possibly die a . . .' I hesitated as her cook came into the room with a courier slip.

'Stop worrying about me. I am quite an independent, self-satisfied woman.' She laughed impishly, her eyes sparkling with amusement.

It was good to see her back to her cheerful, lively self. She may have denied her heart from loving another man, but she surely hadn't denied herself the pleasures of life. The best part about Tanu di was that like the shock-absorbers of a Sumo van she would spring back soon enough after a bumpy stretch.

The cook came back, this time carrying a beautiful bouquet of carefully handpicked red roses. *'Didi, it ij yoer berday?'* inquired the cook in her broken English.

Tanu di said no and the girl retreated to the kitchen.

'*Didi, hu haj shent theej rojes?*' I asked, mimicking the cook, but she was lost reading the little note that came with the flowers.

I will be in town this Friday,
Would love to catch up with you.
If you consider me worthy of company,
I will book a table for two.
—VC

Nostalgia overtook her. I could tell from the youthful exuberance that lit up her face that she was back to her IIT days, reliving a fond memory, possibly of another rose bouquet from Champ.

'Who the fuck is this VC?' I demanded, pulling her out of her reverie, and accusing her of not keeping me updated with her dating diary.

'Vikram Chhacchi.'

'Hmm ... unusual surname! Is he good-looking?'

'Totally! John Abraham types! Tall, lean, handsome, with a smile that makes you go weak in the knees,' she sighed deeply. Coming from Tanu di, it sounded a little fishy. Like most people of her generation, she was more a believer of internal beauty, the body being just a wrapper to the soul. I, of course, liked my presents attractively wrapped.

'You are not ... er ... pulling my leg?' I asked suspiciously.

She shook her head gently and smiled back.

It was hard to imagine that a handsome catch like him was still available. 'I hope he is not married,' I said anxiously. The last thing Tanu di deserved was to become the *'woh'* in a *'pati–patni'* combo.

'Separated,' she replied, arranging the roses carefully in a vase, 'and he drives a Mercedes.'

'Cool! So he is sexy, smart, separated and swanky,' I summarized, getting all excited now.

'Where did you meet him? When were you planning on telling me? Have you guys kissed yet? Do you think . . .' I barraged her with questions.

'Slow down, honey,' she said. 'Your generation is so tuned to one-way dialogues. What happened to the good old you-ask-a-question-and-wait-for-the-reply way of communicating?'

Sometimes Tanu di could get really touchy about her pre-cybersex, snail mail era.

'So, where did you have a face-to-face, two ways, tête-à-tête with him?' I asked again, and waited for her to answer.

She smiled at my deliberate rephrasing of the question.

'I met him during the final round of interviews for the *Businessworld* Hottest Young Entrepreneurs' award in Mumbai, last month. He was one of the panellists.'

'You reached the finals? When will the results come? Did he ask you out in Mumbai?' I was back to my rapid-fire mode.

'You are reading too much into these roses,' she said, bursting the tiny balloons of hope rising in my chest. 'He wants to meet me just for business.'

'How can you be so sure?' I asked. Last I knew, red roses were more a symbol of passion than profession.

She gave me a smug look, and thrust the latest edition of *Businessworld* in my hands.

Tanu di, in a green *tussar* silk suit, was smiling from the cover page. The headline read 'IIT girl proves to be the hottest entrepreneur'. I let out a little shriek, my mouth agape in amazement. I quickly turned to the relevant page and skimmed through the article. It described how she had taken refuge in a corporate job when her first start-up ApproxAir succumbed to the millennium dotcom crash. However, the entrepreneur in her had roared back again and before long she was nurturing her second venture on employability skilling for students. The business now had partnerships with several hundred educational institutes across the nation and had job-trained over one lakh graduates.

I tried to close my mouth, but I couldn't. This was Tanu Di's dream come true. Recognition at the pan-India level was a testimony to her sheer hard work and undying spirit. Today was certainly a day of surprises.

Seeing my shocked expression, she clarified, 'I meant to tell you earlier, but we got Dee-p-stracted.'

I held her in a tight hug as if to let the good news sink in, and screamed excitedly, 'Oh my God, Di. I am so happy for you!'

I saw two drops of tears moisten her eyes, trace their path down her cheeks and disappear. I reckoned one was a tear of joy at having achieved the goal she had set out to conquer a decade ago, when she had refused a Berkeley scholarship and forayed into the real world. The other was a tear of regret at having lost her love in pursuit of her goal.

'So now you see why VC wants to meet me?'

She was the hottest entrepreneur and he was a hot venture capitalist. There was only one possible reason I could fathom. I shook my head in a no.

'Honey, he is a venture capitalist. He wants to invest in my company,' she explained slowly, like she was teaching addition to a first grader.

'Along with a share in your company, you could also offer him a share in your life?' I suggested doing simple logic. Her dream had come true at the hands of this good-looking guy. To my romantic mind, this seemed like the work of Cupid.

'Never put all your eggs in one basket. I prefer not to mix business with pleasure.'

'Why not pursue pleasure with this hunk and find another nerdy investor for your business?' I tried to make her see my POV.

'I don't want to kiss the goose that lays golden eggs,' she declared with finality.

There was not much point in arguing with a Taurean. If Tanu di had made up her mind to wear business attire for VC's dinner, then he was not going to see her cleavage.

My phone burped. There was a message from Mom saying that they were waiting for me for dinner. In the process of reviving Tanu di's love life, I had forgotten about the impending danger to mine. With butterflies, as large as bats, fluttering in my stomach, I trudged back home to face my parents. I couldn't confront Jay about my desire to eat junk, my parents about my passion for painting, even the mail man about dropping junk in my mailbox. How was I going to tell them that I loved Jay and didn't want to marry Deep?

LOVE VS ARRANGED

'Don't listen to Tanu di. Check him out,' encouraged Neha, rejecting Tanu di's idea of Deep-freezing.

I was on my way back home, when I received her call, in response to the SOS SMS I had sent out earlier from office.

'Go on a test drive. You can always say no later if you don't like what you see,' she wisecracked. I could almost see her shrugging her shoulders in her no-big-deal attitude.

'You forget I already have my heart set on an American make,' I quipped.

'Most Americans keep two cars, one for every day, routine life and the other for an occasional fun drive,' she remarked flippantly.

I wondered if Jay was having fun with another girl on the side, while he was formally dating me. The image of Denise snogging Jay flashed before my eyes and I contemplated flirting with Deep just to make Jay jealous. Immediately, Sharmaji's 'bhabhiji' started reverberating in my head, attacking me from all directions, and I dropped the idea.

Unsure, I geared the conversation away from me. 'What are you riding these days?' I asked her playfully.

'A brand new model,' she said, moaning with excitement. 'What power-packed performance! You got to experience it to believe it.'

'Maybe you can bring him along when you visit Delhi next,' I remarked casually.

'You mean like a threesome,' Neha laughed naughtily. 'I have never tried that before!'

What could I expect when it was Neha I was talking to? Of course, Neha could never be serious about boys. They were like toys to her. I smiled at my own slip-up. 'Shift, Del—forget what I said,' I said emphatically.

Neha and I were bosom buddies ever since my first day at play school when she had shared her favourite cookie with me. Two little girls with little ponies bouncing on either side of our heads, we had experienced our first crush together on this cute little boy who would go all red whenever we smiled at him. We even made it together to the junior school student council—she, as the house captain, because she liked to wear the special badge, and me, as the vice-captain, to make my parents proud. A few years later, we tasted our first kiss, on the very same day, with the very same guy. But now, while I thought I would kiss a guy only after falling in love, she would make love to a guy and then decide if he was worth kissing.

'How many more cars will you try before taking the final call?' I demanded.

'Only a couple of hundred more,' she giggled.

'Isn't this exhausting—emotionally and physically?' I was confused by her life's philosophy and concerned for her well-being.

'It might be exhausting but it is also exhilarating.'

Agreed that Neha was lucky to share the burden of parental expectations with her siblings. Also, I agree that you should explore unchartered territories. But that was not all there was to life. You also had to find that one person whom you loved and who loved you back unconditionally. That one soul with whom you wanted to share all your joys. The one face whose smile will brighten your mornings and soothe your pain.' You do need to settle down some time!' I insisted.

'Watch out, Suhaani! You are beginning to sound like your mom,' she warned. 'What happened to the adventurous girl I knew?'

I stopped in my tracks, ruffled my hair, crumpled my kurta, applied some lipstick and reconsidered dating Deep. I couldn't become prim and proper like Mom.

Sensing my discomfort, Neha offered an alternate approach. 'Look, if you don't want to play around with this boss of yours, it's your choice. Why do you want to tell your parents about Jay yet?'

Now she was talking my language. I, too, was unconvinced about going public with Jay. While I wanted to be honest with my parents, I knew telling them about Jay would only fast track their groom hunt.

'Well, Tanu di thought I should . . .'

'Listen, I gotta go,' she said cutting me short. 'But here is something for you to mull over: to seek love, sex and marriage in one specimen is like looking for a car with luxury, speed and mileage. They don't make those models any more. At best you can find a Toyota—it's the world's bestselling car and a compromise on all three parameters.'

Always the idealist, I was about to disagree, when I heard someone whisper her name.

'My car needs oiling. I left the engine on,' she offered by way of explanation, already sounding distant, before the line went dead.

Holy smokes! She was not alone. All the while she was talking to me, her new model was thumping and vibrating beside her!

My heart pined for Jay. Despite the video calls, long-distance romance sucked. You could see his face and hear him say he misses you, but you couldn't smell his aftershave, savour his kiss or feel his warmth. I wondered if Jay could deliver good mileage under rough conditions on a long journey, or was he only fit to be a sports car.

What if Neha was correct and no single sperm source has it all?

Unconsciously, I found myself evaluating all the available blokes I knew on the LSM metrics. Damn! This was tough. How does one ever know if he is THE one for you? I wished there was a website where I could answer twenty simple questions and compare guys. ScoreYourGuy.com! Anyone looking for a SENSEX insensitive business idea to solve an unsolvable problem and mint money?

I pressed the button for the ninth floor. The elevator started moving up. I was still undecided about how to handle Deep and Jay. On one extreme was Tanu di, an epitome of commitment, who was faithful to her first love even in absentia. On the other end of the spectrum was Neha, a serial switcher, who was continuously off to new pastures. Tonight, in my mind, they were waging a tug of war. Should I keep my options open for a while and not shut the door on Deep or should I hit the DEAL button and reveal Jay? With Neha and Tanu di at loggerheads in my head, I reached home.

'I feel terrible,' I heard Pa say, as I entered the dining room.

'Stop blaming yourself. You did nothing. It was meant to be,' Mom consoled Dad, as she laid out the spread of his favourite dishes on the table.

'You always say so,' disagreed my father. 'Even when you conceived Suhaani immediately after marriage, you said the same,' he reminded her.

'I mean, you did do something, but the outcome was unintentional,' she said coyly, blushing at the memory.

'Still, just like that time, I forgot to forewarn,' insisted my dad, refusing to be redeemed of whatever wrong he had done.

'How were you supposed to know what will happen?' demanded Mom. 'Yesterday I planted a crop before going to bed, and by the time I woke up it had ripened and gone to waste.' It was hard to say whether she was blaming or comforting Dad.

'It must have been such a shock,' continued Dad.

'Everything happens for a reason,' said Mom, serving him an extra helping of butter.

Dad was on an unusual guilt trip, and Mom was as always contradicting him. Preoccupied with my private screening of the Neha vs Tanu di match, I didn't even attempt to comprehend their bickering. I quickly washed my hands and attacked the food.

'You think we can let the status quo continue?' Dad was asking Mom.

'For now, at least,' she concurred, and then as if she realized that she had to compulsorily refute Dad, she added, 'Although, something will need to be done once Suhaani is married.'

My ears perked up when I heard marriage and my name being mentioned in the same sentence.

'What's going on?' I asked, disoriented. If this day got any more confusing, then I would have to implicate the cab driver for attacking me with the Confundus Charm in the morning.

'I am so sorry, beta,' said Dad, visibly disturbed.

If he was apologizing for not telling me that Deep works at iTrot. com, it was a little late. I had done the spreadsheet analysis again on my way back home, this time assigning a negative weight to iTrot for Deep's presence. The dotcom had still emerged a winner. 'It's fine, Pa,' I said, and was glad to see the worry wrinkles smoothen on his forehead. Instantly, I knew what I was going to do. Nothing. Don't they say that if a little lie makes everyone happy, then it's okay to see some happy faces around. Dad seemed upset about getting me in a fix so I reasoned that he wouldn't bring up Deep for a while, and Jay could wait in the closet a little longer.

'You don't understand the complications,' Mom was telling me.

What complications? Had I missed something? I replayed my parents' conversation in my head. Conceived, forewarn, shock, complications ... No way! 'Mom, you are not pregnant again? Are you?' I squealed in delight.

'Pregnant!' Mom screamed out loud, her face horror-stricken like I had charged her with adultery, while Dad burst into a fit of uncontrollable laughter.

Unable to handle the joke, and not too pleased with Dad's chuckles, Mom decided to get straight to the point. 'Deepak's mother called. She informed us that you are reporting to Deepak and she wanted us to persuade you to change your project.'

It was my turn to get horrified. I was not even engaged to this guy and his mother was already trying to rule my life. Mom was right. I didn't understand the complications. I closed my eyes and took a few deep breaths.

'Well, his parents said office arguments could . . .' Dad tried to explain but stopped midway. He could tell from the controlled pace of my breathing that I was about to blow my top off. 'Don't worry. We assured them that today's kids are mature enough,' he retracted.

'And Deepak agrees with us,' Mom butted in from the kitchen, as she stacked the dirty dishes in the sink. 'He told his parents that he was not going to let his personal life undermine office work.'

Fuck Deepak! I thought to myself. He was only trying to save his own ass. He must need a resource for the project desperately.

'Oh! But you must change the project if not the company, once a formal ceremony happens,' advised Mom, misconstruing my silence for consent. She was back in the dining room cleaning the table.

'I agree with your mom,' nodded my father. 'After marriage, you will be the real boss. It will be tough for the poor guy to pretend otherwise at work.' Dad was back to his usual, jovial self.

It seemed like a whole family drama had transpired while I had been away at Tanu di's. My present had been debated and my future nailed, without the need to ask for my opinion. This is why I hated arranged marriages.

And Neha thought I could fool around with Deep. She had no clue about arranged affairs. There was no question of flirting with a prospective suitor. Here, I had barely joined the same office project and the two sets of parents were already advising me on its pros and cons. In all likelihood, mamas and mausis had been informed, and taujis and buas were being called. In a few hours, all living leaves of our combined family trees would be actively deliberating upon what I should wear to office, how I should sit in the cubicle, when I should say yes and when, if at all, say no, and how I should tactfully resist any physical advances from my to-be. If I was to listen to Neha and as much as accidentally brush my hands against this to-be, they will perhaps declare me married, grab the MakeMyTrip homemoon special deal, and start applying for our kids' play school admissions. Neha was wrong and Tanu di was right. I had to put an end to this story immediately.

'I am not getting married to Deepak,' I said firmly, without raising my voice. If there was one thing I had learned from Ekta Kapoor's protagonists, it was to stay calm during these emotional arguments.

'C'mon. Don't be ridiculous. You can always find another job,' reprimanded Mom. She had finished wiping the table spotlessly clean and was now reviving her laptop. 'It's so hard to enter all the criteria in those forms and narrow down a suitable prospect. Naukri.com has more job listings in IT than the number of twenty something, vegetarian, baniya guys on BharatMatrimony.com.' My mom might discredit the Internet for spoiling the current generation, but she was certainly tech-savvy.

'I am not getting married to any guy, for the time being,' I asserted, still keeping my volume down.

Mom's eyes widened and her jaw dropped in shock. Pa also looked concerned.

'You want to stay unmarried for life,' scolded Mom, her voice shaking with angst and anger.

'It must be that Tanu's *lagai bujhai*,' she cursed. 'I told you so many times that sinister spinster niece of yours was a bad influence on Suhaani.' Mom was now directing her fury towards Dad.

I had more or less planned that I would not tell them about Jay yet, but I couldn't let Tanu di get it in the neck.

'Tanu di has nothing to do with my decision,' I denied. This time I was a bit louder. 'If at all, I have only learned to appreciate the value of true love from Di,' I said, expunging Tanu di's name.

'Then what's the problem, beta?' asked Dad politely. Himself fond of Tanu di, he was not too happy with this unexpected blame game either.

'I want . . .' I paused briefly to find the right words, when Dad interrupted excitedly.

'Let me guess.' His eyes glowed like he had gone back in time to when I was a little girl and we were playing the *guess what I want* game.

'You want a Barbie dream wedding set with Stacie and Todd.'

'Dad! You already gifted it to me on my seventh birthday,' I reminded, my anger dissipating at the fond memory.

'We are talking about her wedding, not her doll's wedding,' corrected Mom. She was busy planting strawberry crops on her farm, but her ears were clued in on our conversation.

'You want to go on an all girls' tour to Europe,' guessed Dad, taking inspiration from Bollywood movie plots.

'That would indeed be fabulous, but . . .'

'Is it your art? Do you want to take time off and paint for a while?'

I would have loved to take time off and paint forever, but I knew what Mom was about to say.

'The store is already stacked with her canvasses. I get a bigger house if she gets to paint more,' demanded Mom.

'Okay, I think I have nailed it this time,' claimed Dad, banging his fist on the table. 'You want to live by yourself for a year. Like in your own apartment, independently.'

'Why are you putting these rubbish ideas in her mind,' complained Mom, clearly not in favour of unnecessary frivolity or freedom. She had even perfected the land usage on her farm so that every unit of her farm was profitable.

'Don't tell me it's the new age stereotype *I want to be known as someone before getting known as someone's wife*,' remarked Dad.

When I shook my head, he raised his hands in despair to gesture that he had given up.

I rejoiced at my victory, almost forgetting that I now needed to tell him what I wanted. 'I want to marry a guy I love rather than love a guy I marry,' I said, twisting the truth slightly and keeping Jay under wraps.

'Ah, that is a cliché I could never have guessed,' said Dad, waving his hand dismissively.

'Can we get a little more serious here if the father and daughter have finished playing games?' Mom never liked being left out, but she never liked being party to the fun either.

'In our generation, the saying was "it's better to marry a person who loves you than to marry a person you love",' jabbed Dad. It was hard to get him to be serious.

'What does this instant generation know about love?' attacked Mom. 'Food, loans, messages, henna and sex—everything is instant today. This generation needs arranged marriages or else their marriages will result in instant divorces,' she said, expounding her philosophy.

'Arranged marriages are a by-product of the discriminating caste system,' I protested, on behalf of the entire instant generation. 'They were designed to prevent children from marrying outside the community.'

'And love marriages are a by-product of authors' and movie producers' plots,' replied Mom.

I looked at my mom, blew at a ringlet falling carelessly on my face and gave her a 'what do you know about love' dare.

'I remember my first one,' she said, taking the challenge. 'I was only sixteen and his voice had just begun to crack,' she reminisced.

I had never heard Mom talk about her youth before. It was hard to imagine Mom as anything but a mom.

'He would come to his balcony every evening and watch me pick the line-dried laundry. Soon, we moved houses and before I knew, I was skipping classes to have tea with this other guy in college.'

'You never told me about this college fling,' accused Pa.

'It was irrelevant,' justified Mom. 'Out of sight, out of mind, and that's exactly my point. A fling at this age is nothing but a fleeting fluttering of our fragile hearts.'

'Ma, I am not seventeen, and I can tell the difference between a passing crush and true love,' I voiced my defence.

'You love what you see, but it all changes once you are married.' Ma tried to explain how people put up their best foot forward during the courtship period, but it's the worst that we need to be able to live with for a relationship to survive.

Like I don't watch movies and serials. Of course, everyone knows that stuff. 'How do you guarantee that the same doesn't happen in an arranged marriage?' I argued.

'No one can guarantee that a marriage will succeed, but it's about managing risks,' she preached. 'In arranged marriages, since the family and cultural background matches, the chances of incompatibility are minimized.'

Bull shit, I thought to myself. 'Who goes for arranged marriages these days Mom? It is so archaic. Totally pre-Internet.'

'You mean, just because you were born with an email id, you get to choose the email id you will marry?'

Well, technically, I got my email id on my thirteenth birthday, but I knew what she meant. Finally she was seeing my POV. I told you, my mom was smart.

'You will love Deepak,' Dad chimed in confidently, in the hope to strike truce. 'I told you, you were never very receptive to new foods at first.'

I could have let the love vs arranged argument drop, but the mention of Deepak's name left me with no choice. Dad had to know the truth now. The entire truth.

'I love someone else, Pa,' I mumbled, facing the ground. I could not look him in the eye for I had told him otherwise just a few weeks back.

'How can that be? Your FB relationship status says you are single,' intervened Mom, but Dad motioned her to keep quiet. Normally this wouldn't shut Mom up, but her raspberry crops chose the same moment to mature, thus diverting her attention into harvesting them before they went waste.

Dad held my face in his hands and gazed in my eyes as if searching for something. He was not angry with me. He was not hurt either. He was full of love. I wondered if he was experiencing the 'Father of the Bride' moment. 'Oh! But I still get to hug you, and kiss you, and camp out with you, and sleep with you . . . I mean when he is travelling for work,' Dad sought reassurance like an insecure little child who was being left behind at home while his parents went out to party.

I hugged him tight and started planting quick kisses on his cheek. He showered the kisses back, both of us trying to outkiss each other. 'I win the race,' I declared after a while.

'Who is this lucky young gentleman who is going to compete in the kissing race with me?' he asked.

This wasn't going so bad. I felt my confidence rising. 'He is Jayant,' I replied. 'Jayant Guy.' I completed.

'I have never heard that surname,' doubted Ma. 'Which

community does he belong to? Is it a modernized variant of that movie producer Subhash Ghai's surname?'

This was the part I dreaded the most. 'It's G.U.Y as in 'the cable Guy' or 'the Guy next door,' I spelled out. 'He is half Indian, half American,' I elaborated.

I knew Mom would blow her fuse any time now, but it was Pa's approval that mattered to me. I waited for his reaction, his shock, an outrage or even humour at having chosen a funny surname, but all I got was a pin-drop silence. I looked into his eyes and all his dreams for me flashed past me. The dream of playing cricket with his future son-in-law, of creating a family music band, flying kites on 15 August, of finding the fourth bridge partner. Even if Jay learned the technicality and complexity of cricket, and Hindi music, and kite flying, and card playing, he would still be 13,000+ kilometres away in the US. One by one, I saw his dreams die.

'Are you sure this Jay Guy loves you?' Mom asked thoughtfully, a little concerned. She had closed the laptop momentarily and was trying to deal with this sudden twist in the tale.

I nodded.

'Does his mom observe Karwa Chauth?' she inquired. She had figured that if his surname was American, it must be his mom who was Indian.

I told her that his mom was from the south and perhaps not very religious. In any case, I was not a big fan of fasting myself.

'Would he be willing to compromise and settle in India or make the effort to learn the *Hanuman Chalisa*?' she interrogated further.

'I don't know, Ma,' I replied, toying with my ring, slipping it in and out of my finger.

Somewhere in the back of my mind, I knew the answers.

'Everyone falls in love. Falling in love is easy and falling out even easier,' she said, looking compassionately at me. 'What is hard is staying in love. It requires understanding, trust, time and effort.'

I knew what she was saying made sense and it made me uncomfortable.

'What's wrong with Deepak?' she asked, not the one to give up easily.

'For one, he is an IITian,' I wanted to scream, but there was no way I could tell them why I disliked IITians or what had transpired between me and the IIT guy I was dating four years ago.

'Other than the fact that I don't love him, I don't think Indian boys, especially IITians, have the open-mindedness that I am looking for in my life partner,' I reasoned, without getting into the specific details for my bias.

'I was so looking forward to playing with Pappu and Munni,' said my mom in a resigned tone, bearing a forlorn expression. 'I had even planted mango trees for them on my farm.'

'Who are Pappu and Munni?' I couldn't help but ask.

'Your twins, of course,' she replied and retreated to farming. She had just received some mystery eggs notification from her neighbours which were hatching into white, black, brown and gold chickens.

Dad, who had not uttered a word since I mentioned Guy, also rose to leave. 'Every girl eventually becomes a replica of her mom as she ages,' he said. 'Make sure Jayant likes your mom,' he faked a smile and left.

Me become like Mom. Impossible! We were the complete opposite of each other. Where I saw joy, she saw work. Where I liked clutter, she liked order. While I loved experimenting with my looks, she had never even applied nail polish so as to preserve the natural shine of her nails. Her life was a series of well-planned tasks, completed according to schedule, and mine was like an array of open projects, loose ends and unfinished business. Sometimes I felt she was missing out on all the fun on life as it was meant to be lived.

Can a person change so drastically as they grow old? I shivered at the possibility. There was no way I could see myself tending to farms and livestock with the dedication and sincerity my mom exhibited. It must be the doing of all the expectations from an arranged marriage. Good thing I was not going down that path.

I went up to my room, took out a fresh canvas and started painting. My Facebook status read, 'Love vs arranged marriage. What would you choose?'

INDIANIZING JAY

'Come online,' I whispered.

'I will come whichever way you want me to, baby,' he whispered back dreamily.

Involuntarily, a faint smile spread across my lips. Moments later we were connected via the messiah of LDRs—Skype. 'Where were you? I have been pinging you for an hour,' I complained.

'The laptop must be on mute,' murmured Jay.

I saw him rub his eyes and clear the eye dirt. It looked like he had just woken up from deep sleep. His hair was all ruffled and his voice still crummy. Thankfully I couldn't smell the morning breath on video chat.

'Twenty calls!' he cried out, suddenly coming to his senses, as he found his laptop screen flooded with my missed call alerts.

I immediately lowered the speaker volume on my laptop, hoping that Mom hadn't heard him. I knew she was in the next room, perhaps sending return gifts to her farm neighbours.

'Twenty calls are redundant, don't you think? I would see a missed call message even after one call,' said Jay with a grin which soon morphed into a big yawn.

Of course I knew that, but try telling that to a girl who has just gone live about her affair to her parents. She needs to know that her boyfriend loves her more than anything else in the world. Even more than his sleep. And she needs to know it immediately. 'Isn't 1 p.m. on Monday afternoon an unusual time to be sleeping?' I countered.

'Had a fucking submission,' he explained lazily. He then gave me a teasing look and added sulkily, 'Had to stay up the whole night all by myself.'

Just hearing him talk dirty turned me on. I craved to feel the warmth of his hands around me, the tingling of his fingers on my shoulders, and the wetness of his lips on mine. 'I miss you so much,' I said in a low voice, staring longingly at his lips. Oh! But something looked amiss. 'Why do your lips look swollen like you have been to a marathon snogging session?' I asked half jokingly.

He blinked, rubbed his eyes, and then blinked again. 'I was getting kissed by a hot girl in a bikini,' smiled Jay blissfully and stretched his hands up in the air.

I didn't ask him if the girl in the bikini was me, for I knew that even though it was just a dream I would be green-eyed if the girl kissing him wasn't me. Yet the swollen lips were real. I narrowed my eyes suspiciously and searched for lipstick marks on his neck and ears.

'Hon, stop being jealous like I am hiding a blonde in the closet,' chided Jay lightheartedly. 'It's just a bad case of sun burn.'

I had never seen anyone get anything enlarged due to sun exposure before. Why would actresses spend millions on increasing their cup size if sun bathing is all that they needed to do? 'Americans keep a second car for random recreation.' Neha's words echoed in my mind. What if Jay really was cruising a blonde race car? OMG! What if the blonde car was Denise and she was there with him right now. After all, I could only see the upper half of his body on the laptop camera.

He must have seen the doubt and shock splashed on my face. 'You gotta trust me, honey,' he said casually, but I could see from the way he rolled his eyes that he was beginning to get irritated.

Trust. Oh yeah. Mom had said that trust was important to keep the love alive, but then she hadn't met Denise. In her time, the typical other girl in TV serials was a cunning, conspiring, rich and spoiled saree-clad bitch, who would bad mouth about the heroine to the hero's mom. Sometimes she will poison the hero's mind with a photograph of the heroine hugging another man. Rarely, she would let her pallu drop and reveal her biggies imprisoned tightly in her blouse, but she would never actually get down to engaging sexually with the hero. Denise, however, was more like the sultry, skinny dipping Bipasha Basu in *Jism*. Her sex quotient could weaken any guy's defence and make him undo his pants. Anyway, I paused the Jay–Denise movie playing in my mind and assured Jay as well as myself that I trusted him. 'It's just that I have had a most bizarre first day at work,' I explained.

'Do you want to talk about it?' he asked, with typical American courtesy.

Normally, I would have wanted Jay to express concern and ask *'kya hua'* like an Indian boyfriend. I was not very fond of the formality Americans displayed even with their immediate family, but for now it suited me fine. There was no need for him to know about Deep yet. I had more important things on my mind. I informed him that I had told my parents about us.

'Good! Now you can have your nude artwork back. It is sending out wrong signals to the neighbourhood boys,' he chuckled.

I looked at his naked form and felt immense pleasure. It was a fine piece of art, but however much I wanted to, there was no way I could hang it in my bedroom without my mom going berserk.

'Besides, it needs a rework,' added Jay, showing off his guns.

I could tell from the increased size of his biceps that he was spending a lot more time at the gym.

'Are you mad?' I rebuffed in hushed tones. 'This is no time for a joke.'

'Why? Did your parents say no?' he asked thoughtfully.

'No. They never say no to me,' I whined.

He gave me a confused look as if to question what I was fussing about.

'Well, they didn't say a yes either.'

'Cool.'

'Cool, meaning?'

'Cool meaning cool as in fine, okay, no big deal,' he said in an unaffected, poised manner, just like he had reacted to my lay-off news.

'It is a big deal for me, Jay,' I explained earnestly.

'How does it matter what your parents think? It's your life right?'

'It does matter, Jay. To me their happiness matters.'

'I thought only size mattered,' he ribbed me.

There he was doing it again. Regarding this whole issue as a non-issue.

Seeing that I was not amused by his joke, he argued, 'How do parents get to choose who fucks their daughter for the rest of her life?'

Well, I hadn't seen arranged marriages in this light before and I must admit that I found it funny. I told him he had a valid point, but he would need a lot more than American humour in order to win my parents' hearts.

'At your service, ma'am,' he replied dutifully, giving me a mock salute.

Consciously, I stopped myself from imagining the possible services he could offer and got down to work. I had prepared a comprehensive list of things he needed to learn in the next few months.

'Do you know how to fly a kite?' I began with the simple one first.

'Used to be a kite-boarding expert back in high school,' he boasted.

I quickly googled kite boarding and found that it is an adventure sport in which the rider harnesses kite power to propel himself across the water on a surfboard. Flying a multi-line steerable power kite is not quite the same as manually launching a diamond-shaped paper in the air and then keeping it there by constantly tugging on a glass-coated string.

'Pa is more into Khaled Hosseini type kite flying,' I said, discreetly.

'Maybe I could get your dad excited about power kites instead,' he suggested.

Why not? I thought to myself. Dad was open to learning new things and given Jay's passion for sport, I felt confident that Jay and Dad would find a common ground somewhere.

'Hope your old man is not into that game of balls where men keep coming in and going out for hours together,' said Jay. 'I prefer quicker action,' he sniggered.

I knew what Jay meant by quicker action. It was interesting how everything acquired a sexual connotation when I was with Jay. Even cricket!

Cricket could get boring at times, though I quite liked the IPL T20 format, but Dad watched each minute of every match like he was some Zoya factor and the match's outcome depended on his presence in front of the TV.

'Tee hee hee ...' I giggled nervously. 'Naah, Pa is not into bat–ball,' I lied. 'I mean, except when India plays against Pakistan.' One step at a time, I told myself. We will deal with cricket later.

'How about playing cards?' I asked, moving on to the next item on my check list.

'My favourite is blackjack. I once won a hundred bucks on a blackjack table in Vegas,' he claimed. 'I could teach you some gambling tricks.'

I thought he was being really sweet and supportive. 'You need to do a lot of card counting in blackjack. I am sure you would love bridge too.' I crossed my fingers in hope.

'Are you outta your mind?' he remarked. 'I was like four pegs down when I won that game. It was sheer luck.'

I guess I was pinning my hopes too high or maybe crossing my fingers too tightly. When it came to recreation, Jay had a distinct preference for physical activities as opposed to mental exercises. I mean, I could never even get him down to help me with those naughty crosswords that test your SQ (Sex Quotient). I somehow persuaded him to register on an online gaming site and look up bridge rules. We were doing okay so far, but I knew the next one was a hard nut to crack.

'Remember, I told you about the music evenings my dad hosts at our home. It would be nice if you could sing a number or two,' I spoke cautiously. Jay had made it clear to me, very early on, that he would not be enrolling for any Indian language courses.

'You mean like lyrics . . . no way ... you gotta be kidding,' dismissed Jay. 'I can barely say your name correctly after more than a year of dating. In any case, you know I prefer techno music, without words.'

I could never understand how someone can appreciate music without words. I mean words are everything to me. They added the meaning and soul to a song. A song without words was like a life without love, a flower without fragrance, a book without humour and a shampoo without froth.

'It's only a couple of songs,' I insisted and argued that even a first grader can memorize school poems he doesn't understand.

'American schooling doesn't focus on rote learning,' he joshed, and then moving away from the topic, he asked, 'Doesn't your mom have any expectations from me?'

I wasn't planning on going through my mom's groom selection criteria, at least not yet, but just to see Jay's reaction, I casually mentioned that she wanted him to know the *Hanuman Chalisa*.

'What the fuck is Hen-O-Men Char...Lisa?' he asked, laughing out loud. 'Oh wait! I think I know. CharLisa is a moniker for Charlie Sheen and his former girlfriend Lisa, right!' Jay blabbered excitedly. 'I fuckin love that sitcom *Two and a Half Men*.'

I gave him a blank stare.

'Half-A-Men CharLisa? That's cool! Did your mom coin that term?' he inquired fervently, caught up in his own excitement. The only other things that got him so thrilled were sex toys and sports. 'I think your mom and I will really hit it off,' he concluded, with a self-satisfied grin.

Usually I found his Americanization of Indian words hilarious, but today I felt offended. Unknowingly he was mispronouncing and mocking a prayer. His reaction was expected. It was my reaction that I found surprising. It was not like I was very religious. I was, in fact, rather confused about my belief in God. It was one of the many things that I had put off for future contemplation. Yet, I failed to understand why I was feeling uncomfortable. 'Hun—oo—maan Chaa—lee—saa,' I broke it down phonetically on the chat window. 'And it's a prayer for one of our gods,' I explained sombrely.

Jay closed his eyes regretfully for a moment and then sighed, 'Jesus fucking Christ!'

We both looked uneasily at each other for a few seconds. After a brief, awkward silence, in which we both realized that something had gone amiss, he spoke, 'You can't fall in love with a guy and then change him. What if you find that you don't love the changed person?' His voice was soft and clear and his expression glum.

I waited for him to break into a smile like he always did after pulling my leg. Meanwhile, the iPod in my mind smartly selected the song tagged with keywords love, change, person. I heard the song *Ladki kyun na jaane kyun . . . tumhe badalne ko paas wo aati hai . . .* from *Hum Tum* playing in my back office.

'Listen, Suhaani, I am Jay. Don't try to make a Jayant out of me,' he said, a cold tone creeping into his voice.

I had never seen him so humourless before and it made me fidgety. Clearly, I will never do well in Professor McGonagall's class, for instead of Jay-ant, I had transformed him into Jay-no-joke.

'I am sorry, Jay,' I said anxiously. 'It's just that these things will help my parents relate to you.' I said, justifying my failed attempt at the transfiguration charm.

'All that I care for is whether you can relate to me or not.'

'Of course I do.'

'Good, coz I am not a fuckin Shh-R-hook Can from *DDLJ*,' he said, refusing point blank to make any effort to become a suitable boy.

He had been very supportive a while ago. At least I had thought that he was taking the whole kite and bridge stuff sportingly. Why had he suddenly gone berserk? Did he think I was playing a prank until he goofed up with CharLisa, when it finally dawned on him that I was being serious?

'You got to at least try,' I urged.

'Why don't you try turkey for Thanksgiving dinner first? I promise I will do whatever you want after that.'

I didn't look for any hints of playful teasing in his response this time. His eyes were solemn and his face rigid. 'I can't. You know I am eggetarian.'

'And I am an American, not an Indian.'

I thought he was overreacting. I was willing to eat my eggs scrambled rather than sunny side up if that's what his mom liked or drink black tea because his dad preferred it that way, but eating a bird? Urgh. Vegetarianism was like a lifestyle, a habit acquired over a series of years. Telling vegetarians to eat meat was like asking them to change their religion. I had only asked Jay to Google a prayer, not convert to Hinduism.

I saw him get up from his bed and shift his laptop to the dining table. He went about taking some stuff out from the fridge and heating it in the microwave.

Feeling stuffy and uncomfortable, I also got up and opened the window to let in the fresh cool air. On my way back, I bit into a half-eaten Snickers lying on my bedside table. The bitter-sweet taste of the chocolate-covered roasted peanuts mixed with the sweet aroma of caramel helped me relax. I came back to the laptop and found Jay chewing a crisp, clean cherry tomato from his frozen salad meal. Watching his sexy lips nibble on the fully ripened, juicy fruit made me horny. I looked away from his face and saw tiny snowflakes dance past the window pane behind him.

'I miss the snow,' I said softly, remembering how I would rush out into the open, when it began to snow and lift my face up to catch the fresh snowflakes on my tongue.

'I miss hugging you,' he whispered, and flung his arms wide open as if to hug me from within the laptop.

The simple, sweet gesture dissipated the tension hanging in the air. Chocolate and tomato, the natural aphrodisiacs, had done their job.

'You have had a long day,' he spoke kindly. 'Let's sleep over it and then see how you feel. I am sure you will realize that you would rather have me be your playboy than your parents' perfect boy.'

Seeing the naughty, suggestive smile back on his face, an immense feeling of relief swept over me. I noticed a tear fall from my eyes as I smiled a big wide smile back at him.

'SoHoney, SoHoney!' He sang my name, making it rhyme with 'Johnny Johnny'.

'Yes Jay.'

'Eating chocolate?'

'No Jay.'

'Telling a lie?'

'No Jay.'

'Open your shirt.'

'Why? Why? Why?' I asked in surprise. Last time I heard a toddler recite the poem, he was only opening his mouth not his shirt.

'I wanna see where you are storing all the junk that you have been gorging,' he demanded, his eyes dancing with mischief.

'What's there to see,' I said, smiling sheepishly.

'The size, the bulge and the curve,' he said grinning.

'They are like everyone else's.'

'Would you rather I peek at others?' he questioned, narrowing his eyes teasingly.

'No!' I screamed. Denise didn't have much flesh to look at, yet I didn't want to take any chances.

'C'mon, even your Indian saree doesn't hide the curves,' he said persuasively.

I opened two buttons and slowly parted my shirt.

'Jesus fucking Christ,' he hollered, staring at the stomach tyres bulging over my jeans.

I hid them back and quickly pushed away the empty Snickers wrapper outside the range of the camera lens.

'One hour of cardio exercise, five days a week. No sweets and no fried food,' advised Jay. 'Also, tell your mom to use olive oil for cooking.'

'I hate exercising and I love sweets,' I yawped.

'Try dancing,' he suggested, and then realizing that he was getting late, he quickly put on his snow jacket, said bye, and left for his class.

I turned on my iPod and sauntered out to the balcony adjoining my room. I could see parts of the Gurgaon metro line being constructed from my balcony. Further down was NH 8, lined with interestingly shaped office buildings that were defining Gurgaon's new character. A little on the right was MG Road or the Malls of Gurgaon road. No new construction was happening now as the builders were beginning to feel the aftermath of the US real-estate crash. As I stood leaning against the railing, I felt a sudden gush of wind hit my face and cover it with a layer of fine dust. The pure, soft snowflakes caressing Jay's window were a stark contrast to the tiny dust particles that slapped mine. Yet a snowflake was nothing but water vapour condensed around a speck of dust. Was our love strong enough to overpower the cultural differences and keep our hearts bound together?

THE ART OF REJECTION

'Rejecting a guy could be tough,' I thought to myself, adjusting the height of my ergonomic chair, as the computer booted to life.

I mean, especially if you made the advances that led him to believe that you love him. It's almost like taking your best friend out for a treat at Pizza Hut and then telling her that her thighs were bulging out or her under arms sagging, and that she better stick to having salad. The idea is the same. You don't intend to hurt. You do it for the other person's benefit. Although, such benevolent deeds are rarely perceived as kind gestures.

I remember my first time. It was a week before the Class X board exams and I was finding the build up to the D-day quite stressful. This tall, lean guy had moved into the neighbourhood two years ago and we were both part of a study group. I knew he had a soft corner for me, but I didn't feel particularly attracted to him. I was actually besotted with another tall, fair guy in the group. One day we were studying together in his house and I felt this sudden primal desire to kiss. I knew it was wrong for I felt nothing for him, but overwhelmed by the teenage hormones raging through my body, I went ahead and snogged him. Gosh! I feel disgusted now to even think about it. The next day, we went out for a walk in the evening and he sang this romantic number from *Bobby*: *'Mujhe kuch kahna hai, pahle tum, pahle tum'*. The moment of passion was, however, gone and I found myself unable to reciprocate his feelings. I felt suffocated and uncomfortable, but I kept quiet. One day before the exams, when his repeated phone calls began to become a nuisance and I could no longer fake feelings, I confessed that it was all a big mistake. It was painful while the showdown lasted, but I was glad I had done the right thing. Next day, when the teacher called me up after the exam and asked if I knew anything about this guy who hadn't shown up for exam, I discovered to my horror that he had jumped off the building. Luckily, he stayed on the first floor and there was a pile of cut grass below his balcony, so he escaped with a few scratches and a minor fracture in his hand. I have never eaten so much comfort food in my life as I ate that week. Thankfully, he didn't take any names and my parents overlooked my consumption of ten litres of ice cream as board exam stress.

It took me a couple of more accidents to learn that the key to short and sweet, guiltless rejection was in providing the rejected person with a reason. It was not good enough to tell him that he was this extraordinarily handsome, nice and considerate, simply too-good-for-me fellow and actually it was I who didn't deserve him. We all know that 'it's not you, it's me' means exactly the reverse. There has to be a more solid rationale like 'it is too soon after my last break-up', or that 'I can't risk our friendship if this doesn't work out', or even 'you are from Mars and I am from Venus'. Once I had even employed my mom's sensitivity to caste difference as an excuse, though I would suggest you reserve that for the more serious break-ups.

By the way if you think this is all crap and I am fussing over nothing, I suggest you check out rejectionhotline.com. It is a social service to the million of heart-breakers who suffer like me and a fine example of business in the yet unexplored field of PPO, Personal Process Outsourcing. I actually used their hotline to get rid of this get-a-clue challenged desi, back in Michigan. When he called the fake number I had given him, he was humorously, though not so subtly, informed of my non-interest.

Basically rejection is a highly skilled art, very similar to faking an orgasm. You need to pretend a little, maybe even moan a few times, so as to massage the man's ego but be tactful enough not to bare yourself completely and reveal the ugly truth. I know you think I am lucky. I agree. I haven't had to reject men often. Maybe not exactly single digit, but certainly very few, especially compared to poor Neha. She has had to indulge in binge eating every now and then in guilt, both for rejecting and faking.

However, none of my previous showdown experiences seemed applicable in Deep's case. I barely knew him and this was a setting done by our parents. Neha would vouch that fade away works well in the hardly-any-commitment sort of relationship that I had with Deep. Reduced texting, emails, infrequent phone calls and no hanging out. The guy eventually gets the hint. But I guess it's rather tricky to ignore your boss. Tanu di's signature deferral seemed perfect for Deep, but it was not personalized enough. Besides, this was my only chance at rejecting an IITian and I wanted to do it with style, without hurting my FB access. If only I could buy myself a BlackBerry, I would have been spared all this work. But I knew Dad had blown all his savings on the South Africa vacation and Mom would probably want to buy one for herself first so she could nurture her crops while in school.

Feeling the bra band digging into my skin, I shifted in my chair, re-adjusted the height and loosened the chair back a bit more. Then leaning down on the chair in a relaxed, beach position, I surveyed my surroundings. A couple of late-nighters were dozing off on their desks, but the bulk of the employees who availed the office cab facility were not due for another half an hour. I had reached office early today and was glad to get this quiet alone time to engage in some serious soul-searching.

'How to reject your boss,' I had barely typed in my google search bar, when I heard his sultry, seductive voice.

'Coffee?'

Wearing a green striped shirt and khaki trousers, adjusting the lock of black hair that had fallen on his forehead, he stood at the cubicle entrance.

I stood up before he could sneak a peek at my monitor, discreetly closed the browser window with my left hand and followed him out.

There was no one else in the coffee room. 'Should I deliver the blow now?' I pondered silently.

He poured a cup of coffee, handed it to me and started pouring another for himself.

No, morning was not a good time for rejections, I decided. We had just started the day and he could take the frustration out on me. End of the day was bad too as it wouldn't give me any time to gauge his reaction. Some time during the latter half should be good, I concluded. That way I will also get time to work on my strategy during the first half.

'Deep in thought?' he asked, looking intently into my eyes, as he took a sip of his cappuccino.

Oh! yeah, he was very much in my thoughts right now, but I was not going to let him fool me with a double entendre this time. 'I was just thinking about the cleanest way to handle deep . . .' I said, pausing intentionally in order to out-pun him.

He gave me the confused, quizzical look I so wanted to see on his face.

'. . . linking in YouTube videos,' I added, sounding victorious, and broke into a broad smile. Score evened.

'I find the best way to solve a puzzle is by playing with it. So I would suggest you play around with this deep . . . linking,' he quipped quickly.

Before I could think of something clever to say, a short, puny, young guy, with curly hair came rushing in, looking for Deep. He seemed glad to have found him alone. Well almost, if you ignore me.

'Yaar, Deep, I have a major KS issue. You got to help me, man!' He sounded desperate.

'I am all ears,' chuckled Deep lazily.

The hassled guy looked at me uncertainly, stepped closer to Deep, and then continued, 'I am not able to get through, man. It's driving me crazy.'

'These people you are trying to get through, you know them well?' inquired Deep. I was standing behind Deep, so I couldn't see his expression, but I was certain I heard a stifled, mischievous laugh.

The curly hair seemed embarrassed and shocked at Deep's question. 'It's only one person actually,' he said hesitantly, and again looked at me to check if I was listening. I pretended to be lost in the emptiness of my coffee mug so that he could focus on describing his problem. 'And I have only known her for a month,' he whispered awkwardly.

Deep put a reassuring arm around his frail shoulders and smiled. 'There are 3Cs to successful KS,' enumerated Deep confidently, 'Cooperation, commitment and caution.'

I was pretty sure that the third 'C' for Knowledge Sharing was culture and not caution, but it seemed prudent not to interfere in a private conversation.

The guy still looked as lost as before. I thought he needed training in communication.

'Oil the machinery well, buddy,' advised Deep and then explained something in his ears.

The young man's face suddenly brightened into a smile.

'Have faith in your abilities. Girls need time to open up,' remarked Deep, with a wink and a naughty smile.

The guy, now beaming with confidence, thanked him profusely and left.

It was weird for a start-up to have knowledge sharing issues. I told Deep that if there were KS issues in the company, we should bring them to HR's attention. After all, it required proper processes to be put in place.

'Kavita has her own KS problems to deal with, but I will let her know your concern,' dismissed Deep casually.

'But KS is a key foundation for the survival of any institution,' I insisted. I was unhappy that he was not taking my feedback seriously.

'I couldn't agree more with you,' he said, smiling knowingly, before he headed out.

Much to my embarrassment, I was to learn later that the KS advice that Deep was dispensing was regarding the Knowledge of Sex, aka, *Kama Sutra*, and not Knowledge Sharing as I misunderstood it to be. And the third 'C' he referred to as caution was actually condom!

WHOSE LINE IS IT ANYWAY?

Thank God it was Friday! The whole week had gone by with me being trapped in a training room, learning the ABCs of iTrot's business, with other newbies. I didn't get any clean one-on-one timeslot with Deep and I didn't feel like dumping him over email. Finally, after a long four-day wait, I was going to carry out my well-planned rejection. I knew by the way I felt today that this was going to be different. The usual twinges of conscience were subdued under unexpected fireworks of excitement. It's not every day that you get an upper hand over an IITian. For a brief moment, my mind went back to the summer I had spent with that schmuck IIT intern and how it had hurt. Well, tonight was my golden chance to get back at their creed.

I looked at my reflection in the office bathroom mirror one last time and I liked what I saw, especially the hint of the cleavage that peeped out from my strapless, floral dress. Short and seductive, I had carefully chosen the outfit for today's mission. With my hair twirled in a high, puffy top knot to accentuate my bare shoulders and my tummy tucked in to hide the bulge, I sashayed into the office lobby, ready to go for the kill. I noticed Deep give me a long, appreciative once over as I reached close to his car parked in the driveway. He gave me a soft, playful smile and I smiled back flirtingly. As he was about to open the front door of the car for me, I walked past him and hopped onto Sanjeev's bike.

'*Chalen*, Sharmaji,' I said to a startled Sanjeev, who was staring wistfully at Madhuri, now heading towards Deep's car.

Sharmaji kicked hard on the pedal and the bike immediately roared to life. '*Vaise*, by choosing you in his team, Deep bhai has proven that he is a true professional,' said Sanjeev, shouting above the loud roar of his bike.

'How so?' I asked intrigued.

'I would never be able to work with my would-be wife in the same team,' he admitted. 'It's hard to hide feelings, especially for guys, you know,' he explained shyly.

From the corner of my eye, I saw Deep observing us as he got into his car. Deliberately I bent closer to Sanjeev, and holding my breath to avoid inhaling the strong coconut smell from his hair, I whispered, 'That way, every girl who is of marriageable age could be a would-be wife. You must be having a lot of problems, Sharmaji,' I teased.

'You are very naughty, bhabhiji,' he said blushing, the colour of his cheeks blending in with the colour of the tilak on his forehead.

Moments later, Deep's car whizzed by at top speed. Someone was feeling hurt. Touché.

Another half an hour later, after having navigated through dust clouds that seemed to have found a permanent home in Gurgaon, I had a layer of sand on my skin that made it feel itchy. I felt nauseated by the obnoxious smell of exhaust fumes, Sanjeev's sweaty armpits and his hair oil, and I was cursing my decision. By the time we reached the restaurant, we found that the others were comfortably seated and already chugging cool beer. I took the empty seat next to Madhuri, bang opposite Deep, and allowed myself to soak in the refreshing lemon grass scent. While Sanjeev humorously narrated the incident of being caught by a traffic policeman, for taking a pillion-rider without a helmet, and then escaping without a ticket or a bribe, I stole a quick glance at Deep. He was dressed in a collared, lime yellow tee and faded blue Levi's jeans. This was the first time I had seen him in casual Friday attire and he looked surprisingly charming. Good for me, I thought. It would have been tough to lure someone I found unattractive. Tonight, as per the plan, I was going to tease him, flirt with him and tempt him, and then in the end I would leave him high and dry. A perfect KLPD (Khadi land pe danda) in an IITian's lingo.

Madhuri caught me eyeballing Deep and smiled approvingly. *'Who's the hottest girl in the world, my desi girl, my desi girl,'* she hummed in my ears.

I returned the compliment by saying that her boot-cut jeans suited her curvy hips perfectly.

Becoming conscious of her pear shaped body, she said wished she had an hour-glass figure like mine.

I suggested that she wear boat-neck tops with slight embroidery to widen her shoulders and balance her small bust with her full thighs.

Amid the discussion on female body types, I gingerly raised my eyes to check on Deep and catch his attention, but he was engrossed in the office gossip that dominated the conversation around the table. One guy was cribbing about how the salary hike had reduced this year from 100 per cent to 50 per cent while the another guy felt a desperate need to increase the estrogen levels among the staff. It was basically an outing of Deep's close associates from office, all of whom had been with iTrot for at least two years, barring Madhuri and me. First week at work, I had little to complain about other than the boring training, the flat taste of instant coffee and the scarcity of pencil sharpeners. I was playing the role of a passive listener, when I heard Kavita complain about her insensitive, manipulative MIL.

'Doesn't your husband say anything?' I asked, genuinely surprised.

'I guess the poor husband finds himself stretched between his wife and his mom,' empathized Vikas, who was sitting beside me. I had seen him earlier on the first floor a couple of times, but I had never met him before. I noticed that he had a handsome face though the hair on his sides was beginning to thin.

'Indian men,' I said sarcastically, 'They grow up enough to have sex with their wives but never to stop sucking up to their moms.'

Kavita burst out laughing loudly at the crass humour of my comment, but Vikas stared at me like I had slapped him on his cheek. Mission accomplished. I had everyone's attention, including Deep's.

Deep bent forward towards me, pursed his lips in amusement and narrowed his eyebrows suspiciously. 'I am sure you won't stop loving your dad just because you are married and have a different surname,' he challenged.

'You're right, I won't,' I said, staring directly into Deep's eyes, 'and neither will I change my surname,' I declared confidently. 'But I will not have an arranged marriage either. I will marry a guy I love and know well. A guy who will stand by my decisions.' I took a swig of my beer and ran my tongue sensuously across my lips.

'I agree with you, Suhaaniji,' supported Sanjeev. He then took out the picture of a slim girl holding a *matka*, her short choli revealing her fair navel, but her face covered under the *chunri*. 'This is what my parents sent me and expect me to say yes to. Now how can I marry an unknown face, Ji.' He then looked hopefully in Madhuri's direction and said, 'I will also marry a girl I love and know well, Ji.'

I watched Madhuri, waiting for a reaction, but she sat inert, expressionless, studiously ignoring Sanjeev. My girl–guy relationship sense told me something was wrong, but I soon got distracted.

'Arranged or love,' Deep was saying, 'I have no problem whichever way a girl wants to enter my life ... or me.'

His sassy remark was received with a huge applause, especially from the boys.

'I actually had a love marriage,' divulged Kavita to my utter shock. 'Knew the guy for three years, or so I thought.'

'I also fucking thought I understood the girl I married,' retorted Vikas, defending the male of the species.

I caught Vikas smirking at Kavita and felt a strange tension in the air between them. It was weird that both Kavita and Vikas were dissatisfied with their love marriages. If three years wasn't enough to get to know a person, how does one ever figure out whom to marry? Were my ideas about love marriage all wet?

'Understand a woman? Are you kidding me?' Deep chortled mockingly. 'Try complimenting your girlfriend and she will tell you to stop lying. Now try keeping quiet and you will be accused of not noticing her or taking her for granted,' joshed Deep. I smiled inwardly at having similarly blamed Jay for being glib and non-observant on several different occasions.

'Women are too complicated for our simple minds, yaar,' Deep summarized and there was a general chorus of agreement from the men around.

'No, they are not,' I asserted, keeping my eyes locked with Deep's. 'It's just that a woman doesn't only want that ONE thing men are after.'

'You are right. The woman doesn't want one thing alone,' said Deep smugly. 'She wants to be loved, to be respected, to be desired, to be needed, to be listened to, to be trusted, to be praised, and she also wants that ONE thing.'

Despite myself, I found his wickedly honest sense of humour in complete alignment with my spicy single-track mind. I couldn't stand the fake people who thought of sex and said behenji. Grinning, I bit my lower lip suggestively.

Sanjeev, who was fascinated by Deep's knowledge of the fairer sex, asked him if he had ever been in love.

> *'Arz kiya hai,'* said Deep in his deep throaty voice.
> *ye na thee hamaaree qismat ke wisaal-e-yaar hota* [wisaal-e-yaar = meeting with a lover]
> *agar aur jeete rehte yahee intezaar hota*
> *tere waade par jiye ham to ye jaan jhoot jaanaa*
> *ke khushee se mar na jaate agar eitabaar hota* [eitabaar = trust]
> *koee mere dil se pooche tere teer-e-neemkash ko* [teer-e-neemkash = half-piercing arrow]
> *ye khalish kahaan se hotee jo jigar ke paar hota* [khalish = pain]

In a flash, my mind went back to the cool summer nights I had spent with Tanu di. Lying on her terrace, gazing at the starlit sky, and listening to Ghalib playing on her old, rusty tape-recorder. Deep paused in between to explain how the poet would have died with happiness if he had confidence in her love and how he felt the pain of the arrow half piercing his heart, that is, his unfulfilled love. But I who knew the verses by heart, needed no interpretation. Everyone watched Deep weave the magic of words as he melodiously sang Ghalib's soul-stirring ghazal. My mind, however, was searching for a suitable riposte. Lost in a dreamy trance, experiencing the joys and the sorrows as penned by the famous poet, the words traipsed through the memories and fell out of my mouth. Before I knew it, I was reciting a couplet from the another of Ghalib's famous ghazals.

> *mohabbat mein naheen hai farq jeene aur marne kaa*
> *usee ko dekh kar jeete hain jis kaafir pe dam nikle*

'There is no difference between living and dying when you are in love,' I deciphered for the others. Startled at my esoteric music taste, they looked at me with undisguised curiosity, like I was a book with an erotic cover which contained the *shloka*s from the Bhagavad Gita. Impressed by my unexpected rejoinder and making no attempt to hide his surprise, Deep took on the challenge and responded, 'Just because I smile in front of my lover, she thinks that I am all right.'

unke dekhe se jo aa jaati hai munh par raunaq
wo samajhate hain ki bimaar kaa haal achchha hai

I immediately knew what I was going to say. 'Don't ask how I am doing in your absence; see how you are faring in front of me.'

mat pooch ke kya haal hai mera tere peeche ?
too dekh ke kya rang hai tera mere aage ?

The witty repartee continued and people looked from my face to his and back again in awe. It was no longer about putting the other person down. The initial rivalry had transformed into a *jugal-bandi* where we were both experiencing the intangible joy of sharing a common passion. I felt like a part of our souls was connected and somehow this connection was nourishing my existence. It was satisfying my innate social desire to be understood by others, to be told that I was right, and to be assured that I was not alone. It made me feel more complete and alive.

Two hours later, I stood in the washroom, looking at myself in the mirror for the second time during the evening. Ignoring the strange glow adorning my face, I applied a coat of light pink lip gloss and re-adjusted the underwire of my seamless, push-up bra to snugly hold my assets in place. I undid my bun and left my hair open, letting it ripple down loosely over my shoulder skin. The evening had been fabulous and I had thoroughly relished the Mediterranean hummus, falafels, the cool beer and the playful banter. Coming out of the washroom, I was glad to find Deep standing all by himself in the foyer. I was hoping to be able to get a ride back alone with him. It was hot outside and he had opened his t-shirt buttons, revealing a manly tuft of chest hair. What? No, I was not leching at him. Just because I find black body hair more macho than light brown doesn't mean I wanted to get all over him.

'Where are the others?' I asked off-handedly.

'Couldn't take any more Ghalib,' chuckled Deep, as we headed to the car park.

'You have a good voice,' I commended, in what clearly was an understatement of the year.

'You have good taste,' he responded with a complacent smile.

We walked along the pavement in silence, till we reached the car. There was a palpable restlessness and excitement in the air.

'You play any games?' I asked, just to keep the dialogue going.

'Games as in mind games like chess and bridge? Used to be in the hostel team back in college days. Haven't played since though.'

Ting tong! A bell rang in my mind at the mention of bridge. 'Marry him. He can be your fourth bridge partner,' whispered someone from the back of my mind. I quickly shushed my back office and told it to mind its own business.

'I meant more like physical games,' I said out loud.

He smiled at me dubiously.

Realizing the alternate implication of my statement, I soon corrected myself, 'Physical, not as in getting physical, but as in involving exercise ... er ... I mean the other kind of exercise ...' Shucks! Why was I blabbering?

'I play squash regularly. How about you?'

'Not an expert at any, but used to play a bit of tennis earlier,' I said indifferently.

'What about your imagination?' he asked curiously.

'What about it?' I asked cautiously. I had a pretty wild and sexy imagination. I wondered what he was referring to.

'I thought painters preferred playing with their imagination.'

I gave him a startled look. How did he know that I paint?

'Your biodata,' he replied to my unspoken question.

'Oh! Yeah!' I said dismissively, marvelling at how deeply he had read every word in my biodata and how serious he was about getting married to me. I knew I should just dump him and get it over with, but somehow I couldn't bring myself to do it. We chatted about this and that, mostly inconsequential stuff, both of us wanting but neither of us broaching the marriage issue weighing on our minds. He had turned on the car's air conditioning but I was still feeling hot. I saw a tiny drop of sweat lazily trickle down his temple. I bent forward slightly and stretched out my hand to switch on the FM in the car radio. The black hair of his forearm accidentally brushed against my smooth skin as he changed gears. We both felt a spark of electricity run through our bodies in that brief contact. I sat back upright in my seat once again and looked outside the window. The glowing neon signs lighting the front of the multinational business offices, gave a playful, pub-like personality to the national highway. We would be reaching the MG Road any time now and my home was only minutes away from there. I had to do it now. Crossing my fingers, hoping that he wouldn't take the rejection badly and screw my first job, I turned my attention back on the job at hand.

Deep had begun to hum along the chirpy old number '*Hum aapki aankhon mein is dil ko basa dein to . . .*'

'His voice is so titillating that it makes me want to make love to the notes as they come out of his mouth,' babbled my back office. I reminded it that we were here to bewitch Deep, not to captivate ourselves. I had barely hushed the voices within when my libido kicked into top gear. My nipples became hard and tingling, craving for a touch. What was wrong with me? I never had problems being friends with guys or in breaking hearts in the past. Why was I behaving like a novice on a first date, about to experience her first kiss?

I looked at his lips as they parted rhythmically, producing the rich, mellow sound that I wanted to get drowned in. I had to find a way to shut him up if I wanted to accomplish the task I had set out for. Suddenly a light bulb lit up in my head. It was again my back office's brilliant idea. I was going to kiss him so that he couldn't speak and then tell him that I couldn't possible marry him because we were not kiss-compatible. It would not only soften the blow but also minimize any after-effects. At that moment, in my libido-infused mind, the plan seemed flawless.

We were waiting at a traffic light very close to my house now. I looked up at the stop time metre. I had forty seconds.

'Deep,' I uttered softly, gazing into his eyes.

He turned and looked at me. His fingers were drumming the steering wheel and his lips still chanting the magic love spell.

I tucked a stray piece of hair behind my ear. Thirty seconds. On your marks, get, set, go. I lapped my tongue over my lips, wetting them slightly, flung my body forward and landed my lips on his. He resisted the invasion for a brief second, after which he kissed back with the skill of an expert. He slid his tongue gingerly on my lips to warm them and then gently blew air on them, the hot and cold kiss causing an explosion in my body. I caught hold of his lower lip, sucking on it and flicking my tongue at it alternatively. Slowly, our lips parted and our tongues passionately and ruthlessly explored each other's mouth, while the rest of the world melted away.

The signal became green and a bike zoomed past us blaring its horn and snorting at us. Regaining composure, I unlocked our lips and pulled away. Deep steered the car aside and parked in the service lane.

'I have to say something,' he mumbled a bit awkwardly. He had the regretful look of a class teacher who was about to inform his students about the cancellation of a school picnic.

'There is no need for you to be sorry,' I said condescendingly, to spare him the guilt.

'Well, I am not,' he said serenely. 'Not about what just happened. I kind of like the strawberry flavour,' he added with a chuckle.

'It wasn't strawberry. It was a Bobbi Brown raspberry shimmer lip gloss,' I corrected, having forgotten why I was here today.

'Raspberry, hmm? Are you sure?'

'You bet! I applied it,' I said irately, ferreting for the tube in my purse.

'Maybe I ought to taste it again?'

'You might ...' I closed my eyes and lifted my chin to offer him my lips, when I heard him say, 'Just kidding.'

I retreated, abashed at my own impulsiveness. After a few minutes of sitting in silent meditation, I looked up. Deep was blankly staring ahead out of the car windshield. When he spoke, his voice was kind and soft.

'I wanted to apologize on my mom's behalf for calling your parents,' he said. 'She had always wanted a daughter and she got a bit carried away on learning about our working together in the same group.'

I could tell by the disconcerted look on his face that there was more to come. I waited patiently.

'I have been meaning to tell you this whole week, but you have been busy with the training,' he said, in a build up to whatever it was that he was preparing to say.

'You are the one who sent me to those boring information dump sessions,' I complained.

He gestured his assent and then exhaling a deep breath, he said, 'Look, I just wanted to let you know that I am not interested in getting married at the moment.'

'Whose line is it anyway?' I asked, to make doubly sure, for it seemed like our roles had mistakenly been swapped and he was reading out my lines.

'I think mine,' he answered, wearing a decidedly comical expression.

'Are you rejecting me?' I asked dubiously.

'No. I am simply saying that right now is not a good time for me,' he explained.

'That's deferral. A polite and yet insensitive type of rejection,' I argued.

'Look, I am sorry, but please don't take this thing personally,' he said in a humble tone. 'I am actually planning on pursuing my MBA. I have even got the interview calls from A, B and C.'

'You suck!' I hollered.

'I beg your pardon?'

'You have no idea how to reject someone gracefully.'

'Oh! So now I need to take a crash course in the art of rejection from you.'

'You could, for future use, but in any case you can't do this to me.'

'I can't do what to you?' he demanded with a curious mixture of mockery and relish.

'Well, you can't reject me because I was going to reject you.' There, I had said it finally.

'I don't know why, but it appeared more like you were kissing me,' said Deep.

'Yeah, but that was all part of a plan,' I said defensively.

'Wow! I don't mind such seductive rejections,' smiled Deep, as he started the car.

Feeling frustrated and irritated, I stepped out of the car and slammed the door. The apartment complex was only a crossing away. I decided to walk it back. I was so looking forward to rejecting Deep. Worse than getting rejected is getting rejected by the guy you were planning to reject. The only other time I had been dumped, it was by an asshole who I had been dating for a couple of months during my summer training in Bangalore. After a passionate kiss, as we lay in each other's arms in the office cubicle, he had proudly informed me that he was getting married in a month's time to a girl of his parent's choice. At least she would be first hand, he had laughed. I remember feeling humiliated and cheated. He had been an IITian too. I should have known better. My horoscope doesn't gel with that brand.

Lost in my indignation and nursing my hurt pride, I failed to notice the car that waited outside on the road till I safely reached my building.

GIRLS' NIGHT OUT

'Why are you dressed so inconspicuously, like there is going to be a Shiv Sena attack in this pub tonight?' Tanu di asked with a hassled look on her face. 'I went past this table five times before realizing it was you.'

Feeling low after my unceremonial dumping the night before, I was not in the mood to attract attention yet. Tanu di was herself draped in a chic A-line, long, brown skirt and a beige tank-top.

'It's the same dress that you gifted me last year,' I said defensively.

'Since when did you start wearing a salwaar-kameez to a pub, honey? Is everything all right?'

'A most unexpected thing happened to me last night,' I said sombrely.

'You didn't get robbed or anything, right?' Tanu di was suddenly alarmed.

'Hell, no!' I replied immediately.

'Cool then,' she said sinking into the comfortable cushions on the leather couch at the lounge bar. 'I have something unusual to tell you as well,' said Tanu di, giving me a mysterious smile.

Just then, Neha rushed in, wearing a bright red halter with the latest bummer pants.

'You are not going to believe this!' she called out excitedly.

I was still thinking about Tanu di's news. What could possibly happen in a thirty-five-year-old, single woman entrepreneur's life? Another business deal or an award? At best she could meet a forty-something divorcé who takes her out for an exquisite dinner. If he then happens to ask her 'Your place or mine?' I very well knew what Tanu di would say. 'You go to yours, I will go to mine.'

Neha, of course, must be referring to a new hot guy she made out with. Nothing these two had to say could beat getting rejected by the guy you were planning to reject.

'The person with the least shocking news pays the bill,' I declared promptly. Might as well get some free drinks out of my tragedy, I decided, already feeling better.

'Deal,' said Neha, banging the table with her fist, while Tanu di calmly nodded her head.

'You go first,' I told Neha, as she finished giving the order for our drinks.

'Okay . . .' she said, elongating the 'k' to build the suspense. 'I am getting married,' she declared exuberantly, shouting above the din of the live music that had started playing at the pub.

Neha getting married! The idea was as absurd as a free bird willingly flying into a cage or a liquid assuming a fixed shape forever.

'Stop kidding,' I said, laughing it off.

She smiled at me knowingly and coolly placed her left hand right under my nose.

My eyes popped open as I sighted a huge sparkling rock adorning her delicate ring finger. 'When did this happen?' I asked, dumbfounded.

'This afternoon,' she stated confidently.

'But I talked to you like at 10 a.m. this morning and you said you were going out for a family lunch with your parents.'

'I know. It happened all of a sudden, you see. I did go out for lunch with my parents to Hyatt, but it turned out that we were actually meeting an old friend of my dad's and his family. Before

I knew it, I was ushered into a hotel suite with their gorgeously good-looking, one and only son for a tête-à-tête.'

It was clear that Neha's parents had tricked her but it was more bothersome that she did not seem to mind.

'You won't believe what his opening line was!' Neha laughed merrily.

'Can you cook?' I offered.

'Do you sing?' prompted Tanu di.

'He said he was not a virgin,' revealed Neha, bursting into peals of laughter.

'Wow, a frank guy,' I admitted admiringly.

'And experienced too!' remarked Di. 'Looks like hands-on experience has become a valuable asset in the marriage market as well,' Di added mockingly.

Unaffected by Tanu di's sarcasm, Neha continued. 'Mmm ...utterly butterly delicious,' she slurped, licking her lips pleasurably, evidently remembering a sensual experience.

'What! You kissed him already?' I asked, bewildered.

'Hello?' Neha looked at me questioningly. 'When you are buying a car, that too a second-hand model, you have to verify that it has been maintained well and ensure that there are no mechanical glitches.'

Tanu di and I exchanged confused glances at being unable to follow Neha's car–guy analogy.

'Girls, I am getting married to this fellow. I had to check whether we were sexually harmonious,' Neha explicated.

'You mean cum-patible,' I joked and we both burst into girly giggles.

'Let me get this straight,' said Tanu di dubiously. 'You had sex with a potential suitor on your first meeting, to decide whether you would marry him or not?'

'Di! Please don't act like my concerned and well-meaning but old-fashioned mom,' Neha said irritably.

Tanu di was shocked by Neha's brazen attitude towards sex, but I knew Neha could knock boots with a cute chap she just met in a DTC bus. What I couldn't understand was how she could agree to marry a person she barely knew?

'You can't possibly be serious about marrying this guy. You don't love him.' I argued.

'Who said I don't love him? He is the only son of a millionaire. He runs his own chain of five-star hotels in Milan. We are going shopping to Europe next week. I won't have to stay with my mother-in-law, who is quite a social vignette by the way, and he knows how to satisfy a woman. I jolly well love him.'

Neha was already two drinks down.

'That's a very materialistic view of life,' observed Di.

'Ten years into marriage, with two kids, three maids, two drivers, with gymming to stay fit, maintaining a high flying career and a hectic social life, you get a maximum of half an hour with your hubby in a day. As long as he does his job well during that time, it does not matter what he does with the rest of his day.'

Neha had a point. Where was the time to cherish and nurture love in our busy lives? And yet, all the movies and the songs, all the books and the paintings, all the pain and the joy seemed meaningless to me without love.

'What about the remaining 199 cars you were going to test drive?' I teased Neha jokingly.

'I found my Volkswagon GTI, baby. A sexy sports car with mileage. I am calling my bets now,' Neha replied, her eyes gleaming with happiness and the sparks reflecting off the diamond in her ring.

'She can always rent a car even if she owns one,' said Tanu di cheekily. 'Dial a cab. Anywhere, any time. Our services are just a call away.'

Suddenly the happiness disappeared and Neha's face flushed with anger. 'I might not wait a lifetime for my lost love like you,' said Neha, looking directly into Di's eyes and sounding hurt, 'but I am not the kind to cheat either.'

She and Neha might have had dissimilar moral values when it came to physical intimacy—as different as a veiled, village woman and a stripper in a Las Vegas casino—but they were the two most honest people I knew and they were my closest friends.

'I am sorry,' said Tanu di immediately, realizing her mistake.

'It's okay,' said Neha, gulping down another margarita, and smiling once again, her anger dissipating as quickly as public outrage in India after a terrorist attack.

Neha was definitely not paying the bill tonight. Confident that I would be able to beat Tanu di, whatever be her surprise, I downed the rest of my drink and placed the order for another round.

Drumming my fingers on the table and swaying my head to the beat of *Ayyayaye Coco Jambo, ayyayaye*, I looked expectantly at Tanu di and sang, '. . . and make me happy.'

'I went out for dinner with Vikram yesterday,' Tanu di spoke with a meaningful smile.

'Anything less than a kiss and you are paying the bill tonight,' I warned Tanu di jubilantly.

'His firm wants to invest in my company. He offered me a valuation of ten million dollars.'

Ten million dollars was big news but not unusual, especially coming from Tanu di. I could see from the wide-eyed expression on Neha's face that she thought otherwise.

'Everyone knows that Lakshmi and Saraswati have joined hands ever since the dot-com boom,' I said dismissively.

'I agree,' said Tanu di, unfazed. 'I always knew I would make it big one day,' she added with a touch of arrogance.

For once, I didn't mind an IITian's overconfidence. I was buzzing after my third mojito and I slumped down contentedly in my seat. In the joy of being treated to free drinks, I had temporarily forgotten my deep-reciation issues.

'Oh, and there is one more thing,' she said, almost as an afterthought. 'I am going to the North Pole next week.' She said it in such a casual tone, it was as if she was announcing that she was going to the loo.

'Is that a new restaurant or something?' I asked, visibly at a loss to comprehend Tanu di's statement.

'No, it's the northernmost point of the earth, located in the middle of the Arctic Ocean, amidst water that is almost permanently covered with constantly shifting sea ice,' explained Tanu di, still maintaining a poker face.

'Now, that's rather adventurous and very unlike you,' said Neha with a hint of jealousy in her voice. 'Are you going alone?'

To my indescribable shock, Di shook her head and said she was going there with a friend.

'Which friend?' I asked, springing back upright in my seat.

'Vikram, of course,' she replied coolly.

'Fuck, there goes Suhaani's free drinks,' cursed Neha.

'Excuse me! I thought you didn't like mixing business with pleasure,' I challenged Di.

'I am not going out on a date with him. It's only an expedition to the North Pole,' justified Di. 'Besides a whole bunch of CEOs from the companies funded by Vikram's firm will be going as well.'

Date or no date, a trip to the North Pole with a handsome hunk was definitely more unexpected than my reverse rejection.

'What about the snow?' I said in a last-ditch effort to save my pride and purse. 'You freeze even in Delhi winters!'

'I know, the cold weather sucks, but this trip is the key to my suck-cess,' wisecracked Di.

With Neha tying the knot and Di ready to visit Santa Claus town, I felt like I was being subjected to shock treatment. Pissed at my defeat, I was wallowing in self-pity, when an old romantic

Kishore Kumar song, filled the ambience with nostalgia and transported us all to an ethereal dreamlike state.

Tanu di waved at a waiter who promptly rushed to our table. After ordering a margarita, a mojito and a diet Coke for Neha, me and herself respectively, she asked the waiter who had requested this song. The waiter pointed to a guy in a bright red tee, sitting across the dance floor on the other side of the lounge. Leaning back in his chair, his hands behind his head in a disarmingly relaxed posture, he was enjoying the number he had just requested. A pretty, petite girl sat across the table from him, smiling and casually bobbing her head rhythmically to the music. They seemed to be sharing a very close and comfortable friendship.

He seemed like a familiar person in an unfamiliar setting and because of the lighting and the alcohol in my system it took me some time to recognize who my friends were staring at. It was Deep!

'Don't you find him irresistibly attractive?' Tanu di chirped excitedly, her eyes shining with renewed vigour. I was well aware of her weakness for guys in red t-shirts and her association of the colour with Champ.

'Man! He's super hot,' Neha chirped in.

'No, he isn't,' I said defiantly, curbing the urge to eyeball Deep again and unsettled by the jealousy that suddenly hit me at seeing him with another girl.

'Either you are bullshitting me or you need to see a sex therapist,' objected Neha, staring lustfully at Deep. Then she turned towards us and sighed guiltily, 'I wish I wasn't engaged.'

'Aah! I love being single,' said Tanu di, literally drooling over Deep. 'You can go to any party, get drunk, lech at a guy to your heart's content, and not worry that your better half will catch you.' I could see that she was stripping him naked with her piercing gaze.

Of course, Tanu di was all talk and would never do anything.

What was weird was that even Neha found this Suri-like guy of *Rab Ne Bana Di Jodi* sexy.

'Are you sure you don't want to go up and kiss him?' Tanu di asked no one in particular.

'I already did. Last night,' I informed impetuously.

'You know him?' They both squealed in surprise. Neha almost fell off her seat in inebriated excitement, attracting inquisitive looks from the nearby tables.

'He is Deep,' I mumbled contemptuously. 'The suitor-cum-boss I was supposed to reject last night.'

'But you just said that you kissed him,' Neha said, raising one perfect eyebrow in confusion.

'Yeah,' I replied flatly.

'You kissed him means you were physically attracted to him,' deduced Neha asap.

'You kissed him also means that you didn't reject him,' said Tanu di. I could see that Di was now feeling conscience-stricken, for leering at her possible future brother-in-law.

'Well . . . I couldn't,' I said feeling a bit embarrassed at my failure.

'I totally understand,' comforted Tanu di. 'He is quite a temptation to resist,' she added, completely misunderstanding the situation. 'The only time losing is more rewarding than winning is when you are fighting temptation,' she quoted from her quote bank.

'I am never in favour of rejecting guys, at least not without scoring a game or two with them,' said Neha in my support.

'Fuck you, guys,' I said crossly for both of them were both trying to justify why it was okay that I couldn't resist the irresistible Deep. 'I couldn't do it because he beat me to it,' I explained.

They looked at me, flustered and shocked. Then, they looked at Deep with longing admiration and he hadn't even spoken a word yet.

'Poor you,' said Neha feeling sorry for me. 'It's sad that you lost the free trial opportunity to experience mind-blowing sex with him.'

'You'll be fine, honey,' said Di sympathetically. 'Remember you felt like a rained upon, rotting, uneaten fruit when you were ditched last time, but you soon forgot about it when you found Jay,' said Tanu di, lavishing her sisterly concern.

Tanu di knew that I despised all IIT guys because of that one bad experience. It was true that I had moved on quickly to Jay, but she was wrong if she thought I had forgotten or forgiven that IIT schmuck.

'Maybe you should try homosexuality,' suggested Neha with utmost sincerity. 'It's the latest fad among the broken-hearted.'

'Neha!' said Tanu di, aghast at her wild get-over-a-guy therapy. 'We don't need such drastic measures yet. There are plenty of fish in town.'

'Whatever,' said Neha losing interest in my lost opportunity and focusing on hers. 'I wish I wasn't engaged,' she reiterated, gazing wistfully at Deep.

'He sure is hot,' echoed Di.

'I will foot the bill,' offered Neha kindly. 'You win hands down.'

'Your shock is deep-er than ours,' punned Di, and agreed to split the bill with Neha.

'Stop it you two,' I said sharply, bugged by their desperate de(ep) votion.

Even though I didn't have to pay the bill, I felt miffed. It was not their pity that bothered me. Pity was okay. It was welcome actually. I was irritated that they were regarding my rejection as a big deal because they found Deep overwhelmingly charismatic. Why were these women behaving like he had spiked their drinks with a love potion? I stole a quick glance in Deep's direction. He was indeed looking sexier, even more than last night. It was not the way he had half tucked his shirt in his jeans, neither was it the voice, for I couldn't hear him at the moment. It was something else. Something that he had done differently today. Something that I couldn't put my finger on in my tipsy state. Something that made him look unnervingly appealing. What's wrong with you? I scolded myself. Jay is a hundred times more handsome than Deep. Why are you salivating for a dussheri when you have an alphonso?

Indignant and embarrassed, I got up in a huff and walked, unsteady in my high heels, but determinedly, towards his table.

'Hello, Deep,' I said, tilting my head to a side, smiling at him and fluttering my eyelashes.

'Hi,' he said, uneasy at seeing me there.

'Do you want to taste the raspberry from my lips again?' I asked lasciviously, leaning slightly forward, for it was hard to be heard otherwise.

My hair fell around my face and hid both our faces from his dinner date. He shifted uncomfortably in his chair. I giggled teasingly and pulled away.

'Er ... this is Suhaani,' he said haltingly, 'and this is Meeta.'

It was fun watching him falter awkwardly, as he made the formal introductions.

'Hi, Suhaani. Nice to meet you. Deep was just talking about you,' she said, unaffected by my intrusion and my insinuation at having kissed Deep.

Her calmness annoyed me. 'Could I borrow him for a minute? We have some unfinished business to deal with,' I said with a cold artificial politeness.

'He is all yours. I was just leaving,' she replied, not in the least bothered that someone else was hitting on her guy.

With that, Meeta got up, waved goodbye to Deep, winked at him, and said that she would call him later.

This was not a good sign. Meeta's unconcerned attitude either meant that Deep was crazy about her and she was not insecure or that she was actually not interested in him. The latter seemed improbable given how Deep attracted women like festival sales.

I cast a fleeting look at Neha and Tanu di who were watching my progress with curiosity. They gave me a thumbs-up as I settled myself in Meeta's seat.

'Sad that your girlfriend left so suddenly?' I smirked.

'No,' he replied serenely, his discomfort vanishing with Meeta's departure. 'I am quite fond of raspberry lips,' he said, with a playful wink.

I felt my cheeks burn with the heat of his raking gaze.

'Besides she is not my girlfriend,' he added.

Although he seemed to have regained his sense of humour, I could vouch on my years of love-affair experience that he had feelings for her. Feelings that were unreciprocated.

'Is she the reason why you rejected me last night?' I wondered.

I didn't realize that I was thinking out loud till I heard him say, 'I didn't reject you, but I am sorry if it hurt you.'

When a guy who loves you apologizes, it's heartwarming, but when a guy who has just dumped you shows kindness, it's heartwrenching.

Enraged by his superfluous compassion, I retorted. 'Don't BS me. Guys love refusing girls in an arranged marriage set-up so that they can boost their ego.'

'And a girl waits till the guy has fallen in love with her and then crushes his feelings,' he snapped.

'Well, I wanted to tell you on day one that I was not interested in you,' I defended myself.

'Really!' exclaimed Deep. 'Then why didn't you?'

'Well . . . I was waiting . . . you know … for an opportune private moment.'

'Fair enough,' he said encouragingly.

'And then last night when we were alone in your car, I was about to tell you when ...'

'You kissed me instead,' he said, cutting me off. 'Why did you kiss me, Suhaani, when you knew you were going to reject me?' he asked, looking into my eyes, his voice suddenly serious.

One look into his soul, bared through his honest eyes, and I knew I had misjudged him. He was simply being forthright when he said he wasn't ready for marriage. He never intended to put me down. It was childish to feel hurt if you apply for a job and get rejected when the company is not even looking to hire.

Unwilling to admit that I indeed wanted to make him desire me before delivering the blow, I blamed the kiss on the social lubricant, namely beer.

'I had heard of a bear hug before, but I now I have experienced a beer kiss too,' he said, loosening up and adjusting his hair.

It was then that I noticed the difference. He was wearing a snazzy, black, metal hairband. No! The hairband didn't make him look girlish or gay. Rather it added a naughty spunk to his personality. Four drinks down, sitting with a kissable, wickedly funny guy, I found myself stranded on an island, in a two-piece polka-dot bikini. I was wearing a hairband around my neck. He was chasing me around to take it back and I was playing hard to get. He caught up with me and held me tight in his grip. I felt threatened and aroused as his fingers traced a gentle circle over my lips. He was about to kiss me when suddenly I heard a beep.

My phone's SMS tone interrupted my fantasy. 'Don't kiss him again,' read the message from Di. I tried to recall if the guy in my imagination was Deep or Jay but it all seemed hazy. Wary of my heady and intoxicated thoughts, I got up hurriedly.

'I should be going now,' I said, gathering my senses.

'See you on Monday,' he said, smiling.

My head throbbed and I swayed slightly as I took the first step. He immediately rose from his seat and held me steady with his right arm around my waist. I was reminded of the way Jay would hold me in his arms, his heart warming mine, the familiar scent of his aftershave mingling with my perfume and his tongue softly titillating my earlobes, wreaking havoc in my libido.

Aching for Jay, I spontaneously leaned in, closing the distance between our lips, but he gingerly placed his hand in between and said, 'Let's just be friends.'

Before I knew what was happening, I had fallen in Deep's arms and passed out completely.

SEALED WITH A KISS

Jay had just stepped out of the shower after an hour-long game of Frisbee and was wearing only his boxers. His chest gleamed with water dripping from the strands of his hair. With his ripped body and sexy bedroom eyes, he looked like a model any girl would want to drag home. I felt a tingling excitement spread through my whole body as I caught him eyeing my bust. However, the ooohs were soon replaced by urghs as I was overcome with a strong burning sensation in my stomach. A queasy reminder of the large amounts of alcohol I had guzzled in the last two days. The maid came in with a glass of chilled milk and placed it on a table next to the bed. I was craving for my morning cup of tulsi tea, but I knew that caffeine was even more diuretic. Unwillingly, I took a few sips of the cold milk to counter the acids burning my food pipe. The maid smiled coyly on seeing a shirtless gora guy on my laptop screen. '*He ij yuar by-friend?*' she asked sheepishly. I nodded my head slightly. Her eyes widened in awe and she smiled in obvious approval.

'Who is that?' asked Jay.

Hearing the picture talk, the maid squealed in surprise, became self-conscious of her own appearance and left in a hurry. I added the idea of movingpictures.com to my growing list of ingenious, innovative business ideas.

'And where are you?' Jay wondered out loud, while I was lost in my magically real world. Not a very keen observer, he had just realized that I was not sitting in my own room.

I knew I was at Tanu di's place, using her laptop, but I had no recollection of how I'd got there! Last I remembered, Deep was talking about beer kisses and I had noticed his black hairband. I strained my memory to extract further details. My heart did a back flip as I recalled how I had thrown myself at Deep, for the second time in the last twenty-four hours. How could I kiss another guy when I was in love with Jay? I would be furious with Jay if he would do this behind my back. Even when he had only been a passive receptor to Denise's smooch, I had been enraged.

'Have you never ever felt a strong desire for physical contact with someone other than me?' Jay had asked me once, and I had proudly preached to him that it was human to feel attracted to more than one person, but the power of love lay in restraining oneself from succumbing to these temptations. How had I, a strong believer of love, then lost self-control?

A sharp pain shot through my forehead and I flinched. I was having a really bad hangover. Feeling horribly sick and guilty, I wanted to tell Jay all about it, but my inner voice stopped me. 'You do truly love Jay,' it assured me and ascribed my libidinous actions to excessive drinking. Solemnly swearing never to get smashed again, I told Jay briefly about how I had got very drunk last night and had to come to Tanu di's house.

'You look beat, hon,' remarked Jay, noticing my smudged mascara and puffed eyes. 'Should we talk later in the day?' he offered courteously.

'No, I am fine,' I said, smiling despite the throbbing pain in my head. So much had happened since I last chatted with Jay, a week ago, that I was feeling disconnected from him. I desperately wanted to stay online with him. I needed him to tell me that he loved me, that all will be fine, and that my love story will have a happy ending.

'Cool then. I have something important to tell you,' said Jay with unusual seriousness.

'I am sure you would agree that it's hard to keep the romance alive in a long-distance relationship,' he was saying. 'Every day I jog past your apartment and look up at the window, I imagine you standing there waving back at me. The first faint rays of sunlight dancing upon your face, contouring the delicate curve of your cheeks and adding an ethereal glow to your eyes. Every evening as I sit all by myself in front of the TV watching Friends, I miss the warmth of your body next to mine. I miss the crunching sound of chips that you used to eat and I miss telling you the calories it has. Everything here reminds me of you and leaves a deep void in my heart. This existence seems too painful to endure and yet when I think about being one with you, I tell myself it's all worth it.'

OMG! Something was very wrong with Jay. Why was he doing all this pre-climax-type sweet talk? He was not the kind to express his love through words. He was more a man of physical than philosophical love. Could this be a build-up to a break-up? I knew he had been to another one of Ashraf's wild parties. Maybe he met Denise there, wearing a sexy, skimpy dress, and she invited him to undo her strings. What if he wants a way out of our no-walk-only-talk relationship? The thoughts boggled my mind as Jay kept on murmuring the mushiest things he had ever said to me.

'I know things have not been smooth for you at home and I behaved like a jerk last time,' I heard him admit and then he began to sing in his not-so-melodious yet full-of-feelings voice.

Oceans apart, day after day
And I slowly go insane

I hear your voice, on the line
But it doesn't stop the pain
If I see you next to never
how can we say forever

I heard the song *I will be right here waiting for you* playing on his laptop. Jay was singing along with Bryan Adams, his eyes boring into mine and his arms entwined around me in a virtual embrace. This was the most lovey-dovey, Romeo-like thing he had ever said or done. Moved by his unexpected romantic gesture, I found myself crying and longing for his arms.

The guilt weighed even more heavily on my mind and I felt even more scared to confess my deceit for I didn't want to lose him.

'I am sorry that I don't know your language or can't become your bridge partner, but I love you and I will be right here waiting for you,' he said as the song ended.

'I love you too, Jay,' I said, my voice choking with emotion and tears of joy brimming in my eyes. 'Did you plan all this by yourself?' I asked with unmitigated surprise.

'Nope. I borrowed the idea and the speech from Ashraf,' he said frankly. 'But the chips and the calories were mine,' he added with a childish pride.

'I wish I could tell you how much this means to me, Jay,' I said, all starry-eyed and swayed by his lovelogue.

'You could if you wanted to?' he challenged teasingly.

'How?' I asked, eager to play my part as his Juliet. I could see him watch the gentle rise and fall of my breasts as I breathed in and out.

'Virtual sex,' he whispered, his hazel eyes glowing with excitement.

I knew Di had gone out to the market to run some errands

and would take at least an hour to get back, but the maid was in the house.

'Why don't we take off our clothes and chat for a while?' Jay suggested, sensing my hesitation.

My breathing quickened and my nipples hardened in anticipation, as he slowly lowered his shorts and let them drop on the floor.

I quickly got up to shut the bedroom door and drew the curtains across the balcony window. I came back and felt the heat radiating from the laptop as though it could sense the sexual tension in the room.

Uncertain, I listened to my hormones and morals battling it out with each other whether I loved or hated his royal blue, low rise, sheer mesh designer briefs that left almost nothing to the imagination. Conscience-stricken for having given into my de(ep) sire, I agreed to having Skype sex with Jay as a penance. I took off the salwar suit I had worn to the pub last night, but left the bra and the panty on.

Jay's tongue slid unconsciously over his lips as he saw the little heart pendant around my neck, slide down the inviting crevice of my cleavage. Realizing that I was feeling conscious of the webcam, Jay told me to shut my eyes and relax. I did as he said even though I was far from being relaxed.

'Visualize that I am massaging your shoulders like I always do,' he said in a seductive voice, 'and my fingers accidentally brush over the swell of your breasts.'

I found myself arching my back so that my breasts were pushed forward and my thick brown nipples poked at the delicate fabric that was trying desperately to hold together my modesty.

'Now imagine that you are enclosed in my arms and I am blowing warm kisses in your earlobes, nibbling and working my way up to the top of your ear,' he said huskily.

All of a sudden, I was reminded of last night, when I had pictured this very same setting and leaned towards Deep to kiss him. Disturbed by my own reckless behaviour, I opened my eyes.

The heartburn had become better after a few gulps of cold milk, but I could sense a new queasiness developing in the pit of my stomach. I knew I had to do what was right.

'Jay, I have something to tell you,' I said softly.

'I am licking your breasts now and you are melting in my arms,' he whispered, moving his tongue in a circular motion and continuing to fantasize.

'The guerrilla guy whom my dad wanted me to marry is my boss,' I said a little more loudly, somehow controlling the excitement that was threatening to rip me apart.

This time Jay stopped the licking action midway.

'I am really sorry, Jay,' I apologized.

'That's unfair. That arranged suitor gets you to work under him and kiss his ass while I have to make do with cyber sex,' he said slyly.

I was so wrapped up in my remorse that his pun was lost on me. 'I didn't mean to do it. I was too drunk,' I mumbled, almost crying, scared that I would lose him forever.

'Hold on, hon,' said Jay, rolling his eyes, feeling somewhat irritated at the interruption. 'What exactly happened? Did you go to bed with him?'

'Heavens, no!' How could Jay even contemplate something like this? Sitting on Tanu di's bed in my undergarments, I truthfully recounted the highlights of the kiss-n-dump episode, where I had kissed Deep and he had dumped me, and its repeat telecast at the girls' night out yesterday.

'Cool,' said Jay.

'Cool? Aren't you angry?' I asked baffled by his phlegmatic attitude.

'No. I am actually quite turned on,' he said with a salacious grin.

I too baffled to react! Should I have been relieved that Jay was indifferent about, or should I say aroused by, me kissing another guy or I should I have been worried that my kissing another guy did not upset him.

'So you still love me?' I asked incredulously.

'I never stopped, baby,' he said, getting hornier by the minute.

'But you should be angry,' I insisted, concerned that he may take this incident as a carte blanche to kiss other girls, especially Denise.

'Just don't make a habit of this,' he warned playfully, 'or you will have to pay for it.' He was sexily sucking on his middle finger to keep the mood going.

Sometimes we end up encouraging what we know is wrong. *Chalta hai*, we tell ourselves. If you have ever been caught for talking on your mobile phone while driving and then bribed the traffic police guy or offered *chai-paani* to the address verification officer so he would expedite your passport processing, you would know what I mean. Tanu di would perhaps have warned me against Jay's casual disposition but I decided to let the matter rest.

I could hear the aching desire for me in his voice. Absolved of my kis-sins, I responded by cooing, 'Arrest me officer. I have been naughty.'

Half an hour later, we both lay on our respective beds, smiling, spent and satisfied. He got up to go to the loo. I put on my clothes, unlocked the door and called out to the maid to get me some tea. The last two days had been so hectic with drinking, dumping and deep-kissing that I had forgotten my FB world. There were numerous comments on my arranged vs love marriage post. While some Indian guys had expressed a strong preference for an ideal arranged marriage *bahoo,* all my American friends had chosen love marriage. I was surprised that an overwhelming majority from my Indian friends circle was also rooting for ALM—an Arranged Love Marriage. One guy had commented, 'my parents told me, luv tum karo, arrange hum kar denge.'

'How lucky!' I thought as I wistfully looked at Jay, who was also going through his Facebook notifications. I would be the happiest person on earth, if my parents agreed to arrange my marriage with Jay.

'Hey, I just got a friend request from your mom,' said Jay, with a startled look on his face.

'Tell me you rejected it,' I said, freaking out.

'How can I?'

'Just click on REJECT.'

'Ha ha ... thanks for the Facebook 101, but seriously speaking, she is your mom and she is trying to be friendly. Isn't that a good sign?'

It was strange that I was just thinking about my parents arranging my marriage with Jay when I hear about my mom trying to make friends with him. My dadi would have said that this was a sign from the universe. Stop being such a romantic! I scolded myself.

'The only sign I see is that of danger,' I told Jay.

'Too late. I already got a Farmville neighbour request from her.'

'Holy cow!' I cursed and advised him to customize his privacy settings to disallow my mom from seeing the photos or videos he was tagged in.

'Don't you think it's funny to protect your public privacy from your in-laws,' he said, laughing off my concern.

'Suit yourself,' I said and got busy clearing my FB backlog. I was swarmed with 'is everything ok' messages from my online circle of friends. I quickly went through the latest posts, liked thirty of them and commented on another ten.

Jay meanwhile started chatting with someone else. A minute later, he asked me, 'Is your mom into hot car wash babes?'

'Are you mad?'

'Well, she just asked me about car wash hot.'

'Why are you even talking to her?' I demanded, as I searched for any recent posts on Jay's wall that needed to be hidden from my mom.

'Hon! I don't want to be rude to my future mom-in-law.'

'She doesn't want to be your mom-in-law,' I argued.

'I think she is sweet. She just liked my picture.'

'Forget it,' I said exasperatedly, wondering what Mom was trying to do by befriending Jay. Getting to know him better was definitely not the right answer. This was definitely not *Gandhi-giri*, for my mom didn't believe in being kind to her enemies. Jay was naive to take my mom's actions at face value.

'Last time, you only talked about your dad's expectations from me. What about your mom? What does she think of me?' Jay asked curiously.

'Oh! She believes that love marriages are high risk, so you don't even figure in her options list,' I teased.

'What if you fall in love with an arranged suitor? Will she object to it then?'

I hadn't really thought about this before. I was debating if Mom would have an objection if I fell in love with an arranged suitor like Deep, when there was a knock on Jay's door and someone came in. I couldn't see the person but I was certain he was talking to a female voice. I was sure it was not Denise, but my spy antennae went up all the same.

'Who was that?' I asked cautiously when he came back, trying not to sound jealous.

'My mom,' he answered carelessly.

'Why didn't you introduce me to her?' I said. I had always wanted to meet his parents and get to know them better.

'She saw you on the video, but she didn't ask and I didn't tell.'

It is interesting that in America, even your mom won't ask you an intimate question, while in India, your maid considered it her prerogative to know about the goings on in your life.

'Listen, I gotta go drop my mom at the airport,' said Jay. 'Tonight was fun,' he winked.

'Same here,' I said blushing.

'And by the way, car wash hot is a fast observed by married women for the long life of their husbands,' informed Jay.

'That is Karwa Chauth,' I exclaimed, disconcerted that he was still on chat with my mom.

'Yeah, same thing,' he chuckled and hung up.

I could hear Tanu di's voice from the drawing room. I was about to log off from FB when I saw there was a new friend request from Deep. I clicked on accept without any compunctions. I knew I had gone off the deep end, but I didn't feel any regrets. I believed in enjoying life, not fretting over it. What was done was past. What lay ahead was an unknown but definitely exciting future. I liked to live in today, in right now. And right now I knew that Jay loved me and Deep's chapter had been sealed with a kiss!

SECRETS UNVEILED

Being five feet one and a half inches tall is not good for your lower back. None of the usual positions are comfortable when you are small. When the legs align well, the neck gets strained and when the back is well supported, the feet end up dangling in the air.

My personal favourite is the cross-legged position, though I can never get my eyes at the desired top viewing angle. I really wished I didn't have to suffer so much because of my size.

I am talking about office chairs, by the way. And people tell me I have a one-track mind. You see, the office chairs, much like office t-shirts, are ordered in bulk, typically for sizes M and L. So for the likes of us, who are petite, these supposedly ergonomic chairs turn out to be quite a challenge! Anyways, so I was sitting cross-legged in my medium-sized, blue, ergonomic chair, working on my to-do list, when I heard the familiar husky voice.

'Everything in control, Suhaani?' asked Deep, as he entered the cubicle. It had been over a month since we went public as 'just friends'. Yet, every time I heard him say my name, I felt the same nervous excitement as I had felt talking to him the very first time.

'It was, until you came,' I said, trying to hide the fluttering in my heart, and continuing to gaze at the unanswered emails in my inbox.

'I don't like it when girls tell me that,' he said smiling facetiously.

I laughed at his sexual interpretation of coming. 'Well, you came earlier than I was expecting,' I said, playing along.

'Usually I have better control on my timing.'

'Been out of practice?' I teased.

'Looks like,' he admitted. 'In future, I will make sure you get enough time before I come.' Deep winked and plunged himself into the pile of documents on his desk.

I had always been comfortable talking about sex with both my girlfriends and guy friends. I could discuss PMS with my guy friends with the same ease as I could talk cricket with my girl gang. Somehow, most Indian guys mistook my sexual candidness as a loose bolt in my character. This was one of the reasons I was wary about marrying an Indian. Deep, however, seemed different. If there was one thing I had begun to enjoy while working together with him, it was our non-stop raillery. Touchwood, so far, he hadn't misinterpreted it or made any physical advances at me.

Back to work, the top-most item in my to-do list was to classify my email contacts using a newly downloaded email prioritization tool. One hour of uninterrupted, focused effort and BOOM, magically my inbox was reduced from fifty to six VIP mails. Two from Deep, one from the big boss, and one each from SnapDeal.com, FashionAndYou.com and Jay. Facebook, of course, was a category in itself and I was professional enough to only check it once every couple of hours while at work. I was debating whether to write 'Dear Mr Khanna', 'Dear Sir', or 'Dear Rohan Sir' to the big boss, when Deep asked if I wanted to have tea. You can't say no to your manager, especially on status meeting days and definitely not for tea. So I followed him out of the cubicle.

Deep meticulously filled his cup with 4/5th hot water and 1/5th milk, added a teaspoon of sugar and dipped an Earl Grey tea bag in it. Dressed impeccably in a white shirt and black trousers, he looked every bit the serious, sincere and sharp employee that he was admired for being. The black hairband was the only giveaway of his lighter, jovial side that his friends were privy to.

'I hope that since you have undergone the customer sensitization training, you will now respond to all client emails ASAP,' remarked Deep casually, removing the used, soggy tea bag from his cup and throwing it in the bin.

'I have always been good at keeping my inbox empty,' I said haughtily, making a mental note to create 'Clients' as a separate sub-category within my business contacts.

'Really? May I ask what the secret of your efficiency is?' he asked sceptically.

Proudly, I told him about how I organized my contacts in accordance with Steven Covey's 'First Things First' principle.

'What about new contacts?' he asked, this time sounding genuinely interested.

'They go in a new category that I glance through periodically,' I boasted, taking a sip of my readymade masala chai.

'Hmm . . . and which category would you say a random unknown guy lands up in?'

'Pain in the Ass,' I informed him instantly without thinking. PITA was where I kept all my previous boyfriends and the other junk mailers.

He coughed pretentiously a few times, and then said, 'Thanks for the compliment.'

At first I didn't understand what he meant and then it dawned on me that he was referring to the 'random guy from my dad's guitar class' and his first mail that I had purposely not responded to. I looked into his eyes and they smiled back knowingly at me. I knew that he knew that I knew that he had waited for my response and in revenge he had made me go through the wait-in-the-lobby routine on my first day at iTrot.

There was never a dull moment with Deep around! This was

another thing that I was beginning to like about him. I was thinking of a snappy response when suddenly Vikas, the guy from first floor with an unhappy love marriage, barged in and interrupted us.

'So glad you came early,' said Vikas.

Deep looked at me and we both burst out laughing at having shared this joke earlier. Vikas looked confused. He took Deep aside and started talking about some personal stuff. I got busy with my phone. 'Wait the Talk mystery resolved,' I SMSed to Tanu di. I was about to head out of the cafeteria when I heard Deep say to Vikas, 'I thought you have worked out your KS issues?'

I was surprised that even a relatively senior employee like Vikas had knowledge sharing issues.

'Why don't you talk to Kavita about it?' I suggested like a concerned, dedicated employee, obviously oblivious that he was talking about sex.

'I don't think you know what I am talking about,' said Vikas, with the ever-present smirk plastered on his face.

I had met him a number of times in office, during lunch and coffee breaks, since the kiss-n-dump outing. He had come across as a strong ego type of guy who loved to praise himself and subtly put other people down. Certainly not my kind of guy. Before I could argue in my defence, he added, 'In any case, my KS issues are with Kavita, so I can't really talk to her about it.'

Curious to hear what Deep had to say about it, I decided to stay put and listen.

'Did you try using any of the external tools we had discussed last time?' Deep inquired.

'Collaboration tools could be quite an asset,' I promptly offered my two cents, unaware that Deep was referring to pleasure enhancement tools like vibrators and arousal gels.

Deep burst into cubicle laughter while Vikas stood there giving me a 'you-know-nothing' stare.

'Kavita is fucking adverse to any new ideas,' Vikas swore openly, ignoring my presence.

I found myself agreeing with Vikas on this point. With the same stiff bouffant hairstyle every day, Kavita did come across as a person fixed in her ways.

'Besides, there is always the fucking performance pressure,' Vikas sounded pretty peeved.

'Let the lady take charge and lead the game,' advocated Deep with an amused expression. 'Sit back and enjoy.' Deep inhaled and exhaled slowly as if teaching Vikas how to calm down.

'That's the fucking problem, man. I can't let go,' said Vikas. 'I like to be in control.'

It seemed that every time he used the word 'fucking', he derived an orgasmic kick from it. It gave him a sense of freedom and power that he was craving for.

'You are making this an ego issue man,' Deep pointed out.

'Call me old-fashioned if you will but women ought to stay below and not on top of men,' stated Vikas.

I misunderstood Vikas's preference for the missionary sex position as his bias against women rising to upper rungs of the corporate ladder. So far I had been cool about Vikas's views on Kavita, but now I felt he was getting sexist. I started educating him on the inappropriateness of the glass ceiling and how men have to be mature about women in senior positions.

'Aren't you going to stop her?' Vikas urged Deep, who stood calm, peacefully smiling, hearing me preach to Vikas.

'No,' declared Deep defiantly.

'Why not? It's not like she is your wife,' demanded Vikas.

'Didn't you see? She is armed,' said Deep with a serious face and pointed towards my hands.

'Fuck,' cursed Vikas staring at my fingernails. 'These are long. Really long. Veryyyyy long,' he said, looking disgusted.

'I hope you can type with those,' said Deep with a suspicious grin.

'I am getting used to them,' I replied honestly.

'But is this allowed? I mean doesn't our employee handbook say that your fucking fingernails can't be longer than your eyelashes,' blurted Vikas, still in a state of shock. He seemed to have forgotten his own problems.

'As long as I am not her keyboard, it doesn't bother me how she picks a hair out of her eye,' joshed Deep, and walked out of the cafeteria.

OMG! Deep had noticed. I felt like jumping in excitement, but my bowed out platform heels vetoed the idea. Okay. Calm down. He is not your boyfriend. Ya, I know, but when you spend 5,000 rupees getting your nails done, you want everyone around you to notice. I had been so disappointed when I had gone about flashing them for over an hour to Jay without even an acknowledgment from him. I had justified it to myself by saying that nail extensions were such a common sight in the US, that he must have overlooked mine. At the end of our call, I had myself told him how I had found a nail spa through Facebook and gotten artificial nails.

Can you believe what he said when I asked him if he liked them?

'Uh-huh!'

I understand that men usually speak 7,000 words in a day as compared to a woman's whopping 20,000, but 'uh-huh'? Really? It is barely even a word. Even my dad had managed better. 'Are you okay?' Pa had asked, concerned on seeing the bill, but had been glad to hear that this time I had experimented with my looks in a celebration of life rather than as a stress-relieving measure. I, of course, didn't tell him I was celebrating being in love with Jay.

The rest of my day passed by without much fruitful activity, with my nail extensions getting in the way of everything I tried to do from sending SMSes to removing the food particles stuck under them. Finally, it was time for an important video conference call I had been preparing for over a week.

'Welcome to my thinking pod,' said Mr Khanna with an acquired American accent, taking a sip of coffee from a Starbucks takeaway cup. He was an external US-based consultant, hired by iTrot for competitive analysis and digital media strategy, the special project I was lucky to be a part of.

'Morning, Rohan!' Deep greeted back.

I hadn't prepared to meet a strikingly imposing, mysteriously charming man whose grey streaks emphasized his financial stability rather than his age. Equally imposing was the bright, bold red paint on his office walls. It was 8 p.m. our time, but I found myself mentally re-energized and physically awakened. Nothing seems to have as much impact on atmosphere as wall colour. Or was it the high testosterone level in the room?

While we waited for other people to join in, Deep and Rohan started discussing some IIT hostel winning all the trophies this year. Apparently, Rohan was also from IIT Delhi and although they were not around at the same time, they were both from the same hostel.

'How are your guitar classes coming along?' Rohan asked.

'Quite rewarding,' said Deep, giving me a sideways glance. 'How are yours?'

'I just started two weeks back. I am still struggling with the chords.'

'You have to live up to your reputation, sir,' said Deep. 'From what I have heard, you were the champ at picking up any new skill and mastering it in no time.'

Had I been a little more attentive, I would have been able to make the connection between Rohan and Tanu di's Champ. A thirty-five-something ex-IIT-D start-up consultant, with red colour on his walls, and a champ at learning new things. Alas, this story would have to wait a while longer for its happy ending.

'I am sorry it got so late for you guys,' said Rohan when everyone had arrived. 'Let's get started.'

'The biggest problem iTrot is facing currently is the low conversion rate,' pointed out Deep.

'We offer better deals than our competitors and yet others seem to be getting all the business,' said the guy from the holiday package team.

I was surprised to learn that only 2 per cent of the users visiting the iTrot.com website actually bought something. How come I never came back empty-handed from a shop? I guess, when you go to a store, you end up buying at least one thing in order to justify the driving and parking hassles. A website was, however, only a click away. I was racking my brains to find an intelligent answer, when a fresh MBA graduate explained that having better deals was not enough and what we really needed to do was to offer better targeted deals. His idea was well received.

'The other important aspect is social media marketing,' Rohan emphasized.

'Facebook is so new. No one knows what works in that domain,' cribbed a sixties'-born, senior marketing guy.

'Well, I understand that she is a new lady in town and I myself don't date her often,' admitted Rohan, smiling handsomely. Everyone in the room laughed at his joke. 'But we ought to learn how to woo her,' Rohan added, looking expectantly at the younger team members.

My face lit up at the opportunity. I was certainly the most active FB user among those present. I should be able to say something smart. I had barely begun to formulate my strategy to woo 100,000+ fans on iTrot FB page, when Deep proposed an FB community around work pressures and mean bosses that could be used to offer our travel packages. Everyone, including Rohan, acclaimed his Boss Bashing campaign.

The meeting went on but I was unable to contribute anything useful. I was beginning to feel lost and out-of-place like a 4XL-sized woman looking for clothes in a petite-size store.

'I would like you guys to watch out for any issues within the organization that could hamper its growth,' said Rohan in his closing statement.

'Sure, thanks, bye,' people said and filed out of the room one by one.

Nobody had said anything about me being a mute spectator in the two-hour meeting, but somehow I felt compelled to prove to others that I could speak. This 'am I good enough' was a rare phenomenon for me as I am a very positive person. I was grappling with my insignificance, when I saw a chat message pop up on Deep's laptop. 'Are you done? Need urgent KS help.'

'Voila!' I thought. Surely this was an organizational issue. I told Rohan about the various people I had seen approach Deep with knowledge sharing concerns.

'Knowledge sharing problems in a start-up? That's strange!' Rohan expressed surprise.

I looked at Deep for support, but he seemed irritated with me. 'It's not a big deal,' said Deep, giving me a mildly disgruntled look. 'I think Suhaani has misunderstood.'

Over the last few weeks, I had come to admire Deep's sensitivity to his juniors, even the non-IIT ones and respect for others' ideas. Why was he behaving like this today?

Insistent on making a point, I reiterated that it was a real concern and people even had these issues with HR.

Rohan was visibly miffed now. 'Is there something you are trying to hide, Deep?' he asked mildly but sternly.

Deep had to come clean now. To my utmost embarrassment,

he revealed that the cases I was talking about were not related to knowledge sharing but to first timers and beginners of Kama Sutra.

'Trying to increase the conversion rate of random dates to reproductive mates,' paraphrased Deep.

I could see Rohan trying hard to control his laughter. I didn't know where to look. Not only was I now a plus-sized misfit in a dainty store, I had also made a fool of myself by mistaking maternity clothes for large-size clothes.

'Thankfully for now I have only one mistress,' Rohan said, looking lovingly at his BlackBerry. 'My heart begins to beat fast when it vibrates and my eyes light up when it signals invitingly, but I will surely seek your advice, when I need it,' winked Rohan and signed out.

And in case you are wondering how Vikas had sex issues, mouse years after marriage, and that too with Kavita, you will be happy to know that they were unhappily married to each other.

Back to me. Stuck to my seat with invisible glue, I mumbled an inaudible bye. The last thing I wanted now was to make eye contact with Deep. Looking down at my notebook, I sneaked a sideways glance at him. He was busy on chat, presumably dispensing gyan on client penetration. I got up gingerly and started tiptoeing out. I was almost at the door when this huge 24" x 36" picture frame hung on the wall caught my attention. It showed a guy in a white shirt and black suit, leaping in the air. His head was tilted backwards and his hands were stretched out with a briefcase in one hand. At the bottom was a quotation by Cynthia Heimel that read, 'When in doubt, make a fool of yourself. There is a microscopically thin line between being brilliantly creative and acting like the most gigantic idiot on earth. So what the hell, leap.' Perfect! I thought. It didn't give any advice about what you should do if you take the leap and end up falling on your face. What did I say earlier, about the happening work environment when Deep is around? I take back my words.

There was another learning that I wanted to share with all my friends though. So I updated my Facebook status to, 'Never wear platform heels if you expect to get stuck in a situation that requires a stealthy escape.'

KUCH KUCH HOTA HAI

Even before I opened the latch, I knew who was standing outside. I could hear Deep humming from the other side of the door. My heart skipped a beat at the thought of last night's KS blunder. Blushing with embarrassment, I unlocked and held the door open.

'Hi. How was your day?' I asked, trying my best to keep my voice to sound normal as Deep walked in.

'It was quite an experience,' he responded, widening his eyes in emphasis.

'I have heard that IIM interviews can be quite gruelling,' I commented, walking back to the drawing room.

'Oh! The interview was the usual mix of behavioural and business aptitude assessment,' Deep said carelessly as he followed me in. 'But you won't believe whom I met while I was waiting for my turn,' he said fervently.

'Your long-lost twin brother?' I hazarded a filmy guess; dropping down on Sanjeev's newly bought plush loveseat.

Sanjeev had just purchased a house and since he didn't have many relatives in Delhi, he'd invited all of us for the house warming. I had a feeling it had also to do with him trying to impress Madhuri who was yet to arrive. It was just the three of us for now.

Sitting across the handcrafted ivory centre-table from me, Deep looked at me with a dazed expression. I knew by the way his eyes sparkled that the interesting part of the story was yet to begin.

'I met the most beautiful girl I have ever seen in my life!' Deep gushed, lost in a trance.

'Had she also come for the interview?' I asked, interested.

He nodded his head dreamily, still captivated by her beauty.

'So what happened?' I prodded curiously.

'Nothing,' he sighed heavily, letting his shoulders droop.

'Nothing? But you just said you had "quite an experience" with this pretty woman,' I asked, intrigued by the uneventful end.

'Do you believe in love at first sight or should I walk by again?' said Deep, suddenly getting up from his chair.

'That's an outdated pick-up line!' I said, taken by surprise at his flirtatious remark.

'That was exactly my reaction when this really hot girl, sitting next to me in the waiting lounge, got up from her seat, sashayed past me once and then came back and sat down next to me, her long lovely tresses falling on her delicate shoulders.'

'Did she know you from before?'

'Hello? Didn't you hear she said she fell in love with me at first sight?'

'But that was a real quick fall,' I said, not bothering to camouflage the bewilderment in my voice.

'No,' he denied.

'No?' I asked baffled.

'Not if you compare it with her swiftness as she threw herself on me the moment we were inside my car.'

For a moment I thought Deep was pulling my leg. I peered into his eyes, but found him looking right through me, perhaps reflecting on what had transpired back in his car.

'What was she doing in your car?' The words came out automatically.

'She wanted . . .'

'Forget it. Don't answer that,' I said abruptly, before he could finish the sentence.

'. . . a ride back home,' he completed despite my interruption.

'It's enough, Deep. I don't want to talk any more,' I said, knowing but not wanting to hear what happened next.

'That's exactly what she told me, fluttering her long eyelashes. She told me to shut up and get up after we had chatted for a while.'

Typically, I had no problems listening to my guy friends talk about their dates. Rather I had always enjoyed these tales. Unable to understand why I was feeling uncomfortable today, I was glad when I heard Sanjeev shout from the kitchen, above the whistling sound of the pressure cooker, 'I will be with you in a minute, bhabhiji.'

For some queer reason, known only to him, Sanjeev had continued calling me bhabhiji even after Deep had informed the people in office that he was not looking to get married in the near future. By now, I had also gotten used to Sanjeev's unique, affectionate greeting style. I got up from the sofa and played the Golden Collection CD I had selected just before Deep had rung the doorbell.

'Would you like to dance with me?' Deep said, as the latest blockbuster songs echoed in the double-ceilinged living room.

'Now?' I was flustered.

He shook his head and said, 'Not you. I asked Ms Gorgeous if she would like to dance with me when we reached my house,' said Deep, continuing his story.

'So, you took her to your home? All men are the same,' I sneered.

'Hello? Were you listening? She was the one coming on to me.'

'Well, you must have encouraged her in some way.'

'I can hardly help it if women find me irresistible,' Deep said smugly.

'You are quite a flirt, Deep,' I said teasingly.

'Thanks for the compliment. I always try my best,' he wisecracked.

Okay. I admit I was feeling jealous, but not because I had any feelings for Deep. It was because I was feeling aroused by Deep's literotica narration and beginning to miss my Jay.

'Please stop, Deep,' I said desperately.

'I wish she had pleaded to me to stop. Sadly, it didn't get that far,' said Deep, dejected.

'What happened?' I asked, curiosity getting the better of me.

'I told you, nothing happened. I was about to make a move when she took out a *sutta* and asked me if I had a lighter,' said Deep with a devastated expression.

'Poor you!' I said pitifully. 'The beast kept waiting for the true love, while the beauty danced, smoked and left,' I kidded.

He threw a small pillow lightly at me. I caught it and smiled back, a real smile this time, for I knew that Deep was allergic to cigarette smoke.

'Next time try drinking the lucky potion, Felix Felicis,' I recommended but my Potter joke was lost on Deep.

'I am sorry to keep you waiting, bhabhiji,' said Sanjeev guiltily, coming out of the kitchen.

It was a very hot day and Sanjeev was sweating like a pig. I noticed a lock of his oily hair stuck across his forehead. His tilak was all smeared and the heavy gold chain around his neck glistened with sweat. He looked more like a Raja Babu type rich, country bumpkin than a sharp-minded IITian. He turned on the air conditioning to the maximum.

'I thought I heard Deep bhai. Where is he?'

I pointed outside, to the balcony, where Deep was standing, busy on his phone, giving directions for Sanjeev's house to someone.

'Have some p*rasad*,' he offered, holding a box of freshly cooked *boondi* laddoos in one hand and adjusting his La-Z-Boy recliner with another.

The sweet appetizing smell filled my nostrils as Sanjeev popped one full piece into his mouth.

I was very tempted. I bent forward slightly and extended my hand to pick one when I noticed Sanjeev's fingers smeared in yellow oily syrup as he generously helped himself to another piece.

'No, thanks, Sharmaji,' I refused reluctantly.

'Don't mind, but we Indian men prefer fat ladies. I mean more the fat, more there is to love, right?' Sanjeev laughed loudly and a few pieces of laddoo stuck in his mouth flew out and landed on his cream trousers.

I didn't want to get into the biological nitty gritty of where men liked fat on women, but I found myself nodding in agreement.

'I feel that this dieting is all wrong. One day you are eating salads to lose calories and the other day you immerse yourself in chocolate pie, gaining back more than you could lose,' Sanjeev continued his lecture, gorging on the laddoos all by himself.

Salivating at the thought of the delicious, sugary, yellow balls dissolving on my tongue, I couldn't agree with him more. I was a live example of the yoyo dieting he was talking about. 'Bigger snacks, bigger slacks,' I quietly repeated Jay's latest dieting mantra to myself.

'Fattest people are often the happiest,' Sanjeev stated firmly. 'Research has shown that an increase in your BMI causes a rise in the quantity of serotonin, the feel-good hormone in your body, which leads to a happy state.'

With convincing arguments like these, Sanjeev could easily put VLCC weight management programmes out of business.

'Do you not like sweets?' He asked incredulously as he devoured his fifth laddoo.

I looked at the sinfully delicious contents of the box in his hand and wondered why the things that you desire are always the ones you ought not to be having. A holiday from school, a dance with your boyfriend's roomy, an ice cream in winters and your dad's credit card.

There was only one piece left now. I couldn't resist any more. I quickly made a dive for the last laddoo but before I could get my hands on it, Sanjeev closed the lid.

'Madhuri ji likes these laddoos. Let's leave this one for her,' he said and put the box away.

Just then the bell rang. Sanjeev got up eagerly to get the door hoping that it would be MD. We were both disappointed to hear Kammo's honey sugared voice as she walked into the drawing room.

'That is a very interesting tee you are wearing, Deep,' said Kammo as Deep walked inside from the balcony.

I turned around to see what was printed on Deep's t-shirt. I was stunned to see that it had inverted commas drawn in various different poses like 69, 99 etc., and at the bottom it said 'Comma Sutra'.

Holy cow! How I had not noticed this before? I looked up to read the expression on Deep's face and found him smiling suggestively at me. I bit my lips sheepishly and prayed silently that he would not tell everyone about my KS misunderstanding and make fun of me. For good or bad, right now he seemed more interested in Kamini.

'I am glad you found your way,' remarked Deep, reclaiming the seat opposite mine.

'I can always find my way to you,' Kammo replied coquettishly, in her high-pitched voice, and sat down on the sofa next to Deep.

She was wearing a green *patiala salwar* with a short yellow *kurti*. A green chiffon *chunni* adorned her bosom. With her long flowing hair, dangling silver earrings and a small green bindi, she looked quite the epitome of Indian beauty.

Ignoring Sanjeev and me, she looked into Deep's eyes and said, 'I am so excited about singing with you at the annual staff meet.'

'Yeah. Should be fun,' replied Deep, echoing her enthusiasm.

'I have already shortlisted the songs,' she squealed excitedly, and started crooning '*Gum hai kisi ke pyaar mein dil subah shaam . . .*' She lifted her eyes to look into Deep's, pouted and then coyly looked down again as Deep joined her in the romantic, playful duet.

Oh! She was such a show-off. To be fair, she was an amazing singer, perhaps even better than Deep, but I couldn't stand her self-important attitude. No, I didn't have any feelings for Deep. It was just that her affected manner of speaking made me pukish.

Luckily, Madhuri, Vikas and Kavita arrived by the time their song finished. I saw Sanjeev take MD aside and offer her the last laddoo. She smiled demurely and followed him into the kitchen to get the snacks organized. A while later, we were all sitting comfortably, sipping on cold coffee and munching *gobhi* pakoras. Everyone listened with rapt attention as Deep retold the story of how a sexily innocent-looking girl came up to him and asked him for a lift.

Having heard it before, I was sitting on the swanky sofa, admiring Sanjeev's beautiful house and its luxurious furnishing, when Kammo asked why Sanjeev had purchased such a huge place.

'*Abe sooli pe to nahin chad raha na?*' Vikas jibed.

Sanjeev's fair cheeks turned a ripe tomato red at the mention of marriage. 'I want my parents to come and stay with me,' he replied with a cherubic smile.

'That could be stifling,' warned Kavita.

'He is talking about his parents, not his in-laws.' Vikas took a jab at Kavita and she gave him a disgruntled stare.

I thought Vikas was being funny, but then I wasn't married to him. I pursed my lips to stifle the laughter.

'Whole day TV, non-stop nagging, and *pooja-paath*. Retired parents are a pain, yaar,' cribbed Kammo.

Although I could relate to Kavita's preference for an independent life, I was shocked at Kammo's disregard for the elders.

'*Wah Kammoji! Kya doodh ka karz ada kiya hai apne*,' said MD mockingly.

'I wasn't breast-fed,' Kammo shot back angrily.

A small laugh escaped from my lips and I quickly covered my mouth with my hand.

'Even if your mother didn't breast-feed you, I am sure your parents helped you walk the first steps of your life,' said Madhuri in a soft, calm voice, bobbing her head up and down like Dev Anand.

'Everyone's parents do,' said Kammo with a simper.

'Shouldn't you then help them walk their last?' MD snapped, delivering her punch line in *Baghban* style.

Kammo was now lost for words. She looked at Deep for help. Given that Deep had returned to India for his parents' sake, it was no surprise when he also supported Madhuri's viewpoint. Kammo was dumbfounded. The swaggering smile painted on her face vanished like Deep had applied a nail polish remover on it.

'I don't mind the *Aastha* channel or the "come home soon, eat more, don't ride a bike" instructions as much,' intervened Sanjeev. 'I am more worried because my parents are getting old,' he clarified, deep furrows materializing between his bushy eyebrows. 'I need to find a girl, fall in love with her, convince her to marry me and then . . .' Sanjeev paused and smiled shyly before continuing, '. . . fulfil my parents' desire for grand kids. And I have to do all this within a year.'

Wow! And I thought our project had tough deadlines!

'Why waste time looking for love?' Vikas remarked.

Kavita gave him another mean look, but Vikas ignored her and added, 'Simply marry a girl your parents like. You will get more even options to choose from.'

'And you can ensure that the girl is not qualified enough to ever exceed your salary, but is educated enough to be able to handle the kids' homework,' Kavita replied cuttingly.

Vikas just continued to grin. I was beginning to get irritated by the arrogant, stupid smirk on his face. I couldn't believe how the sweet nothings of love had been reduced to nothing sweet in Vikas and Kavita's life. The bitterness in their marriage could put bitter gourd to shame and make a girl think twice before proposing to her love. Yet MD surprised me by siding with Vikas.

'Looking for love is like a temporary employment,' she said. 'You can't seek other options, there is no guarantee of becoming permanent, and the other party can end the contract any time and hire your best friend instead.'

I knew where MD was coming from. If my college-time boyfriend of two years had ditched me and hooked up with my best friend, I too, would end up hating love. I mean, for a little while perhaps. But you don't stop drinking because of a bad hangover. You just make sure you get better liquor the next time.

I was about to tell MD that you don't give up on good things in life because of a single bad experience, when she said, pointing explicitly at Kammo, 'If a good-looking girl, from a good college like LSR wants to marry an analyst in McKinsey, how does she meet him? Arranged marriage is the only way.'

Kammo was nonplussed. She knew that Deep had received an arranged marriage proposal for me and she was not too eager to encourage arranged marriages, definitely not Deep's, but MD had called her good-looking so she had to play along.

I, too, was confused. I had never viewed arranged marriages as social dating services that helped to bring together people who otherwise would not have met. I didn't think arranged marriages did anything more useful than increasing India's population. 'Aren't there any dating services in India?' I wondered out aloud.

Kammo gave me a 'you stupid FRI (Foreign Returned Indian)'

stare. 'The girl ends up looking desperate if she goes on a random date in India.' She spoke with the look of someone who had been there, done that.

'Deep can help make your random dates more fruitful,' I joked, and cast a knowing look at Deep who smiled back warmly.

Kammo was not too pleased to see Deep and me share private jokes, but I was having the time of my life. It was hugely satisfying to watch Kammo getting hammered. But, I wasn't happy with MD's negative opinion on love marriage. I had to convince MD to give love another chance.

Before I could say anything to convince MD to give love another chance, she started humming, '*Kya karoon hai, kuch kuch hota hai*,' hinting at Deep and me, even though she knew there was nothing brewing between us. Okay, partly it was my fault as I hadn't told anyone about Jay yet, but why was MD adding fuel to Kammo's fire? I was beginning to wonder if MD disliked Kammo only due to her conceited attitude or did it have anything to do with Kammo's recent shift to Sanjeev's team?

'Will you marry a rich, fat guy, if your parents found one?' Kammo challenged MD, unable to control her anger. Sanjeev looked like he had been stabbed in his heart. The colour drained from his chubby cheeks.

'I don't mind fat,' replied MD coolly, and the immediately the colour returned to Sanjeev's face.

If it was up to Tanu di to do matchmaking, she would have declared Sanjeev and MD man and wife right now. I was happy to see a faint spark between Sanjeev and MD, but I couldn't just let everyone bash love marriages. I seriously felt that matches in arranged marriages were based on hard facts rather than feelings.

'An arranged marriage may give you more choices, but at the end of the day, you basically do "Inky Pinky Ponky" and randomly select a donkey. How else do you decide whether to marry the person who loves to read fiction or non-fiction?' I asked good-naturedly.

'Choose the opposite of what you like. Opposites attract,' opined Kavita.

'I would say birds of a feather flock together,' Vikas contradicted.

'No two people can have the same taste in books or music,' MD generalized.

'Or lipstick flavour,' said Deep naughtily, and added, 'My personal favourite is strawberry.'

'It's raspberry,' I corrected unconsciously.

'Oh, sorry. Yeah, its raspberry,' agreed Deep mischievously.

Everyone looked from me to Deep and back, puzzled how I knew Deep's lipstick flavour preference.

I could almost feel my skin burn under Kammo's intense glare. Before she could attack me, Sanjeev butted in.

'I know arranged marriages are much simpler for boys,' he said, 'but I want someone who will marry me for me and not for my money or education. I don't want to land up marrying a pear.'

Pear? What did Sanjeev mean by that? Everyone seemed confused. Madhuri looked uncomfortably at her heavy bottom and B cup-size top.

'Pear as in *naashpati*,' translated Sanjeev.

We were still not able to understand what he was trying to say.

'*Arre bhai, naashpati matlab pati ka naash karne waali,*' Sanjeev explained and everyone burst into hysterical laughter.

I was lazying outside in Sanjeev's little private garden, a luxury for those of us who live in high-rise buildings. The sun seemed reluctant to wind up its art class and was colouring the sky in a left-over pinkish hue. I could tell from the clinking of the plates and beep of the microwave timer, coming from kitchen, that MD and Sanjeev were busy preparing dinner. Kavita was standing on the first floor balcony, talking on the phone with her mom. Vikas and Deep were watching

WWE inside and Kammo was trying to become the ultimate cool babe by giving them company. I closed my eyes and meditatively listened to the birds rest in their nests, and engage in after-dinner chirping. I wondered if they were tweeting about the reducing green cover in the NCR or the increased pollution in the Yamuna which was discouraging their migratory friends from visiting them. I must have been lulled to sleep by the relaxing sounds of nature, coz I was startled by the ringing of my phone.

'Hello,' I said, in a sleepy voice.

'There is an unprecedented Buy 1, Get 1 offer on a dark brown Paris Hilton handbag. Should I get you one?' It was Neha calling from a showroom in Milan.

'As long as you let me keep the free one,' I cracked up. I was so excited to hear her bubbly voice. She had been on a never-ending pre-engagement shopping tour for the last three weeks.

'I wish you were here, honey. These Italian boys are so touchy feely sexy.'

'Is there a deal on them as well?' I asked, and we both started giggling like we were back in the school courtyard, secretly ogling senior boys and passing remarks on them.

'Um ... actually, I need some help,' she said seriously.

Surprised by her sudden change of mood, I asked if everything was okay.

'I am having sex issues with my fiancé,' she spoke in a hushed voice.

'I thought you had already established that you were sex-patible,' I said, worried. 'Hope you are not breaking up?'

'No, no. But I need your help.'

What possible help could I offer in this area? I thought to myself.

'The problem is that he is an early morning guy and I am a late night gal. Can you ask your sex-pert boss about how to manage this timing mismatch?'

I told her I would connect her to Deep so she could directly seek his help. 'Anything else?' I asked.

'Ya. Give him a kiss from my side,' she said, back to her playful self, and hung up the phone.

Friends and their unique demands!

SUITOR # 2

When Deep informed Dad that he was not ready for marriage yet, Dad had first joked about men being never ready to get tied down. When he realized that Deep was going ahead with further studies, he had suggested that we explore other suitors. We were sitting in the living room, Dad on the sofa and I on the cool marble floor below. It was Friday evening and Ma was busy buying cows and lambs from a one-hour yard sale on Farmville.

'You need to be sure about your feelings for this American guy,' Dad said, filling his palms with Parachute hair oil and vigorously rubbing it into my scalp. 'Meet other guys. See if you still love him.'

Who would refuse a blanket flirting permission? Still, I warned him, 'Dad, you know when I really like something or someone, it's hard to get me to like anything else.'

He nodded and looked lovingly at me. 'First we have to ascertain if you really like this Jay Guy as much as the powdered milk. Maybe he is just a mashed banana in your taste-building experience?'

I smiled at the analogy. I distinctly remembered watching a childhood video of my first year. Dad was trying to feed me mashed banana. I had proudly overturned the bowl on the floor, dipped my fingers into the mess and applied it all over my face and his like a face pack, but not a spoon had gone inside my mouth. Finally, Dad had given me Cerelac mixed with my favourite Parle-G biscuits which

I had happily devoured. This was Dad. I could be myself with him.

'Dad, you really think one meeting with a stranger is enough?' I asked earnestly, without any fear of being scorned.

'You always know the sandal you want to buy within five minutes of stepping into a store,' Dad replied.

'Well, yeah. But I do spend the next half an hour browsing around before buying what I initially chose,' I countered. 'And these are sandals not husbands. I buy ten of these every year.'

'All human behaviour is an attempt to remove doubt from our lives,' Dad theorized. 'That is precisely why I want you to meet other boys.'

I was still missing the point. Dad seemed to agree that you can't make the decision of your life in a single meeting, and yet, he wanted me to go through the motions.

'You shouldn't have any regrets later,' Dad explained further. 'There are seven vows to eternal bonding but there is no seven-day return policy.'

It was weird comparing shoe shopping to a groom hunt, but I think I finally knew what Dad was saying.

'So you want me to evaluate other prospects to make sure Jay is the right choice?' I asked baffled, still not sure what Dad had to gain from this exercise.

Dad spread out his hands, his palms facing upwards in a 'now you get it' gesture.

'There is also a slim chance that you might stumble upon a soulmate in the process,' revealed Dad, his eyes gleaming with hope. 'A glass slipper that fits you like you were Cinderella.'

I wasn't a huge believer of matches made in heaven, but I needed to buy time till I got a job offer from the US or Jay visited India. I agreed to browse brawny bachelors in search for a sole-mate.

The day arrived when I was going to meet the first of the seven suitors that Dad had lined up for me. The idea was to spend a month with each prospect to get to know him well before moving on to the next. Dad was following the same principle that is used to introduce new foods to a baby. I sat in front of my dressing table, wrapped in a soft, light pink dressing gown, listening to AIR FM radio. No matter what the occasion, I loved getting ready. I always found this time in front of the mirror, experimenting on my face with different colours and strokes, as creatively satisfying as painting on a canvas. I picked up an angled eye-shadow brush from my array of make-up brushes and dipped it in dark brown liquid eyeliner. Holding the skin of my upper eyelid taut, I was working on creating the bold dramatic eye effect, when Deep called. We had gotten into a routine of calling each other and hanging out together with the office gang, especially on weekends. However, I wasn't expecting his call today for he knew that I had an arranged date. Surprised, I pressed the talk button with the hard tip of my extended nail and put him on loudspeaker.

'Nervous?' he asked.

'No, just feeling weird,' I replied.

'This isn't your cup of tea, then why taste it?' he asked curiously.

'For my dad, I guess.'

'Will you marry this fellow if you like him?'

'I doubt I will, but I hope he does like me.'

'Rejection phobia, huh?'

'Big time!' I acceded. I was a self-proclaimed rejection guru, but only when I was not on the receiving end.

'He surely will,' said Deep with a conviction that scared me, 'especially if you tell him you are good at smashing balls.'

'Now, why does that sound sleazy?' I jibed. I knew Deep was referring to the chance smash I had managed in the after-hours office volleyball match last evening. It was nice to banter with him. Deep had come a long way from being a monstrous picture on my laptop screen, from becoming a keep-you-on-your-toes boss, to the guy who dumped me before I could, to the now PJ pal.

'Because you have a dirty mind,' he stated in a matter-of-fact manner.

'Look who is talking! I thought you are the one who operates a sex-advice vending machine in office.'

I heard his raspy, chuckling laugh echo loudly on the speakerphone.

'I am organizing a "KS for beginners" session next week at Vikas's place in case you are interested.'

'What? Really! Is that why you called?' I asked, astonished.

'No. I actually called to say sorry.' His voice was suddenly soft and apologetic.

'For?' I asked while using a medium-sized flat brush to add colour to my cheekbones.

'For accidentally touching your . . . er . . . your t-shirt,' he stuttered.

I figured he was talking about when his hand had grazed over my chest while playing volleyball. I remembered being aware of his hand and feeling a momentary rush of excitement, but used to playing sports with boys, I hadn't given it another thought. It was surprising that Deep had registered the incident and felt awkward about it. The only time a guy noticed such things was when his wife or girlfriend pointed it out and she was not the one being touched. I assumed he was just being a decent boss.

'I haven't been very decent myself, trying to kiss you in the car and then again in the bar,' I replied sportingly. 'I say we are even.'

'I say we are not,' snapped Deep immediately, his voice no longer wavering. 'You tried to kiss me twice. Technically, I can have one more go at it.'

'High hopes,' I said lightly. 'Did you forget about dumping me? I would say that neutralized my second attempt at kissing you.'

'Whatever,' said Deep indifferently, not interested in getting into the 'I didn't dump you' argument again.

'Suhaani, are you ready?' I heard Mom's voice calling me from the kitchen.

'I gotta go,' I said, applying the last layer of make-up.

'Do this suitor a favour. Don't kiss him if you want to dismiss him,' said Deep, laughing out loud at his own joke.

I didn't like the way he was making fun of me. 'Will call you later,' I said hurriedly as I heard the doorbell ring.

'Don't bother,' said Deep airily. 'I am going out for a movie with Come-in-i. I will call you when I am free.'

Hearing him talk about Kamini irritated me further. 'Who are you playing hard to get with? No one is coming to get you anyway,' I riposted.

'She is nice, you know.' Deep continued.

'She is a girl after all. The least she could be for an IITian is nice.' I shot back calmly and disconnected.

I felt a shiver as the cool air from the AC caressed my skin through the slit in my gown, reminding me that I still had to get dressed. I could tell from the increase in the activity level and sounds coming from the living area that the guests had arrived. Mom had strictly instructed me to wear only traditional clothes. No bold colours, no noodle straps and definitely no halternecks. Sifting through the contents of my wardrobe, I found that there was only one dress meeting her criteria. It was not that I didn't like non-bold colours. Rather, I loved wearing earthen, pastel shades in summer, but who wears sleeves in summer these days? I pulled out the pale green, cotton suit with three-fourth sleeves that I had bought three years ago from a Pragati Maidan expo. After much tugging, pulling and arm twisting, when I finally managed to fit in, I could barely breathe without my tyres noticeably breathing with me. I looked like I was wearing two swimming rings beneath my costume. These tyres were a fashion disaster. I had to get rid of them, if not for any other reason, then for the sake of my dress sense, which I was very particular about. I knew everyone was waiting for me and I knew that Mom would be furious if I wore one of my choices, but I figured I needed to breathe to be able to survive or get married. This was all happening because of Jay. If only he would agree to come down and meet my parents, I could be spared this drama. And that hideous Kameenee. And how could Deep be so naive as to fall for her. I cursed them all as I somehow managed to wriggle out of the tight-wrap and changed into a comfortable noodle strap, yellow kurta with a blue churidar. I covered my exposed shoulders with a crinkled blue dupatta. Just to keep Mom happy, I also wore my dad's grandmother's gold jhumkis that Mom had taken out of the locker for the occasion.

My phone beeped. It was a message from Deep: 'Best of luck. P.S. You look Very Nice in Indian dresses.'

A happy smile slowly replaced the frown on my face.

My phone beeped again.

Message from Dad: 'Come down, *beta*. We are all waiting for you.'

I gave myself one last look in the mirror and sprinted down the corridor. I was only a few steps away, when I realized that ten pairs of eyes were keenly following my movement. I immediately slowed down and lowered my head, which was anyway being pulled downwards by the weight of stones tearing at my ears. Ignoring my mom's disapproving glare, I readjusted the dupatta that had slid aside exposing my transparent bra-straps and started walking delicately.

I am going to skip the details of the girl serving a tray of tea to the prospective groom's party, walking shakily like she had just learned to walk, her eyes lowered to make it convenient to check out the guy's package, while the guy sneakily sizes her bust. You must have all experienced this scene either in the main role or a side role. Frankly though, other than the gulab jamuns and samosas, nothing else is worth mentioning.

Next day, I was watching the previous night's recording of KBC with my parents. It was a scorching hot Sunday afternoon. The air conditioner was running on full blast, but I could still feel the sweat on my palms. Looking debonair in a black bandhgala suit, Amitabh was discussing the everyday life of a peon's daughter from a remote village in Madhya Pradesh, who was on the hot seat, when my phone burped.

Message from Deep: 'I have decided not to go for an MBA.'

In today's paper, I had read an article on how the average salary across top tier B-schools had dropped by 25 per cent, wiping out the record 20 per cent to 22 per cent salary gains students made last year.

'Good choice, but I am not available now,' I replied.

The very next instant, my phone started vibrating vehemently. My parents were a big fan of Big B, so all our mobile phones were kept in silent mode while they watched KBC. This was the only time Mom entrusted her farm with the Farmville cheats application to automatically plough, plant and harvest her crops.

'Big boss calling,' my phone's screen read.

'Are you planning to take part in that ridiculous reality show?' Mom asked disdainfully, staring at my phone.

Mom really had a wild imagination. I must have inherited it from her. I shook my head, picked up the phone and went inside my room.

'Hi,' I said.

'Congratulations,' said Deep.

'For?'

'Your marriage.'

'With whom?'

'To the arranged suitor #2.'

'Who told you?'

'You just said you were unavailable, so I deduced that you have decided to marry the guy you were seeing yesterday.'

'Are you jealous?'

'Hell no, poor guy!'

'I agree. Can you believe I was the fifty-first prospect he was evaluating in the last two years?'

'Fifty-first! Are you sure he was not looking for a reliable, fully trained maid who can read his mind and receive his couriers?'

'You mean like a soul-maid,' I punned and we both cracked up.

'So I take it that you told him that you guys were not "maid for each other".'

'No.'

'No?'

Was there a sense of disappointment in Deep's voice or did I just imagine it? 'I didn't but Dad did. The moment Mr Suitor #2 uttered that he was exploring opportunities abroad, I knew his game was over.'

'Hmm. So technically you are still available then.'

'Technically, yes. I am still waiting for my Mr Right to sweep me off my feet.' I could have told Deep about Jay, but it was fun to flirt like a not-in-relationship-with-anyone single. At least, till you turned thirty, after which "wow, she is single" became "why is she still single" and you would rather pretend to be seeing someone than not.

'Do you have a list of questions to ask these suitors?' Deep asked curiously.

'Of course!' I had laboriously prepared a twenty-five point list after viewing ten YouTube videos on arranged marriages. How else was I supposed to convince my parents and the guy that we were not compatible?

'You mind emailing it to me?' he said seriously.

'Wo ho ho. Now we are talking. So who do you want to test your compatibility with?'

'Kamini.'

I almost choked on the water I was drinking directly from the bottle.

Deep obviously couldn't see my reaction. 'She sang a love song for me last night, after the movie and then she proposed,' he explained.

'Cool!'

'I know, I am flattered but I am also confused.'

I didn't know what to say. I was also feeling confused. 'She is the kind of diamond that shines so much that you wonder if its fake. And she seems allergic to old parents, but otherwise she will suit you,' I offered my candid opinion.

Deep burst out laughing at my description. He seemed unperturbed by Kamini's *'Main apni favourite hoon'* attitude. He also told me that he had informed her that she was expected to stay with his parents after marriage and she had said she was fine with it.

'She even came over and met them this morning,' he said in her defence.

That was super quick. Our generation really was instant. 'Is that why you dropped the MBA idea?' I asked surprised.

'No. That credit goes to you,' I heard him chuckle softly. 'Remember the other day when I told you that I wanted to be an entrepreneur and you said that a start-up doesn't require an MBA?'

WTF! I had rambled off some GQ about Mark Zuckerberg, Bill Gates, Steve Jobs and our very own Baba Ramdev being college dropouts and even the Google founders Page and Brin being only engineering graduates. How was I supposed to know that he would take me seriously and drop the idea of an MBA or that Kammo would grab the opportunity to dip her biscuit in his chai? Well, as long as Deep doesn't blame me for the mush at the bottom of his teacup due to Kamini's dissolved biscuit, I was happy with my hazelnut-flavoured Jay-caffee. As Tanu di would say, it's not practically possible for a girl and a guy to be friends forever. Of course, Deep was going to get married and of course, I was going to get married and we all know that friendships change after marriage.

I could hear Amitabh Bachchan's powerful voice asking for an audience poll in the drawing room outside. Not in the mood to listen to Kammo's proposal story or interact with anyone in the offline world, I hung up the phone and decided to engage in some quasi-socializing and logged on to FB.

Neetu's status read, 'Two more weeks to the wedding. I wonder if it will feel any different doing it as husband and wife.' I thought about a typical Indian bride in a red and golden lehenga, sitting on a bed decorated with rose petals, waiting for her husband to come in and deflower her. *Suhaag raat* had such a special meaning in her life. It was her freedom from the social constraints to finally explore and enjoy sex with a socially approved partner. It was something she had been dreaming about and preparing for ever since she first saw the hot steamy scene on the big screen. And here was Neetu for whom the wedding night was like having yet another bite of the wicked brownie. It left me wondering if it was better to dig into a tried and tasted pie or if the whole virgin experience was really worth the wait. I added some smilies on her post.

Jay had sent me a 'mis u, luv u, can't wait 2 kis u' message. I replied saying 'me 2' and urged him to come to India for the Neetu–Ashraf wedding and meet my parents as well.

I was impressed to see an update even from the not so FB savvy MD. 'One day someone will walk in your life and make you see why it never worked out with anyone else,' she had written. Looks like someone is falling in love all over again. Good for Sanjeev. I thought. His 'parents to grandparents in one year' project was really on a tight schedule.

What really got me excited was the message from Neha about a cool new FB application called Crushaider. I went to its page and it had this bold white lettering on a red background that read, 'Does your crush have a crush on you?' Finally, somebody had come up with a cool, innovative, fast and embarrassment-free way of finding out if the person you loved, loves you back. Curious, I logged on their web page and sent out a 'I have a crush on you' message to Jay. It promised to send a mail to both of us in case Jay responded with my email address. It also assured me that in case Jay had a crush on some other email address, then he will never know who sent him this crush message, saving me the embarrassment. Not that it mattered in this case. I was just testing their service, not our love. Next, on a crazy impulse, I sent another crush message, this time to Deep. With Kammo having proposed to him and his mysterious non-girlfriend date Meeta whom he never talked about, he would never guess it was me.

CAN'T TAKE ANOTHER REJECTION

I was sitting all by myself in a secluded treehouse, a few minutes' walk from the main camp in Chakrata. Chakrata is a beautiful place 70 kilometres from Dehradun. Nestling in the lap of nature, set amidst the stepped farms overlooking a valley, with magnificent views of the snow-capped Himalayan peaks, Chakrata had divine beauty. Coming from the high-rise concrete jungle where my daily contact with nature was the pigeon shit scattered all over my balcony, I felt spoilt for choice. I took a long, deep breath of fresh, naturally purified air and then slowly exhaled it. I could feel the cobwebs in my mind getting sucked out by oxygen-rich air. Feeling rejuvenated, I picked up my sketch book and started capturing the pristine beauty of nature, untouched by mankind. My detoxification however was interrupted by the Airtel's *atoot network*.

Message from Mom: 'Jay is going trekking with his friends.'

I replied saying, 'Stale news'. Ever since Mom had befriended Jay on FB, she had become a 24 x 7 spy looking for gossip to turn me against him. Initially, when she had started digging up Jay's older posts, she had been shocked to learn that I had started dating Jay within a month of reaching Michigan. Confident that Jay had been my way to cope with homesickness and convinced that an

American tofu was no replacement for the Indian paneer, she had been feeding me scandalous titbits from his past like the time he had been caught jerking off under the desk by his biology teacher or the sophomore year V-day when he had dated ten different girls in the same cafe at one-hour intervals.

I had just deleted Mom's message when I saw another new message icon.

Message from Mom: 'Denise is also going with him.'

This time my heart stopped beating and my hands froze. Most of Mum's news was like the repeat telecast of the Jay-covery channel, but this was sensational 'Denise' *Tehelka*. Jay had told me that a bunch of guys from his gym group were going for a weekend bike trail, but he hadn't mentioned any of them being girls or specifically Denise. My imagination ran amok. I could see Jay sitting on a log in a forest, lifting Denise's smooth, sexy legs to his lap and tenderly massaging her lovely feet with his firm fingers. Moments later, he was watching her bathe Mandakini-style under a waterfall, only now the white saree seemed to be missing. Suddenly the scene changed and he was sitting beside me up in this treehouse, rubbing the sides of my back with his thumbs. His legs were dangling down the wooden plank, occasionally playing footsie with mine. He cracked a joke about a man-sitting-up vs a miss-under-standing. I was giggling madly at his KS joke and . . . wait. KS joke? Something was amiss. How did my hazelnut-flavoured Jay-caffe become KS-spiked D-caffe? 'Looks like you have been smitten with the *Jaane Tu Ya Jaane Na* bug, teased my back office. 'Thinking friendship, feeling love'—this was a common condition afflicting teenagers with little or no experience. But this couldn't be happening to me! Urgh, this was so humiliating. Neha would kill me for this blasphemy. This couldn't be happening!

'It must be due to the excessive parental pressure that I was having to deal with,' I consoled myself. I had met with two more prospective *paneer*s (you could call them *murga*s if you are a non-vegetarian) in the last two weeks and my ear lobes were threatening me with a regional split if I didn't stop the jhumkis invasion soon enough. Suitor #3 had been kicked out by my mom as he had asked for all her Farmville assets in my dowry while suitor #4 had rejected me on grounds of being a control freak. I had just asked him if he liked doing it in the bathroom or was he open to doing it on the dining table instead. Guess some people are rather touchy about where they read their newspaper. Thankfully I was spared this weekend as I had to come away for an official team-building trip.

I wished that finding your life partner was easier. That, there was one fixed, easy-to-find soulmate for everyone and that one just knew the person one ought to love and marry. For instance, you could be born with a unique number on your navel that your parents could post in a worldwide database the moment you were born and search for the only other person with the matching number. Oh! That might not work, as it would require too many digits with the increasing world population. Besides, some parts of the world still didn't have Internet access. Well, then maybe if you met someone who was your destined life partner, you could both develop a matching pattern, almost like an allergic reaction, only in the nice way. It could be a matching eyebrow pattern, or the love line in your palms, or something like that. See I was so confused now.

I picked up a fern lying nearby and started plucking its leaves. J, D, J, D ... I mumbled alternately as I picked each leaf. The last leaf had ended with D. C'mon, what did that mean now? Did I love D or J? Why was I finding love so elusive, like finding a star in the daylight or tomato in the ketchup? I really needed to talk to Tanu di. She was a master of these 'one for sorrow, two for joy, three for letter, four for boy' type natural love signals. I was turning my phone at different angles to see where the signal reach was better when it slipped from my fake, decorative nails and fell down.

'Caught it,' said Deep, as I was about to go down in search of my phone's pieces.

His voice was so close that I almost lost my balance and fell off the wooden plank. Standing a few rungs below the treehouse, he held me with one solid arm, holding my lifeline in the other. I smiled with relief and climbed back up.

'What are you doing up here?' he asked curiously.

I couldn't tell him that I had been daydreaming about him playing footsie with me. 'Seeking myself,' I replied and leaned back against the treetrunk.

'Did I spoil the fun by seeking you out?' he smiled. He had settled himself beside me, his legs also dangling. I felt a shiver run up my spine as his leg accidentally touched mine.

'What are you doing up here?' I asked to distract myself.

'Hiding myself,' he said in a soft, low voice and winked mischievously at me.

Suddenly, my mind-Pod selected a hide-and-seek song and started playing it in my head.

'Hum aapki aankon mein is dil ko basa dein to . . . hum moond ke palkon ko is dil ko saja de to.'

I must have been lost in the song and singing it out loud, because I felt the warmth of his hand on my lips as he covered my mouth. Startled, I gestured with my eyes to ask what happened? In response, he tapped his ears indicating me to listen. I heard the sound of footsteps rustle the fallen leaves and then I spotted Kammo right below our treehouse. He put his free hand's finger to his mouth telling me to keep quiet like I had a choice in the matter. It had been two weeks since Kamini had proposed to Deep. She had since been away for a family wedding to Australia. Having returned yesterday, she was obviously expecting Deep to announce his love for her.

'I thought you liked her,' I whispered, once I was sure she had retreated back to the main camp.

'I like her and she is nice, but she is not Very Nice.' He was simple and to the point, like only a guy can be.

I felt a small air of jubilance and relief wash over me. 'Have you told her so?' I asked, faking concern.

'Wouldn't be hanging from here like a monkey if I had.'

'No,' I joshed. 'You would be lying down there, trampled, like those crushed leaves.'

He winced at the thought. 'I don't have a lot of experience with breaking hearts,' he said, with a childlike naiveté.

'And I can write a whole thesis on the topic,' I laughed again.

'So what's the most effective and least painful method of rejecting someone?' he asked half jokingly.

'KISS.'

'You mean like the way you kissed me before you could dump me?' he accused charmingly.

'Alas! I never got the opportunity!' I sighed haughtily.

He made a pitiable face at me and laughed. Unmindful of his teasing, I laughed with him.

'Anyways, I didn't mean that you actually kiss her,' I clarified. 'I meant, "Keep it simple, stupid!"'

'And what would be simple for a girl?' he asked.

'For example, you could tell her that she sings better than you. It could lead to post-marital rivalry like it happened to Jaya and Amitabh in that movie *Abhimaan*. She may end up losing her mental balance like Jaya does in that movie and you don't want to do this to her, and hence you can't marry her.'

'Hmm ... that's rather simple! I get the idea,' he said and gave me a mock salute. He then took out his iPod and started listening to some songs. I picked up my sketch book and began doodling, while my back office was busy determining the probability of a kiss given that a sexually active female sat five inches away from a sexually active male on an isolated treehouse. I sneaked a glance at Deep. His eyes were closed and he seemed very absorbed in the music. Assured that my love for Jay was not under any threat from Deep, I slumped down in a relaxed position and began capturing the shadow of the treehouse on the farm below.

We had played some cool icebreaker games after breakfast in the morning like group juggle and categories followed by more back-breaking and adrenalin-pumping stuff like rock climbing and rappelling. Most lean guys like Deep had been able to climb up the wall with relative ease. Sanjeev, of course, kept slipping down due to his weight and also his oily hands. After the initial couple of steps, I had found it very hard to get a grip of the stone above and lift my body straight up. The team, however, had cheered and I had managed to scale about one third of the wall before my hands finally gave up and I slipped down. Rappelling had been quite scary too although more doable, except that I thought my back would break.

Lunch had been simple dal roti, and sabji but it had tasted delicious especially after the workout. Feeling drowsy after the overnight train journey, the physical activities and a wholesome lunch, I had walked up a few hundred metres away from the camp, found this lovely little treehouse with a hanging rope ladder and climbed up. Of course, all my sleepiness had vanished the moment I saw the panoramic view of the hills and the river Yamuna flowing through the picturesque valley below. There was still an hour before we would drive down for wide-water river-rafting in the Yamuna.

A while later, I felt a warm wisp of air on my neck and found Deep peeping into my sketch book, over my shoulder.

'Why did you join iTrot?' asked Deep.

Feeling conscious of his peering eyes, I straightened the neckline of my top, which had slid down due to my slouching.

'To get a good base for my career and to have some fun,' I replied candidly.

Deep gave me this most funny, quizzical look.

'What? Why are you giving me that "Don't BS me" stare? What do you want me to say? *Saat saumder paar main tere peeche peeche aa gayi*,' I cracked lightly.

'Show me your palm,' he said inquisitively.

I stretched my left hand, palm facing up. He held my hand gently, his thumb gingerly placed above my fingers. He then started to blabber the usual palm reader's bluff. You are a happy-go-lucky person and you don't think before you act but you can pull yourself through a crisis, you are best motivated around deadlines, you have strong perseverance but you sometimes give up too soon etc. If you are surprised how all this describes you perfectly too, it is because it is meant to. Guys love to practice chiromancy on girls so as to get a chance to hold their hands. Well-versed with these tactics, I wasn't taken aback by the aptness of his predictions about me. However, every time he traced my lines with his forefinger, I felt a strange tingling on my skin and every time he said something nice about me, I felt an uncontrollable urge to reward him with a kiss.

'You are experiencing chaos because your heart is elsewhere,' he concluded, his voice calm and controlled, a stark contrast to the conflicting emotions churning inside me.

This time he had managed to unnerve me. Did he know about my relationship with Jay? I hadn't checked my FB or mails for over eighteen hours. Had there been any post on my wall that gave it away?

'When you see a curved, zigzag line, you don't see the company's sales graph going up and down, you see a river winding through a valley,' he added further.

'Is this written on my hand?' I asked, startled.

'No, but it's drawn here.' He smiled, dropping my hand aside and pointing to my sketch book. 'You are awesome at art! Why don't you paint the rainbow of your dreams on a canvas rather than PowerPoint?'

It felt so good hearing him praise my work. Excitedly I told him about my dream to add nude artworks to the New York Met museum. 'But unlike M.F. Hussain, not everyone can make money by painting nudes,' I sighed. I intentionally left out the male part as I didn't want him to think that I was asking him to model nude for me. Though that would have been fun!

'I have never seen or bought a Hussain and I know practically nothing about nude paintings, though I wouldn't mind one in my bedroom,' he said, tickled by the idea. 'But I know a senior of mine from IIT, who left her corporate career and found passion in art. She is now a full-time art curator in Gurgaon. I am sure she would love to exhibit your paintings.'

I didn't know what to say or do. I was elated to find a place to dump my canvasses. I wouldn't have to look at Dad's small, helpless face every time I got a new canvas and Mom cribbed about her need for a bigger house. Ecstatic, I hugged Deep.

'One hug for every painting sold,' he bargained playfully.

'Deal,' I smiled gleefully.

He went back to listening to songs and I to my sketching. Minutes later, I felt his hand on my shoulder. I hadn't realized when he had stood up. I thought he must be gesturing to return. I checked my phone clock. It was almost time for river rafting. I started to pack my pencils when he lifted me by the waist, placed an earplug in my ear, and started turning me around.

A fast-beat, romantic song was playing on his iPod. We had learnt some basic ballroom dance steps on this song for the ASM last week. I was still struggling to learn the nuances of salsa; Deep however seemed a pro. I closed my eyes and let myself flow with his rhythm. He swayed me around with the slightest pressure on my back and gentle push to my arms. I had never experienced anything so romantic in my life before. Nothing about this was real—the cast, the location or the wild excitement that I was experiencing. And then the music changed and a slow number started playing. Deep pulled me closer and I sidled up to him, feeling safer and confident that I wouldn't fall off the treehouse plank.

'Remember the day at the pub, when you had collapsed in my arms?' he said, gazing directly into my eyes. The music continued in the background in our ears.

'Yeah. That was quite embarrassing,' I said, and looked away, feeling shy.

'I was with this girl called Meeta.'

I could vividly recall Meeta. In fact, I had debated many a times later to ask Deep about her, but could never gather the courage. Deep had told me about his close circle of IIT friends and their girlfriends but he had never brought up Meeta before.

'I have known her ever since I got to know the difference between a boy and a girl. We went to the same school. She was my best friend and I was hers.'

I had guessed that much. I wondered why he was telling me this story now.

'That day in the pub, I had proposed to her.'

I remembered the hurt look in Deep's eyes and knew what might have ensued. I waited for him to say it.

'She didn't think I was her Mr Right.' Deep's voice was solemn and pain-stricken.

No wonder he had been so enraged that night about girls playing with guys' feelings. 'Deep, I am so sorry,' I said in order to empathize.

'Let me finish,' he said gravely. There was a strange sadness in his eyes. The kind that I had never seen in anyone's eyes before. The kind that made me scared.

'I don't want to burn my fingers again,' he said. 'So I want to ask you one last time if you are interested in exploring a future with me?'

He wasn't proposing to me or telling me that he loved me. He was simply asking if there was a road for us to be together in the future or was it a dead end. I knew I ought to have said a straight no. I ought to have told him about Jay. This was not about flirting and having fun any more. This was serious. Yet, I found my lips sewn with an invisible thread.

'You don't have to tell me now, but please let me know as soon as you know,' he said softly, and loosened his grip around my waist.

I felt so close and yet so far away from him.

Even though his face had become a blur now, and it didn't matter how he looked, I couldn't possibly get serious about him. I was supposed to be in love with Jay. I was in love with Jay, I corrected myself. My hesitation to reject him must be because he was a good friend and it hurts to hurt friends, I told myself.

When we got back from river rafting, I saw the tears in Kammo's eyes and figured that Deep must have delivered the blow. Better sooner than later. She seemed to be handling it quite well. I found Madhuri and Sanjeev merrily playing cat's cradle in a corner. A bonfire was being lit in the open courtyard, and the guys were getting ready to drink and dance. Deep was busy on his phone and I was lost in my own web of confusion.

I came back home more exhausted than ever. Experiencing web withdrawal symptoms, I immediately logged on to Gmail and saw a 'crush confirmed' new message from Crushaider.com. This was exactly what I needed right now. A confirmation from Jay that he loved me. I clicked open the mail and it said, 'Congrats! dgblahblahl@gmail.com has confirmed a crush on you. We offer you a discount coupon of 25 per cent on your next dinner date.

Please click here to book a restaurant through Crushaider.com.'

OH MY GOD! I checked the mail delivery time. It was yesterday morning. Deep must have already seen the email on his phone before he came over to the treehouse. WTF!

IS HE THE GUY?

Sipping a glass of wine and nibbling on different varieties of amazingly mouth-watering cheese that I had no idea were available in Gurgaon, I was passively observing the surge in demand for contemporary, affordable and aesthetically appealing art in this suburb. It was the opening eve of an art exhibition, at Epicentre, curated by the same art curator that Deep had kindly connected me with. The exhibition hall was bubbling with artsy excitement and overflowing with colour. While some were looking for provocative, catchy art to go with the theme of their upcoming summer bonanza party, others just needed to break the monotony of the expansive cream walls in their recently purchased 5000-square-foot apartment. A serious few were exploring art as alternative investment and a fraction thereof were seeking moments of contemplation, to unlock the worlds inside their soul. Largely it was folks who came along because a friend was coming and they had nothing better to do. The good part was that this majority had a huge discretionary income and were prone to whimsical purchases.

I stood in a corner, looking at the painting of a young girl draped in a Maharashtrian-style saree, the fabric tucked between the legs, with a backless choli. She was walking on a dirt track in a dense forest, towards the ray of hope, her partly bare back facing the viewer.

'She seems to evoke a feeling of definite purpose in my consciousness,' remarked a woman standing beside me and admiring the painting. She was herself dressed in an elegant, designer saree. From the few whites sprinkled in her hair, she seemed to be in her late thirties.

'Me too,' I admitted.

'This artist has never displayed earlier, but I see potential in her works,' observed an older, seemingly art-worldly-wise lady.

'I would like to have her on my bedroom wall, so that every morning she would give me the courage to keep pursuing my dreams in life,' said the first woman. She was definitely interested in buying the painting.

'Sorry, but she is going in my den,' informed the proud owner, a dashingly handsome, forty-something executive in formal business attire.

'Congrats, Suhaani,' he said addressing me, 'Love your work.'

'Thanks for the encouragement, Vikram, but you don't have to buy,' I said, gathering appreciative glances from the women around as they realized I was the artist.

'Trust me, it's not for you, it's for me that I am buying,' he assured me with the ease and poise of a lawyer. 'At least I will have some company to watch TV and discuss stocks with,' he added, and broke into a soft chortle.

With his endearing smile and captivating eyes, he must have been quite some catch in his college days. I wondered why his first wife had left him and if he was buying my painting because he wanted to impress Tanu di?

Just then, we heard an announcement about the chief guest's arrival and headed for the lamp lighting ceremony. Tanu di was already standing at the forefront of the crowd, clicking pictures of Shovana Narayan, the most renowned kathak dancer in the world, as she lit the diyas. Tanu di's passion for kathak was like her love for Champ, subdued under her career aspirations, but still longing for fulfilment. I watched her animatedly discuss the intricacies of footwork and mudras with the legendary dancer. Vikram had to leave so he told me to tell Tanu di that he had a business call to attend and would catch up with Di later. Realizing that Tanu di was not going to be free any time soon, I decided to take a walk up to the snacks table and sample some more cheese and crackers. I was disappointed to learn that my favourite oregano-flavoured cheese was finished but I was thrilled to see red dots against five of my paintings.

It had all happened very suddenly. I had shown Deep's IIT senior my paintings and she had liked them so much, that she decided to accommodate me at the last minute in a exhibition she was organizing the same week.

I wanted to share my ebullience at having sold so many of my works on day one with someone close. Someone who would be able to understand what it meant to me. I selected Deep's number and then feeling guilty, I clicked on cancel. I still hadn't disclosed to him the half-red dot placed against my heart, reserving me for Jay. I somehow wanted to hold on to Deep without giving up Jay. While women are in general adept at multi-tasking, this shared love account was bothering me. I needed to discuss this with Tanu di. Now! I found her outside in the lobby, listening raptly to the Padmashree awardee give sound bites to the media people. I pulled her away from the noisy exhibition hall to the quaint little coffee shop in the building. Ordering a chocolate chip muffin for myself and a double espresso for Di, I asked her about her expedition to Santa's town. I hadn't had a chance to talk to Di since she got back from the North Pole.

'Santa Claus was complaining about the latest size-zero fad,' smiled Di. 'He is under pressure to get rid of his wobbling belly and set a good example for children.'

'Jay is so not getting a gift from Santa this year,' I sniggered, digging into my scrumptious muffin.

'He was also upset with the companies cashing in on his popularity by running weight loss programmes like "How to get rid of a Santa belly" that doesn't benefit him in any way.'

'So Chetan Bhagat isn't the only one having credit issues,' I teased.

Di gave a knowing smile for Chetan was her batchmate from IIT. 'Oh! There are far more serious, financial repercussions,' informed Di, dismissing CB's publicity stunt. 'With Kareena importing the size-zero fad to India, Sensex has also become figure conscious and gone on a crash diet, trying to shed the extra pounds it had gained,' said Di. She was rocking her shoulders back and forth, her chin resting on her hands pensively.

Indians have always been besotted with what America does. With Indian retailers now aping the West and offering upto 50 per cent ' markdowns every change of season, it was not surprising that *market down* had also become a regular phenomenon with the Indian stock market. But I felt that there was an unknown hand in the timing of the market crash that couldn't be attributed to Santa's discontent with Kareena's figure or the 10 per cent off on the La Senza push-up bra.

'You don't think it is Champ's curse, do you?' I surmised.

She smiled at my implication that every time she was looking to raise money, markets went down like it was a curse on her success.

'Vikram's firm has still agreed to fund my company,' she revealed lackadaisically, like it was yet another compliment on her Pantene-advertisement-like long, flowing hair. One would think a ten million dollars' funding in a bear market deserved a bit more enthusiasm. These IIT types! They get so used to big successes so soon that they forget how to enjoy the little pleasures of life.

'That's fabulous, right! You don't have to go to the Himalayas any more looking for sanjeevani booti,' I cheered.

She didn't seem pleased. 'Vikram proposed,' she said, this time sounding peeved like he had asked her for sexual favours.

'You are making it sound like he is asking you to marry him in exchange for the investment. Look at it this way. He is giving you the funding in dowry,' I joked.

'What if I am unable to forget Champ even after I marry Vikram? I don't want to end up screwing VC's life,' she said, twirling her hair around her index finger nervously.

'There is very little chance of you doing that,' I comforted her. 'As of now he is planning to spend his evenings with the painting of a girl with her back towards him. At least you would be a face he would be looking at and a lovely dimpled one at that,' I complimented. 'Besides, Champ had only placed a green dot against your heart,' I reasoned in art jargon. 'A green dot reserves a painting for a collector for a limited time. You have already given Champ over a decade of your life. It is high time you moved on and said yes to Vikram,' I advised.

'I wish I could meet Champ once, just once,' said Di, with apparent longing in her eyes. 'If only I had the Marauder map to locate him,' she pined.

'Sadly Muggles only use RFID locator tags for high-value items in a supermarket,' I kidded and then asked curiously, 'What would you do with him if you did find him? He is married, after all.'

'Punch him in the face, kick him in the balls and ask him why he couldn't wait a few years for the love I have waited my entire life for,' she said, her voice charged with emotions. A cold, vengeful determination had replaced the soft, desirous look in her eyes.

I was taken aback at how a romantic comedy had suddenly transformed into an action thriller.

'We don't have the magical map, but we have FB. Why don't you tell me his name and we will look him up?' I offered eagerly, hopeful that a dramatic encounter with Champ would help her close this chapter for good. I, of course, didn't know Champ's real name else this story would have ended pages ago.

'I told you he is not on FB,' she said, dejected.

'Let's locate Piya then,' I suggested. Tanu di liked the idea. We logged on using Di's BlackBerry. Di searched for Champ's wife, Piya Khanna. After scanning through some fifty-plus results without any luck, I proposed we search using her maiden name as many women from the earlier generation, wanting to get in touch with friends, had stuck to maiden names. This time we easily found the right Piya. Her profile had a picture of her with her ten-year-old son. Tanu di's face turned pale on seeing the child's picture. She perhaps saw Champ's reflection in the chubby, fair boy, though I could bet my nude painting on the fact that he resembled Sharmaji or any other Punjabi *puttar* as much as anyone else. Yet, it was intriguing how love could hurt even after so many years.

'Now you see why I can't marry VC?' she said, taking a gulp of water to swallow her tears.

I could see nothing of that sort. All I could see was that her nose was red as a clown and that Champ had filled her heart with pain and VC was eager to fill it with his love.

'I know I let go of the right guy for my ambition, but I can't marry the wrong guy to fulfil those same dreams.' Di gave me some convoluted BS, but there was no point arguing further. The action thriller had now become an emotional drama. Although I was a sucker for the quintessential Bollywood-styled *'Mere paas ma hai'* histrionics, I had my own pressing matters to discuss. I updated her on Dad's so far unsuccessful suitor shopping and then told her what had transpired back in Chakrata on the lonely treetop with Deep.

'Why didn't I say no to him straight away?' I asked puzzled.

'It can't be because you care for him. You are not the selfless, *mahatma* kind,' Di stated, with absolute confidence in my imperfect humanness. Her eyes were still sombre but I was glad that she had regained her sense of humour.

'Yeah, I know,' I promptly agreed, relieved to be able to talk without any façade. Being the only child, I had always felt this pressure of being extra good, of doing what my parents would deem right. Yet, I was a normal human being with my own set of weaknesses. I liked to splurge on my shoes even though I knew that there were kids living on the street that roamed barefoot. I often judged people by their clothes and I sometimes picked my nose and threw the booger on the ground. Di, however, was one person with whom I could be just me, without having to be an idle daughter, the perfect girlfriend or a good, moral citizen.

'Do you think I simply wanted to keep my options open?' I speculated.

'If you were in high school or college, I would say yes. A long-term relationship for the vast majority of kids these days lasts a semester or two. You break up with one guy and hook up with another. It's almost like picking up a new mobile phone,' stated Di.

I found myself agreeing with Di that the affairs of the current generation were more like accessories. A clear proof was the popular chartbuster *'Peechle saat dino mein'* which compared losing one's heart to losing a denim jacket, a silver ring, a half-read novel and a new pair of sunglasses. I mean, nothing could have captured the commodification of love better than this song.

'A college fling is like a Friday evening plan,' Di continued. 'You need plan B and plan C in case plan A doesn't work out as you don't want to be home alone. Love, however, is like the smile you want to wear every day for the rest of your life. You don't want options when you are in love,' she concluded.

'Are you saying that I am not in love with Jay because I am keeping my options open?' I asked, even more puzzled than before.

'Is that how you feel?' she asked, sipping her double espresso, bouncing the question back at me.

'I don't know what I feel, Di,' I said, feeling all muddled up. 'How do I know if I love Jay?' I implored.

'Love is like a child, hon. Just like a single exam paper cannot gauge a child's knowledge, it's hard to devise a test for love,' Di philosophized. 'Like a child, love also blossoms best when left alone to wander, make mistakes and learn. For your love to prosper, it's important that you feel free with your loved one,' Di expounded.

I knew she was warming up and soon she would help me think aloud through this dilemma like many others in the past.

'Can you be yourself with Jay?' she asked, with a thoughtful expression on her face.

'That's a bookish dialogue, Di,' I frowned.

'Yes, and all that we need to know in life has already been documented in books by someone or the other,' she rationalized. 'Anyway, let me rephrase. Do you feel compelled to follow the low carb diet or do you do it because you know that it will benefit you?'

'You know how I love my chocolates and fries,' I said picking the leftover crumbs of my muffin. 'Of course I do it for Jay's sake, but that doesn't mean I don't love Jay. I do so many things for Ma and Pa as well and I know that I love them.'

'That's a different relation. With parents you are designed to obey and respect, while in love you ought to understand and respect.'

Her love feel-osophy was going over my head now. 'I am confused, Di,' I sighed wearily.

Di reassuringly wrapped her arms around my shoulder and said, 'Now this is going to sound absurd coming from a non-experienced person like myself, but do you feel complete after having sex with him?'

I looked at Di uncomfortably. It is not that I couldn't talk about sex with Di, but I didn't know how to admit it openly that while I had kissed many guys, I had never had sex with any. Not even Jay. Consider this a mental block, an unspoken promise to my dad, or a Tanu di effect, the maximum I had allowed Jay was to embrace me without clothes or indulge in cyber sex. Jay, of course, found this to be an absurd manifestation of my Indianness.

'This is going to sound unbelievable coming from a vagabond like myself, but we have never done it,' I said meekly.

'What? I mean, really? I always thought you were the any person, any time breed rather than the right person, right time generation,' she laughed mockingly.

'C'mon now, does it mean I don't love him because I didn't go all the way or does it mean that I love him because I could stand up for myself in front of him?'

'I am confused, hon,' admitted Di comically.

Seeing the exasperated expression on my face, she donned a serious-look face, and asked what it was that I wanted in a guy.

Now, this was something I was very clear about. My ideal guy had to be physically attractive, have a good sense of humour and be cool about my previous affairs. He had to be comfortable with my social drinking, spaghetti tops, shorts and off-shoulder dresses in everyday life and not only on vacations away from in-laws. He also needed to be multi-talented, have an interest in sports, have a cultural bend of mind (music/dance/drama/art) as well as a decent IQ. Helping in household chores, respect for my career and treating me as an equal, all the things that the nineties' women wanted, were the obvious musts.

'Balike, are you sure you are not a re-incarnation of Mahabharata's Draupadi looking for her five Pandav husbands?' Di joshed as I listed the must-haves.

'I bet Champ was all this,' I challenged indignantly.

'Yes, Champ was all this and more,' said Di and I saw a glimmer of pride momentarily flicker in her eyes.

'But he lacked faith in our love,' she added dolefully, the spark leaving a dull ache behind.

I already knew Jay met my eligibility criteria, but did he have faith in our love? More importantly, did I have faith in our love?

While Di went up to the cash counter to order another espresso for herself and a cafe mocha for me, I re-read the last message on my phone.

'Congrats. Looks like I have already earned five hugs. Am wondering if I should have negotiated a better deal—Deep :)'

Something about the message made me happy and something about being happy bothered me.

'Do you think I might be developing feelings for Deep?' I voiced the possibility that had been silently nibbling at my conscience all through the week.

'One hundred per cent, ma'am,' Di confirmed. 'The real question is whom do you love more—Jay or Deep?'

'Why didn't you say so before? How can I fall for Deep if I really love Jay? Doesn't this mean that there is something lacking in my relationship with Jay?' I badgered her with multiple questions.

Di smiled at my impatience. 'You are now talking like Puja,' she reminisced about the good old times spent with her gang of girls at IIT and a colon-dash-bracket spread over her face. Di had been especially close to Puja, but their friendship had suffered a setback when Puja's sister Piya had allegedly lured Champ.

'Puja used to believe that you only look out for opportunities if you are unhappy in your current situation,' recalled Di.

'I thought that is what you believed as well or so you told me,' I asked baffled, for I had acquired all my love fundas from Di.

'I do,' professed Di, 'but there is an exception to the rule.'

I hated exceptions. They would pop up unexpectedly in your well-planned-out code and hang the whole programme. Taking a sip of warm chocolate-flavoured milk froth, I waited for Di to elaborate on the exception causing my life to go haywire.

'Soulmates!' she exclaimed, unravelling the mysterious exception. 'Soulmates are two people who are drawn together by a very strong connection that often defies human explanation.'

This was outrageous! Was Di trying to tell me that Deep-Ache Go-Yell was my soulmate? Could that explain the undeniable attraction I felt towards him, the indescribable appiness I experienced when he was around, or the inexplicable whim that had made me send him the Crushaider mail?

'Do you mean that I really love Jay but I am attracted to Deep because he is my soulmate?' I asked, dumbfounded by the absurdity of my own conclusion.

'Or Deep is not your soulmate but then you don't really love Jay either?' Di verbalized the alternative.

I threw my hands up in the air and looked beseechingly at Di to show me a way out of this 'either both or none' XOR gate.

'You can't possibly expect me to decide whether you like an impeccable, American-style, self-sufficient apartment with a 4★ TripAdvisor rating across 300 reviews or a speciality lodging with a warm, loving, Indian touch having a 5★ rating but only 30 reviews?' Di replied.

Di loved using metaphors to pepper her language. I smiled at how eloquently she had given Deep a higher rating than Jay and at the same time incorporated the fact that I had known Jay for much longer than I knew Deep in the number of reviews. Typically, when planning vacations, I would just choose the accommodation with better pictures, but here we were talking about life-long residence. Besides, Deep's monster face had magically disappeared. I heard him and laughed with him, but I didn't see his face any more. Anyway, I waited eagerly for Di to make the decision for me. To tell me what to do.

'Hon, you are not in fifth grade and it's not about choosing whether to sit by the window to enjoy the outside scenery or hide in the back row to pass around notes. This is not about whiling away time in a boring history lecture. Its about whom you want to spend the good and bad times of the rest of your life with,' Di chided lightly.

Oh! How I wished I was in the fifth grade! Although back then, every instruction from Mom used to be a reminder that I was too young to know what was right for me. *Call me when you reach your friend's house, come back before its dark, don't speak with your mouth full* and *keep the speaker volume down*. I had craved to grow up quickly and take charge of my life. Alas! Now I realize the value of those blessed, carefree days when all I had to worry about was how to keep my paper boat afloat in puddles of rainwater.

I looked at Di and sighed in despair. It was evident that she was not going to tell me the answer. I had brought upon myself the curse of being a grown-up and would have to solve the equation myself.

'I think better when I am relaxed. Let's go for a full body massage. There is a 90 per cent off from a SnapDeal offer,' I proposed.

'I don't like random girls touching me,' squirmed Di, remembering the last time I had taken her to a spa.

'Just tell them not to touch your breasts,' I spoke loud enough to draw curious glances from the guys at the next table, and Di was out of the coffee shop in no time.

Later in the day, I updated my Facebook status to say, 'Love is like a game of poker. The longer you play, the higher your stakes become and the harder it is to give up.'

CHECKMATE

'How do you decide who is the right person to spend a lifetime and all your nights with?' I had spent the whole day calling my close friends, who were either engaged or married, and asked them this question. While one girl had honestly admitted that she had just got too used to her boyfriend driving her around and paying for her shopping bills, and another had said that he had had many live-in girlfriends and this was the first girl who didn't ask him to clean before or after, most people had said that 'you just know when it happens' or 'it's basically a gut feeling'. Hello? I was talking about love emotions, not loose motions.

After a hard day's work, I was disappointed that hardly anyone was able to give me a meaningful answer, one I could use to sort out my life. It was understandable if these people I talked to were in arranged marriages. When instead of only you, the whole family, often extended, is involved in fact-based, comparison shopping, it's hard to add the right size, fun-in-bed or sexy looking columns in the comparison table. You just hope that your elders would look after your interests, like they had hoped from their elders, and so on. After all, they say, *'Umeed pe duniya kayam hai.'* But I had specifically selected friends with love marriages. How could they not explain the most important decision of their lives? Was I the only one fussy about whom to share the TV remote, bathroom and *papri-chaat* with? Now, it was possible that they were scared that I might disclose their responses to their spouses (which I did, actually) or were afraid to analyse their feelings and discover that they might have made a mistake. Although, they all seemed happy and content in their relationships.

The only plausible explanation was that there was no tangible explanation for love. I deduced that love was largely a collection of feel-good moments which kept growing over a period of time and then one fine day, when you had enough happiness in your emotional bank, you took the big plunge.

Yet being a numbers person, and a baniya at that, I knew that rational decision-making could not be based on sunk costs. Just because I had invested some time of my life gathering memories in a relationship with Jay, didn't justify my sticking with him if Deep was indeed my soulmate. But was he? I knew that Deep had been in love with another girl. What if that other girl was his soulmate? I wasn't entirely convinced that I had a *sambhar–idli* or chai–toast type made-for-each-other connection with Deep.

It was 9 p.m. on a Sunday night. Dad was practising his guitar in our TV-room-cum-den and Ma was sitting at the dining table, preparing the next week's meal chart for the cook. I had been in and out of my room, calling friends, meeting suitors and ruminating over the week-long parantha vs pizza tussle ensuing in my mind. Unable to get any useful insight from the more evolved among my friends, I decided to surf the net on how animals choose their mates. Everyone knows that in the animal kingdom males have to flaunt themselves to mate. 'Animal's Got Talent' had the usual entries for who has the loudest roar, the most colourful tail, the strongest tusks, the best croak, the finest nest and the best dancing shoes. But I had never heard of poop-flinging talent before! I was grossed out to learn how a male hippo flings a mixture of its faeces and urine to win a female's heart (Fart for the heart!).

To change my mood, I started reading about animal sex. Soon I was looking at the sex videos of Bonobo monkeys, humanity's closest relative in the animal kingdom. It was amazing how sex for Bonobos was a simple act like a smile for humans. Or a wink, or clearing of the throat, or a handshake. Their entire societal structure revolved around sex, be it conflict resolution, barter trade, or celebration. Wow! I was just wondering if sex eight hours a day could possibly be the new world peace mantra, when Jay called.

He was wearing a sporty, sleeveless tee and loose shorts, showing off the 'heart with a broken arrow' tattoo on his right shoulder. One look at his chiselled body and my artistic soul felt recharged and rejuvenated. All the confusion crowding my back office cleared up and the sunk cost turned into an asset. I would let Deep know first thing tomorrow morning that I was just not into him. Of course, I would apologize for sending him the misleading crush mail and give him the hugs for the sold paintings. Maybe I will let him kiss me one last time. I decided I would even give him my raspberry lipstick as a parting gift. Having worked out a satisfactory severance package for Deep, I shifted my attention on Jay—my KS partner for life. There was so much to say, discuss and plan.

'I love you, Jay. I really do,' I said, starting with the basics. I needed to hear it out loud as much as he did.

'I am glad we got that one cleared,' joked Jay in his usual, carefree tone. 'BTW, you look awfully sexy in that Indian costume,' said Jay drooling over the cleavage as my pallu slipped aside.

I had forgotten that I was still wearing the georgette saree from the Birla Mandir visit to meet Suitor #5 earlier in the evening. I could see that Jay was feeling aroused and it made me feel even more seductive.

'How did your family date go?' he asked curiously.

'Awesome! I finally got to reject a suitor,' I said, pumping my fists excitedly. With my parents and the suitors calling the shots so far, I was beginning to feel like the President.

'Why? Did he not have a good enough body for a nude painting?' Jay asked provocatively, sexily rolling his eyes.

'I barely got to see him as his mom kept jostling him aside, hiding him behind her huge frame,' I complained jokingly. 'Besides, he really was looking for a reversible, double-sided jacket. A bold, hip look that he could wear to his drink and dance parties and a plain, traditional side to be displayed at home in front of his parents.'

'You mean he wanted you to make both him and his parents happy?' Jay said with a sarcastic smile.

'I am really sorry, Jay,' I said, with utmost sincerity. One thing I had realized in the process of meeting suitors was that your life partner was not like a painting that you could re-colour, touch-up or whitewash to suit your parents' requirements. It was like a picture seen through a camera lens. What you saw at the beginning was what you got. I had also realized that I had been unfair in asking Jay to wear an Indian mask to please my parents.

'But you shouldn't pester me about the calories either,' I stressed, trying to be myself with him.

'I only do it for your health, hon,' Jay clarified. 'I would still love you if you were a size 10. Maybe even 12 or 14. Though you ought to agree that a three-month pregnant look can be a put off during sex.'

This was going good. I was all for an attractive look myself. Di was right. Love needed freedom to grow. I could already feel the love overflowing and filling up my boobs.

I was going to ask him about the Crushaider mail I had sent to him, when a chat window popped up on my laptop screen.

Mom: 'Jay shared a tent with Denise.'

I was irked that Ma was spoiling my feeling of oneness with

Jay. Whatever happened to the 'trust is important for love' gyaan she had given me?

But I was pleasantly surprised that my mind hadn't switched to a porn channel on hearing about Jay going near Denise. 'You know it is true love when you don't feel jealous,' I updated my status on FB.

Me: 'Stop snooping around Ma. I know Jay loves me.'

I closed the chat window.

'How was your trek?' I asked Jay nonchalantly. I had been so absorbed with the art exhibition that I hadn't talked to Jay since he got back from his trek.

'Oh! It was fun. Did I tell you that Bob sprained his ankle at the eleventh hour? Luckily, Denise was sporting enough to fill in at a short notice. It sure saved us a few hundred bucks,' Jay told coolly.

You can't suspect your boyfriend when he compares his ex to a discount coupon. For the first time, I could see how Denise was like any other guy friend to Jay, as he had assured me so many times before, and nothing more.

'Did you share the tent with her?' I asked just for the sake of it.

'Oh! Yeah. She didn't know the others. Besides, I couldn't trust those guys with a beautiful body like hers.'

Jay was still as cool as the other side of the pillow, but I was disappointed that he was being protective about Denise. I was trying hard not to read between the lines or see between the sheets, when Ma sent me a link to a picture of Jay and Denise sitting cosily together on Jay's bike. Jay was sitting on the seat, his hands on the handlebar, while Denise was sitting on the crossbar, facing him, her face inches from him and her arms around his neck. Sitting at a higher level than her, he had a clear view inside her blouse. This was getting too much for me. I just copy-pasted the link for Jay to see, closed my eyes and practised deep breathing.

'She struck the same pose with all the guys. It's no big deal, hon,' comforted Jay.

Sometimes I wondered if anything at all was a big deal for him and feared that one day I would also get assigned to his 'don't care' cupboard. I opened my eyes and looked directly into his, searching for the truth. He could tell from the controlled pace of my breathing and hard, fixed stare that the water was beginning to boil.

'Don't start getting all jealous now like a Bollywood movie actress. You also went on a trip with that snogger boss of yours. Am I asking you if he touched your curves or kissed your lips?'

'Then why aren't you asking, Jay?' I demanded. I wanted him to assert his right on me. To be possessive about me like he was about his iPhone.

'Because I trust you,' Jay reasoned.

'Then why don't you tell me what really happened on the trek between you and Denise?'

'Nothing happened. At least nothing that you wouldn't do with other guys.'

I wondered if he was referring to me kissing Deep? 'You know how even a simple high five between you and her bothers me. Why can't you just stay away from her? She is such a lech.' I was back to feeling envious and slandering Denise vehemently.

'You need to have faith in me,' said Jay earnestly, without raising his voice.

'I need you here with me, to be able to have faith,' I said, almost pleadingly. 'Do you think you could come to India for a short while?' I was confident that once my parents got to know him, they would love him as he was and there would be no need to change him.

'Well, I was planning to surprise you at Neetu's wedding reception,' disclosed Jay, his mesmerizing hazel eyes smiling lovingly at me.

I didn't know what to say. I was overwhelmed with joy. I immediately started thinking about the places I wanted to show him and people I wanted him to meet—my room and all my childhood pictures, my paintings, my kindergarten school, Neha, Tanu di, MD and Sanjeev, and may be even Deep. Right now though, I wanted to compensate for my unwarranted fury from moments ago. 'Do you want me to read aloud a "wild one-on-one consensual sex" story from literotica?' I offered willingly.

Jay, who was always up for kinky stuff, immediately agreed and I started browsing through the vast collection of erotic titles on the site. I narrowed down on one about an unusual encounter with a masseur. I had barely read the first line when Mom pinged again.

Mom: 'How are you, beta?'

'Horny! In the middle of cyber sex,' I wanted to type but I controlled the urge to shock her. I knew she was concerned, having seen Denise's lewd picture with Jay.

Me: 'I am fine, Ma.'
Mom: 'You are a strong girl, beta.'
Me: 'Yeah.'
Mom: 'I know you will be able to survive this.'
Me: 'Thanks. Bye.'

I felt like Mom was trying to prepare me for some bad news like she had done when she had broken my favourite photo frame during one of her obsessive cleaning sessions or before giving me the news of my grandma's death.

But eager to get back to the girl who had just entered the massage parlour, I hurriedly cut her off.

The masseur offered the delicate, dainty girl a glass of exquisite wine. He then blindfolded himself and asked the girl to remove her clothes and lie down on the table. He dipped his hands in oil and asked the girl to place them on her navel. He was about to navigate his fingers up to her swells when the chat window popped up yet again. Mom had sent me some YouTube link this time. Before I could tell her that her spy job was interfering with my blow job, she wrote, 'Watch this video once and you have my permission to marry Jay.'

I couldn't let the opportunity pass. I told Jay to wait as my mom wanted to chat and promptly clicked on the video link. It was a clip from Jay's biking trip last week. Jay and Denise were sitting on chairs, chatting like long-time friends. Denise was even wearing a dull grey, full sleeved, unrevealing sweater. If Mom thought this could dissuade me from loving Jay, she needed to get out of her seventies' 'boys only want one thing from a girl' mindset.

I was going to pause the video for later viewing, when the screen went blank. I could barely see their silhouettes, but I could hear her moan, ask for more and then scream in ecstasy while he groaned her name time and time again.

'What are you doing?' asked Jay, who had heard the video playing on my laptop and recognized the voices.

'Why don't you tell me Jay, what you are doing?' I asked, my voice stiff and offended.

'She is nothing more than an old pair of jeans that I have no emotional attachment to, but I might wear it once in a while in moments of despair,' Jay explained with amazing poise.

As always, he was as calm as the middle of the ocean when the coast is tsunami-struck. He must have been a mortuary manager in his previous life, to be able to keep such a calm countenance when people around him were burying their dead.

'Don't try to do a snow job on me, Jay,' I challenged coldly.

'We were just chugging beer outside our tents in the moonlight, chatting and chilling after a tough day of physical activity,' he began recounting the incident. 'After a while, the others retired to their tents and it was just the two of us. She asked me if I missed you and I said yes. She said I was very lucky to have found you. Then I asked if she was happy with her boyfriend and she said they broke up last month because he thought her boobs weren't big enough. Next minute, she took off her top and asked me what I thought her cup size was. She was wearing this black crochet lingerie that came around her neck like a deep halter, barely covering her nipples. I have to admit that I had forgotten how soft and succulent her breasts looked and got an instant hard on. She started rubbing herself on me and I lost all self-restraint. So when she asked if I was game for some bridge sex, I couldn't say no. I really wasn't planning to cheat on you or anything. Besides, it's not like we are married. I know many guys who have made out with multiple, random girls at their bachelor's party.'

'So was this your bachelor's party?' I asked, aghast at how casually he had justified his one-night stand with Denise.

'If that makes is easy for you to accept it, sure!' he offered magnanimously.

'What if you got similar opportunities after we are married? What would you do, Jay?' I asked, feeling hurt, angry and jealous all at the same time.

He simply shrugged his shoulders in response.

'I would like it if we played Dumb-C at another time, Jay. I really need verbal answers here,' I said furiously.

'Frankly, I don't know,' said Jay. 'Sometimes you are out in the market, strolling aimlessly. You see a fancy car and you get enticed into taking a free trial ride. I don't see what's wrong in that. It can happen to you too.'

I heard him legitimize his actions and suddenly it occurred to me that the differences between us were more than IST and EST time zones now. There was a whole generation gap between him and me. Sex for him was like eating. While he was serious about his relationship with me the way he enjoyed his meat and potatoes, a one-night stand was akin to a hot fudge sundae for dinner. I was the healthy option that would nourish him while Denise was his break from the regular monotony of marriage. However, like most Indians, though I loved variety in my cuisine and culture, I believed in monogamous mating for life.

In Neha's 'boys are like cars' world, Jay was an American car, incapable of delivering speed and mileage on Indian roads.

'Checkmate, Jay. Game is over, Jay,' I said firmly.

'What do you mean, hon? I love you,' claimed a thoroughly disoriented Jay like he had just woken up from sleep.

'I don't know about you, but I can never be myself with you, Jay,' I replied with the same calmness that he had displayed moments ago. 'Kadai paneer, cricket, karwa chauth and Kishore Kumar are all a part of me. I do want you, but I want you with a lot of modifications—with Hindi, with love for parents, with Indian values and without Denise. Besides, Suhaani Guy sounds more like a beautiful and tame cow.'

'Like So-Honey Egg-R-Wall makes any sense?' Jay mocked. 'Denise was right that you never loved me. Jesus fucking Christ, I can't believe I fell for your trap.' His voice was no longer soft and loving.

'What do you mean Denise knew I didn't love you? I didn't know it myself till five minutes ago.'

'Because we never did it.'

'That's ridiculous! Anyone who doesn't do IT is "not in love"? I am sure LGBT could sue Denise for making allegations like these.'

'You just get into relationships with guys to legitimize getting physical with them, but you don't want to go all the way because you don't love them,' accused Jay. 'You played around with that IITian during the summer internship and then dumped him when he tried to make love,' he added.

'He dumped me, after making out with me. He said he wanted a virginal wife,' I refuted.

'All the better for you. You didn't have to cook up a reason to get rid of him. Remember the poor guy at school whom you tricked into kissing and then ditched after a week when you had had your fill? You never even owned up to him or your parents that you were the reason he had tried committing suicide.'

'I didn't do anything wrong. Everyone says I love you in moments of passion.'

'Yes, but you say I love you to justify the moments of passion. You have double standards for everything. You can only truly make love when you fall in love. I wish you all the luck for that. But stop fooling guys till then and spare them the agony.'

Wow! So it was okay to have a sex video of fucking your ex on YouTube, but it was treachery if you kissed a guy and said you loved him but weren't ready to make love to him!

It was painful to hear such harsh words from someone who had been pledging his love to me seconds ago. I shuddered to think that I had been ready to hurt my parents for him. There was one last thing I wanted to know.

'Why did you not respond to my Crush mail?' I asked.

'Oh! It was you then? I assumed it was Denise,' he said, sounding genuinely startled.

I had nothing more left to say or tell. 'Goodbye, Jay,' I said with decisive finality.

'Well, what should I do about this nude painting?' he asked indifferently.

I saw his nude painting peek from behind him and remembered how exhausting it had been to control my excitement while making it. Presently, I felt nothing for him. After having gone through the ups and downs of the emotional rollercoaster in the last one hour, I was now feeling strangely serene.

'Gift it to that fucking Denise. I am sure she will be able to put it to good use,' I replied and disconnected.

My updated status read. 'Sometimes, all it takes is a trek to test if your boyfriend really loves you.'

LOVE AAJ KAL

'My current girlfriend and ex swapped places and I am loving it!' Jay had proudly broadcasted our break-up news to all his Facebook friends.

I felt nauseated on seeing his FB status the next morning. I wasn't expecting him to feel remorseful, send me 'I am sorry, let's patch up' messages, or eat fudge topping out of the jar, but I didn't expect him to hook back with Denise and celebrate it either. It was like he had erased our relationship of two years with a Ctrl+Z, like an undo in an editor and gone back to the previous text in a flick.

While most people had congratulated him saying 'Old is gold' and 'Sweet deal', my mail box was flooded with private condolence messages from our common friends. I knew it was good in a way because it was already out there for everyone to know, yet I couldn't help feeling cheated. I mean, how dare he take all the credit? After all, it was me who had done a checkmate. 'I had dumped the bugger,' I wanted to tell everyone. Instead, I just posted the link to his YouTube video in a comment. Let everyone see what a piece of shit he was.

I also decided it was best that I went through the post break-up rituals to exorcise my ex. So I deleted all his lovely SMSes that I had saved in my mobile, the emails from my Gmail and the chat history from Skype. I hid him from the IM buddy list, altered my Facebook settings to hide all future posts from Jay and unfollowed his tweet.

I also downgraded his email address to the PITA category in my email prioritization tool. I still had to go back home and delete all our joyful JPEGs—arm linked, kissing, drinking and sharing a salad—that were lying inside a secret folder in my laptop. And then there were photos of us tagged together on FB that I didn't know how to deal with.

Heck, break-ups are not as easy as shredding photos and burning a box full of love notes any more. It can be quite a challenging task in today's multimedia age.

Sitting in my oversized ergonomic chair, I was busy severing all communication channels with Jay, when Deep asked me for the usual first round of coffee. Oblivious to the storm raging in my heart, Deep eagerly talked about Rohan sir's visit to our office for the ASM next month and how we needed to show him some improvement on the customer conversion rate. Although the sketch of a purchase funnel typically reminded me of a weaver bird's nest hanging upside down, today, for a change, I wanted to talk business. Anything to take my mind off the urge to squeeze and crush Jay's testicles.

I put myself in a casual web browser's mouse, focused all my energies and started to think. What would get me excited enough to buy a holiday package online? I guess, other people telling me how great the resort was and how iTrot took care of all their needs. And of course, like most people wary of Internet deals, I would feel more comfortable if I could undo my action. 'Please check your order details carefully, before you get redirected to payment gateway' was the worst message to give to someone who was still in two minds. It was like putting him on the spot and telling him that this was his last chance to back out.

I told Deep that we should actively promote the customer testimonials with our holiday packages and offer free cancellation for online bookings. Deep was pleasantly surprised by my insightful propositions and said he would promptly discuss them with the others. We were about to head back, when a harried-looking guy who hadn't slept the whole weekend came up to Deep seeking his sexpert advice. Deep caught the sly smile on my face as I pretended to look inside the bottom of my coffee cup. It had become almost a routine every Monday morning. With 9 to 5 office hours becoming a thing of the past and twelve-hour workdays being the new norm across the industry, marriages had also been reduced to being functional only during the weekends. Weekends were the only time people got around to trying to or having sex with their partners.

I overheard the poor guy tell Deep that his scooter had a low pick-up and how he would be pressing on the accelerator for hours before his scooter's engine would have barely lubricated. He obviously didn't know that I had heard several similar stories by now and knew that the scooter he was having start-up issues with was his wife/girlfriend.

Deep patiently explained that he was wrong in expecting his sensitive scooter to behave like a macho motorcycle. 'A motorcycle gets into action immediately while a scooter takes its sweet time to warm up and pick speed,' Deep elaborated. The guy's face lit up as it dawned on him that while both men and women were two-wheelers, there was as much difference between them when it came to pick-up and horsepower as between a motorcycle and a scooter. He went away humming cheerfully, looking forward to slowly and lovingly servicing his scooter next weekend.

'I think I should create an online KS FAQ,' said Deep, his face radiant with the satisfaction that comes from giving happiness to others. 'My knowledge can benefit so many more people if it's available on the net.'

'Excellent thought,' I seconded his idea, 'but I would look at monetizing these pearls of sexology.' I had had the business idea in my mind for some time now. 'Confidential, online sex advice—try us for free and pay only if it brings you ecstasy.'

'Finally! Someone sees the true potential in me,' exclaimed Deep enthusiastically. 'Are you ready to become my partner in crime?' he asked eagerly.

'Me?'

'You are nearly an expert yourself, now that you have been eavesdropping into my sessions for a few months. Besides, I am sure there are aspects of female psychology and physiology that you understand better.'

It was evident from Deep's tone that he meant business, but I couldn't take any chances. I bit my lips nervously. I knew I had to tell him now.

'I am sorry Deep, but I don't think there is a future for us together,' I said regretfully.

He looked me in the eyes, wondering if I meant what he thought I meant. For a brief second, I saw disappointment in his eyes as he tried to absorb the gravity of my statement. Then it was gone.

'Ah well, I see that you couldn't handle my sex quotient,' he joked, going back to his charming, smiling self.

I could feel the hot tears welling up inside my eyes and a lump beginning to form in my throat. I excused myself, went to the bathroom, and cried—for a relationship I thought was love but turned out not to be and for a relationship I thought was nothing but was hurting like love.

Last night after the split-up with Jay, I had looked at my bare face, without any make-up, in the mirror. It had been my moment of truth. Devastated at having discovered that Jay was not the everlasting love I sought, my heart craved for a keeper. It was clear that I didn't love Jay, but who knew if Deep was my soulmate either. Deep could have been only a distraction I was looking out for in my unsuccessful relation with Jay.

After three rejections in the last thirty-six hours— Suitor #5, Jay and Deep—I badly needed to nourish my shattered soul. I went back to my seat, sent Deep a mail that I was going out for some personal work, picked up my purse and walked out. I headed straight to MG Road for some quick retail and tattoo therapy.

After two hours, when I returned to the cubicle, having substituted the pain from multiple rejections by that from tattoo needles, I found MD's face exuding the unmistakable pregnancy glow. Was she already? Had Sanjeev fast-tracked the plan and skipped some minor formalities? I gave her a quizzical look as she crooned the song, '*Tujh mein rab dikta hai, yaara main kya karoon*' to the customer acquisition bar graph on her monitor. Moments later, I heard Sanjeev's fingers snapping to the same tune. I watched him keenly as he sauntered leisurely to his seat and there was a halo of happiness above his head too. I was aware that tattoos cause the release of endorphins in our system, which can induce feelings of euphoria, but I had no idea it could have delusionary effects like this. Sanjeev caught me staring blankly at him and smiled. He said he had something to tell me and asked me to sit down. I hadn't even realized that I had been standing all this while. Feeling dizzy with vague doubts clouding my already overworked brain, I did as I was directed. 'Here's the recap of what happened this weekend in *ghar ghar ki kahani*,' said Sanjeev.

He then brought his seat closer to MD's, took her hand gently in his, and said, '*Suniye.*'

Madhuri turned around, brimming with a beatific, I-am-in-love smile, and replied, *'Kahiye, kahiya na?'*

For a few minutes they kept looking into each other's eyes like they were playing the who-will-blink-the-eyelids-first game.

Sanjeev then started saying the famous dialogue from *Silsila*, '*Main aur meri tanhai, . . . tum ye kahti, tum is baat pe naraaz hoteen . . .*'

MD looked coyly at him and said, '*Haath chodo mera, ab itni bhi khoobsorat nahin hoon main.'*

Sanjeev then responded with, '*Aapko kisme rab dikhta hain Madhuri ji?*'

MD promptly replied with her rehearsed dialogue, '*Main apnee favourite hoon, Sharmaji.*'

Sanjeev then bent down on his knees and asked, '*Mujhse shaadi karogi?*'

MD looked lovingly at the guy kneeling before her in a white t-shirt, cream pants and white shoes, his hair soaked in *shuddh* coconut oil, a heavy gold chain hanging around his neck, and a tilak prominent on his forehead. Sanjeev started singing,

'Cutlet-ketchup, bread-butter jaisa apna pyaar
Lena hoga janam hame kai kai baar.'

MD laughed and mumbled indistinctly but I lip-read her and guessed that she was singing, *'Hum dil de chuke sanam . . . teri kasam.'*

Despite the severe pain in my heart, and the tattoo carved in the soft skin above my heart, I couldn't help but feel overjoyed for Sanjeev and MD. I congratulated them, went to the loo and cried a bit more. Sitting in the loo, I sent a message to Di.

Me: 'Said no to both Jay and Deep.'

Di: 'I said no to VC too, but he wants me to reconsider.'

Me: 'I am so sad.'

Di: 'Me too. Michael Jackson is dead.'

Me: 'I just got my heart tattooed to deal with post-rejection stress.'

Di: 'I prefer watching *Jaane Bhi do Yaaron,* though I have to admit that the last guy I rejected was a decade ago.'

Me: 'See you on the ASM. You have to come.'

Di: 'Won't miss it for the world. Am dying to hear Deep.'

Me: 'Why?'

Di: 'You only said he was too good.'

Me: 'Why the hell did I reject him then?'

Di: 'I am trying to find an answer to that question for the last fifteen years.'

Later in the day, Deep and I were sitting together in a meeting room having a video conference with Rohan sir. Once again I found myself bewildered at how a sparkling gem like Rohan sir could stay undiscovered. Maybe he was also unsuccessful in love, like me? Only a broken heart can understand the pain of another broken heart. Pity that he was rather old for my taste. Perhaps, I should connect him to Tanu di when he comes down to India? After all he was from IIT-D. Oh! And his surname was Khanna too. My thought process was however interrupted when I heard Deep speak out my name. It was high time I got over his husky, sexy voice. He told me to put forth my ideas on increasing the width of the purchase funnel. It was very satisfying to see my suggestions being appreciated by others, especially Rohan sir, yet I could only manage a weak smile. I was trying hard to behave normally, but something was wrong with my eyes for they kept refilling their tank of tears every few hours. I stole a glance at Deep who was laughing and cracking jokes with the others. He seemed to be managing with such ease that it broke my heart to see my rejection didn't matter to him. I really wanted some time alone with my back office. At last the meeting came to an end, everyone left, and we were left alone in the room.

'You are not your normal self today. Did you have a fight with your BF?' Deep asked affectionately.

Flummoxed that he should know about Jay, I gave him a perplexed look and asked, 'Boyfriend?'

'I figured that if you are so much in favour of love marriage, you must be in love with someone,' Deep reasoned.

'Love is a big mirage,' I replied sceptically. 'A score of zero in tennis. A figment of authors' imagination.'

He looked dubiously at me. I saw tenderness in his eyes and

it filled me with pain. I wanted to reach out to him, hug him and kiss him. Instead, I got up to leave. On my way out, I noticed the frame hung on the wall. It had a quote from Robert McCloskey on confusion. 'I know that you believe you understand what you think I said, but I'm not sure you realize that what you heard is not what I meant.'

For the last couple of weeks, many of us had been staying back in office almost every evening for ASM preparations. I didn't really need to stay back that evening as I was only part of the ballroom dance, which was rehearsed on Tuesdays and Thursdays. But while I was busy applying ointment on my tattoo, the office cab had left without me. So, I aimlessly walked down to the basement where the practice sessions were held. Deep was singing my favourite Kishore song, *'Khwab ho tum ya koi haqeeqat, kaun ho tum batlao.'* I sat spellbound on the stairs outside, not wanting to face Deep, but wanting to believe that he was singing the song for me. I was so lost in my thoughts that I was startled when Deep came out and tapped me on my shoulders. He offered to drop me back home. No way! I didn't want to go kissing him again. This time I wouldn't even have the beer excuse. But I didn't want him to think anything had changed between us either, so I agreed. Well, if anything happened, I could always blame it on the post-tattoo endorphin high.

Sitting in his car, I saw a rose lying on his dashboard, waiting to be caressed by a loving hand and kissed by soft lips. I expected him to stop the car any time on the roadside, offer me the red rose, pledge his love for me and ask me to become his for a lifetime. I know I had only rejected him some time back but girls can be really weird at times. A while later, he stopped the car, and I waited for him to make a move, but nothing happened.

'Your home has come,' he reminded me gently.

I cast one final longing look at the flower, reluctantly opened the car door and got out. He drove away without so much as a backward glance. Maybe the rose was for someone else? Maybe he was off to meet his school-time love Meeta?

Some days you just feel so sad and worthless, like your life has no meaning. Like you can do nothing, and you want to cry, but the tears don't come. Partly because you have already spent your month's supply of tears crying in the bathroom. Your heart is full of emotions and pain and you don't know why. You just wish you could go back to being a child and someone would tell you what to do next, and you cry some more. You hate your laziness for doing nothing but sitting idle, and you wish ... but you don't even know what to wish for. Finally, sleep takes over and you can dream what you want because dreams follow no logic.

My FB status read, 'The best way to deal with a break-up is a good night's sleep.'

LOST AND FOUND

I peeped out from behind the curtain and saw scores of people sitting in the auditorium, chatting, and eagerly waiting for the performance to begin. The front row, reserved for the founders and the various COs, was nearly full. The initial speeches were over. The overall mood of the crowd was jubiliant. iTrot had gained a significant market share in the online travel industry in the last one year and drinks were on the house. I spotted Rohan sir lounging on the front row corner seat. Dressed in a casual half-sleeved red shirt with the top two buttons unbuttoned and dark blue jeans, he looked unexpectedly handsome and young. I eagerly scanned the audience looking for my parents and found them smugly seated at the centre of the hall. While Dad was adjusting his SLR hoping to catch a perfectly timed shot, Mom, armed with her latest Nokia N95, was feverishly looking forward to upload my dance on FB. Under immense pressure from her elder sisters in Pune and Ambala to find a suitable boy for me, I think she wanted to show off Deep to them. I noticed that Dad had kept the programme card to reserve a seat for Tanu di next to him. She had promised to reach by 7 p.m., in time to see my dance. I unlocked my mobile and checked the time. She was expected to come any minute.

I glanced at the slide projected on the screen. Kavita was on her last slide, talking about the aggressive hiring plans and about making iTrot a women-friendly company. Our ballroom dance was the next item on the agenda. I knew Deep would be standing across the stage, behind the curtain on the other side, as we were the lead pair. A tiny shiver of excitement trailed down my spine at the thought of him holding me in public. I had thoroughly enjoyed every moment of our practice sessions, enjoying the touch of his strong hands and savouring the spicy scent of his aftershave. My favourite part in the sequence was when he swung me around and let me loose so I swayed away from him, and then he grabbed my arm the next instant, pulling me close in a tight embrace. It made me feel wanted and desired. However, off the dance floor, Deep had been behaving very strangely, very official—boss-like. No morning round of coffee, no KS talk, and no casual flirting. Sometimes, a whole day would go by and he wouldn't even say my name. I was beginning to wonder if the mischievous smile in his eyes, his husky laugh and our repartee sessions had all been a fabrication of my back office.

Kavita finished her speech, left the stage and went back to her seat next to Rohan sir. The MC announced our programme and the stage lights went dim. We all quickly moved in and took our positions. I was glad when I saw Tanu di walk in from the rear entrance. It was too late for her to wend her way through the audience and take the seat next to Pa. She walked straight down the aisle and sat down below on the carpeted step, right next to Rohan sir. She waved wildly at me and I gave her a childish grin in return. Seconds later, I saw Vikram walk down and join her on the step. He was still pursuing her.

Before I could feel the butterflies in my stomach, Deep grabbed my right hand with his left hand and held my waist with his right. I gently placed my left hand on his shoulder and the show began. While Deep effortlessly twirled me around the floor, another drama was unfolding in the front row corner.

'Nice presentation!' complimented Rohan as Kavita came down

from the dais. 'I agree with your views on increasing the company oestrogen levels.'

'Thanks,' Kavita smiled. 'I hope your airport pick-up and hotel arrangements were in order.'

'Yes, they were perfect,' he thanked and added, 'I am sorry to hear about you and Vikas. Is he going to continue working at iTrot?'

'I don't think so. He was never very comfortable with me earning more than him,' she said, disparagingly.

I was not the only one going through 'love is for losers' phase. Along with mine, another love story had ended. Vikas and Kavita's divorce decision had rocked the small world that iTrot was and everyone was speculating who would leave the company.

'I personally feel that women are far more superior to men,' whispered Rohan secretively.

Flattered, Kavita asked in a soft, teasing voice, 'Is that why you never married?'

He gave her a wide, friendly smile and quickly changed the topic. 'That's a very intricate lace on your dress,' he said.

(This was the instant when Tanu di came and sat down on the step next to Rohan sir.)

Startled by Rohan's observation and interest in lace, Kavita raised an eyebrow at him.

'I can't make something half as beautiful,' he admitted humbly.

(Tanu di turned abruptly at hearing the familiar voice and intently listened in on the conversation, her heart beating as loud as thunder when she finally realized who she was sitting next to.)

This time Kavita shook her head in total incredulity, like he had revealed he was homosexual. 'You can crochet?' she asked, fascinated.

'Now that women are running companies, men better learn to . . .'

'. . . bake and embroider,' said Tanu di, completing Rohan's line. It had been over fifteen years when he had said those very same words to her, while sipping coconut water on a beach. She hadn't forgotten a single minute of her time spent with him.

Recognizing the voice, he turned around to face her. He still remembered the first time he had seen her during a ragging session. She had been so beautiful, so naive, and yet so confident that he had immediately fallen in love with her. But then he had lost her somewhere in the battle of heart and mind. How he had pined for her and waited for her to come back to him, all in vain. And now, when he had least expected it, she had appeared from nowhere.

His eyes were beaming with the happiness of a child who had finally found his rainbow, after years of standing and waiting in the rain.

'You still remember what I said?' he asked, rather surprised.

'You are still using the same old pick-up lines?' Tanu di countered half-teasingly, her face shining with the radiance of love that had only strengthened by their time apart.

'Actually, I have ten more lines stored in my BlackBerry for easy reference. I just use the one that best suits the situation,' he wisecracked.

'You haven't changed at all. Ready to flirt with anyone, as long as it is a girl,' she said lightly.

'Not all girls. Only the ones with long, lustrous hair,' he quipped, his endearing smile making her stomach flip and giving her the goosebumps.

'Still wearing a red t-shirt?' she teased further, knowing well that he believed that the red colour enhanced sexual desire in the opposite sex.

'It's not the same one that I wore to the 1994 Rendezvous, I promise,' he joked.

'Gosh! You are already on the wrong side of thirty-five. You must feel old,' she pulled his leg, like she was still nineteen.

'But you are a very young-looking thirty-four,' he said charmingly.

She had done some research on men and she knew that if there was something that became three times its size when a man was excited, it was his pupils. She gazed deeply into his eyes and she knew that he was as thrilled to meet her as she was to meet him. They both floated back in time to the evenings they had spent together, sitting on a broken rickshaw outside the IIT girls' hostel, sharing jokes, discussing their present and planning their future. The moonlit Rajpath where he had confessed his love and the low, brick wall, in the baski courts, behind which they had first kissed.

'I missed you, Champ,' she muttered, having momentarily forgotten that he was a dad to a ten-year-old boy and that VC was sitting beside her, watching her make romantic overtures towards a stranger.

'I missed you too, Tanu,' he said in a soft, intimate voice.

'So, how have you been?' he asked tenderly.

'Just like you left me,' she replied, her voice cracking with emotions.

'Oh! But I never left you,' he said, suddenly getting all defensive. 'It was you who didn't think the time was right, remember?'

'Well, you could have waited for the right time,' she said accusingly, her eyes searching his for the spark she thought she had seen moments ago. 'You never came back.'

'You were busy chasing your dreams. There was no one to come back to,' he argued.

What did he mean there was no one to come back to? What had she been doing if not waiting for him for the last 5000 days of her life? Besides, he had not even waited for her to finish her engineering. He had gotten engaged to Piya at the drop of a hat.

Perhaps she never really understood that he was looking

for an unambitious, educated girl with beautiful, long hair to carry his progeny. Long hair so he would be enticed to make love and have kids with her, educated so she could manage the kids' homework and unambitious so she wouldn't leave the kids at home and go career trotting. She, the women entrepreneur of India, could never really be the girl of his dreams.

Now she knew why they never met for all these years. It was because they were not meant to be together. They were not the pieces of the same puzzle. They were randomly juxtaposed, seemingly befitting pieces of two different puzzles.

'You were right. There was no one waiting for you,' concluded Tanu di with steely resolve. 'Meet Vikram,' she said, holding VC's hand like a prized trophy. 'He is my husband,' she lied and snogged a most astonished Vikram passionately. Then she turned to VC and said, 'Meet Rohan. He is the asshole whom I loved and wanted to marry when I was twenty-one. Back then, I thought it was the wrong time, but today I realized it was the wrong guy.' With that, she punched Rohan hard and square on the face, got up in a huff and stomped away, with VC eagerly following, wagging his tail.

The music finally stopped and we all stood still like statues striking a pose. I was positioned with my upper body arched backwards, my weight resting on Deep's arms and my hands outstretched horizontally. With my head upside down, I saw Tanu di stomp away hastily and Rohan sir sitting, mouth agape and holding a bleeding nose. Kavita, who had stepped out to talk to her daughter on the phone, didn't notice anything. The auditorium was filled with thunderous applause. Everyone loved the foot-tapping music, the synchronization and the youthful energy on the floor.

I changed out of the jazzy dance costume, took the car keys from Dad, told him I was going out to get some flowers for a play and zoomed away. Twenty minutes later, I was parked outside Tanu di's apartment in someone else's reserved parking.

'What the fuck do you think you are doing?' I shouted, as I barged through her living room into her bedroom. I bet you all must have figured out by now that the mysterious, single and handsome Rohan sir was none other than Tanu di's Champ.

'Something I should have done ages ago,' Di replied.

I could tell from her red nose and matching blotchy red eyes that she had been crying. *I surveyed the apartment, but VC was nowhere to be seen.*

'Crying a river and burning a bridge to get over Champ,' Di added.

'Don't burn the bridge. You may want to go back,' I teased. I knew something about Champ that she didn't.

'It's over. I am done masturbating with his picture,' Di declared.

'Cool! It's time you experienced the real thing,' I encouraged, with an amused expression in my eyes.

'Yes. I am getting married to VC,' Di informed. 'I even smooched him in front of Champ.'

'OMG! You didn't.' I stared at her in shock. Saliva exchanging, a tongue kiss, unless done in dreams, was akin to exchanging garlands for Tanu di.

'What? You look like I told you that Hermione is marrying Harry rather than Ron? Don't you think Vikram is nice? Oh God! Don't tell me you met his ex-wife and she told you he is gay, because he didn't really respond to my kiss?'

'Hey, Di, what happened to the good old *'you ask a question and wait for the reply'* communication?' I mocked lightly.

Tanu di folded her arms and pouted like a child. Then, she sat down with her back to me and sulked.

She looked so cute that I couldn't stop myself from breaking into a guffaw. I knew it was sort of mean, but I found the whole situation very funny. Besides, I was just going to tell her something that would make her happy beyond words. I wrapped my arms around her and whispered softly in her ears, 'Rohan sir is not married.'

She immediately spun around and gazed at me wide-eyed. Then she zapped open her laptop, logged on to Facebook and opened Piya's profile picture.

Fuck! The boy did look exactly like Rohan sir. 'Maybe they got engaged, made love, she got pregnant and then later decided not to marry?' I hypothesized, in response to Di's questioning stare. What the heck! I didn't have an account of the girls Rohan sir had slept with. I just knew that he was at the beck and call of his BlackBerry whom he openly referred to as his sole mistress. Feeling a bit stupid, I watched Di's face for a reaction. There was a wild and vengeful look in her eyes. The encounter with Champ had lifted the veil of false hope she was hiding behind—it unleashed the fighter within. Warily, I waited for the anticipated outburst. To my utter surprise, Di clicked 'Add Friend' on Piya's FB page and as luck would have it, Piya instantly accepted her request with a message saying, 'I didn't steal your red. I only borrowed it for a while. Gotta go. Let's talk later at length.'

A gleam of hope sprang in Di's eyes again as she expectantly browsed over Piya's profile details. There it was, etched in grey coloured, 11px, Ariel font— 'Relationship status: Unmarried.'

'Let's go find your Rohan sir. I need to rewrite the ending of my book on IIT girls,' she said calmly, but I could see a smile slowly spreading across her face.

It took us multiple phone calls including a call to the company's CEO (we said we had an urgent message for Rohan sir) to locate Rohan sir, half an hour of persuading, pleading, cajoling and seducing the hotel bellboy to tell us Rohan Khanna's room number (we later realized that a couple of 500-rupee notes would have saved us the effort), and finger cramps from incessantly ringing a doorbell to finally locating a bleary-eyed, jetlagged and confused Champ.

'Are you married to Piya?' Tanu di demanded the moment Rohan sir opened the door.

'No,' he replied and then asked, 'Are you married to Vikram?'

'No,' she answered and in turn queried, 'Are you Piya's son's father?'

He shook his head and asked, 'Why did you stop taking my phone calls?'

'Piya told me she was getting engaged to you.'

'How come you never bothered to check with me?'

'I asked Puja and she confirmed the news.'

'Piya was pregnant with a baby from her previous boyfriend who ditched her and ran away as soon as he saw the two red lines appear in the home pregnancy test. She didn't want to abort and her parents didn't want Piya's situation to impact Puja's engagement. So she asked me if I would pretend to be her beau till Puja's wedding.'

'Why didn't you tell me?'

'I had no way of telepathically telling you and you never answered my calls or read my emails.'

'Why did Puja lie to me? I was her best friend. Didn't she have faith in me?'

'I think both Puja and Piya got a little carried away, hoping that I would actually end up marrying Piya if you stopped loving me.'

'But I never did stop loving you.'

'And I never did end up marrying anyone else.'

'I love you.'

'I love you more.'

'Are you ready to be my Horcrux?'

'You already implanted a part of your soul within me years ago.'

Jesus fucking Christ! I couldn't believe that Rohan sir was also a Harry Potter fan. Now this is what you call a match made in Hogwarts!

I saw him take out a thin, beaten band of gold from his wallet. From the starry-eyed look in Tanu di's eyes, it seemed like this was the same ring that he had proposed with a lifetime ago. She promptly offered her hand and he speedily slipped the ring into her finger. I am sure you can all guess what happened afterwards. She grabbed his wand and he entered her chamber of secrets and they made some magic together. Well, your mind is as one-tracked as mine because they closed the door behind them, leaving me guessing and standing outside the hotel room.

IT JUST HAPPENS

It was Tanu di's wedding reception. I was standing next to the chaat stall with my cousins, gulping down spicy golgappas and wishing that Jay was around to stop me. I never thought that I would ever miss his constant, watchful reminder of the calories I had consumed. Okay, I admit it, I also missed his luscious lips and his perfectly chiselled body. Fuck it. What I really, really regretted was having given away his nude painting to Denise. I mean, it was my hard work after all.

It had been two months since I parted ways with Jay and I had had a lot of time to reason why it ended the way it did. I had realized that Jay was largely a homesickness pill, a temporary anti-depressant, which I had misunderstood to be my mood elevator for life. Yet, when I had snooped on Jay's FB status last month, and it said, 'These days I am always on the Deniscovery channel,' I had been so denisgusted and denisturbed, that I had consumed a whole box of kaju katli that week. So while Jay was busy ensuring that Denise got a balanced sex diet, I had gained five kilos in the last two months. Now I was hoping that Sharmaji had been truthful when he said that Indian men loved well-endowed women.

I saw Tanu di and Rohan walk around lovingly, hand-in-hand, basking in the glow of newly wed bliss and mingle around with each other's relatives. They were a living proof of the existence and endurance of true love, and yet I wondered if in today's adulterated world where Diwali sweets were made with toilet paper, milk and white paint, love was anything but 95 per cent lust and 5 per cent pure affection.

Standing, in the covered patio, I heard the pitter patter of the raindrops on the paved path leading from the air-conditioned party hall to the open lawns. I saw an old peepal tree behind the building, its trunk and branches covered with uncountable rounds of puja thread. I remembered my dadi once telling me how women tied cotton thread around the sacred tree 108 times to strengthen their marriage. She had explained that the thread represented the fragile nature of life, love, trust, faith and all things that went on to make up a relationship. A single thread might be weak, but when it was wound many times around the trunk, it became strong. 'Oh, God! You are so kind-hearted and loving. You look after everyone. You must have made a soulmate for me too. Please help me find my kiss-patible life partner,' I prayed.

I looked away from the tree, went inside, and there he was, standing across the hall from me, at the gaily decorated City Club entrance. Dressed in a cream, lightly embroidered kurta pyjama, holding a bouquet of dazzling red roses, stood Deep. For the brief moment that our eyes met, I felt like I was the most beautiful girl in this world. And then, he looked away and wandered off towards the other office folks whom Rohan had invited.

Ever since I said no to him, there had been so many instances when I had felt like going up to Deep and telling him all about Jay. How I was confused about this whole soulmate deal and perhaps even though I was unsure, I actually loved him. However, Deep had sort of enclosed himself in a cocoon and even though we talked and laughed at work, his eyes didn't have the same playful smile or the mischievousness. Today, for a few unguarded moments when his eyes had bared his soul, I felt the same spark of destined togetherness that I had experienced on the treehouse in Chakrata. It made me feel alive and complete. Alas! It was over before it began. The flow of feelings from my soul encountered a 'No Entry' barrier on reaching Deep's. I stood there like a statue, wishing I was as invisible as he was making me feel. MD who was gorging on boondi laddoos while Sanjeev dutifully held the plate for her, gave me a wicked, teasing smile and started crooning, '*Ho gaya hai tujko to pyaar sajna, lakh karle tu inkar sajna . . . ye hai pyaar sajna.*'

'What rubbish?' I challenged defiantly.

'I don't understand why you are denying a fact?' asked Madhuri.

'Because I don't want a one-sided love story. You can see that Deep clearly is not interested in me.'

'Maybe Deep sir doesn't want a one-sided story either. Remember, you said no to him?'

'But you know girls never mean no as no,' I defended.

'But don't you know that guys take no as no?' she countered calmly.

'Champ didn't. He waited for Tanu di all these years despite her no.' I persisted, yearning for a love like Di's.

'C'mon, you don't find that kind of *mohabbat* these days,' remarked MD. '*Arz kiya hai,*' she said, replaying SRK's dialogue from *Kabhi Alvida Na Kehna*.

Mohabbaton ke jamaane gujar gaye janaab
Ab chhote mote pyar se hi kaam chalaa leejiye aap.

'You mean to say you don't truly love Sanjeev?' I asked, surprised. She had barely been married a few months. She couldn't possibly be already disillusioned with love.

'Of course I love him, but if I say that I would have waited a decade, or even a few years, for him, I would be lying,' replied Madhuri without any sham.

Her frank declaration startled me, but I sort of figured that this was a reality of the instant age we lived in. I mean why would you waste a decade to find out that your love is still waiting for you when you could just ping on FB and ask? In our instant world, magical *mohabbat* had been replaced by a more practical *pyaar*.

'Are you saying that you married Sanjeev because you thought it would be better to marry a friend than a stranger?' I asked, just as an afterthought.

'Partially yes, and partially because I believe that one size doesn't fit all. For me it was enough that Sanjeev loved me while for him it was enough that I was not a naashpati,' MD explained jokingly, and got distracted by the assorted kabab platter Sanjeev had just brought.

Gosh! I never knew she had such a huge appetite. Madhuri was getting tired of standing and eating so Sanjeev got her a chair from the nearby table. Did I not tell you that they were expecting a baby? Oh, yeah, Sharmaji was sticking to his schedule for the timely project delivery. I watched them contentedly enjoy a comfortable companionship. I had seen the same glow on my mom's face every time Dad appreciated her cooking and the same satisfaction on my dad's face every time he got mom's car serviced or the cooker valve repaired. Was this true love or just marriage?

People who derive their definition of love from Bollywood might not realize this but the magic of eternal mohabbat was actually in the everyday expression of practical pyaar.

I saw Neha walk in through the main entrance in an exquisite green and yellow Rohit Bal spring collection creation and decided to leave the two food-lovers alone. She was carrying a Louis Vuitton handbag and 5-inch sexy stilettos.

'Hi! You look like the home page of Fashionandyou.com,' I remarked jovially, hesitant to hug her lest I cause a hundred-dollar stain on her outfit.

Neha ignored my wisecrack and hugged me chirpily like in the good old school days.

'I never thought this day would come in Tanu di's life,' she squealed happily. 'I am so glad she is finally getting some real hands-on experience.'

She was not alone in feeling that sentiment. None of the 500 people present in the room could have imagined this day would come and were all happy for the couple. I filled her in on all that had transpired since our office ASM and how the two lovers separated for more than a decade were at last united.

'But you look sad, honey. Are you feeling lonely on the singles' platform?' she teased as both Di and she had moved on to the couple's bogey.

'I miss our girls' night outs but I am okay,' I said truthfully, for Neha had seen me in worse mess.

'Is your boss engaging you in overtime and night duties?' she slyly smiled.

'Deep and I . . .' I almost choked with emotions taking our names together like that in a sentence. 'He has been avoiding me ever since I said no to him.'

'You said what you deemed right at that time, babe,' she consoled me. 'Are you seeing any more suitors these days?'

I shook my head. As the imminent danger from Jay had receded, my parents had slowed down the groom hunt. Just then, I heard Deep walk by and greet Neha, and my face flushed with eager anticipation. But he simply ignored me and walked off.

'Gosh! You are still attracted to him, aren't you?' Neha jumped excitedly at seeing my reaction to Deep's physical proximity.

'Yes, but how do I know if this attraction will last a lifetime of day-to-day adjustments?' I asked.

Neha offered to give me a rapid, quick fire cum-patibility quiz.

'Do you still cherish the special moments you shared with Deep?' she asked.

'Yes.'

'Does he really care for what you do?'

'Certainly,' I had managed to earn more from my paintings sold in the last three months than my salary at iTrot because of Deep.

'How does he make you feel about yourself?'

'Like SUHAANI—Special, Unique, Hot, Attractive, Able, Needed and Interesting,' I replied proudly. 'He makes me feel comfortable in my own skin.'

'Do you both enjoy your kisses?'

'No doubt about it.'

'And I know that you can talk dirty with him. Cool, then Deep it is for you!' Neha concluded with the certainty of a weatherman.

'What about your no car being good on LSM metrics funda?' I asked, eager to believe her prediction and yet scared to think that it could be wrong.

'Don't worry. Deep is a Harley Davidson bike, not a car,' Neha winked merrily, 'and bikes can deliver (luxury)love, (speed)sex and (mileage)marriage all in the same model.'

My face lit up at the approving nod from Neha. She had known me since we both toddled around together in cloth diapers. I trusted her to know if the boy I was planning to share my tiffin with would be nice enough to help me with my maths homework. I wanted her to tell me what to do next, when her fiancé called from Venice and she got busy in coochicooing with him.

Just then, I heard my mausi call me. I scanned the crowd for her and found her doing *khus-phus* with my mother in a corner. As I reached the secretive duo, my mausi pulled me close to her heaving bosom and whispered, 'If you are not interested in Deep, can I check him out for your cousin sisters?'

Pinki, Chinki and Dinki, my mausi's *sarvgun-sampan* heir production factories, I mean daughters, stood nearby, ogling at Deep with XXX-rated glasses.

I allowed myself a fleeting look in Deep's direction. He was sitting on a chair, next to the *mehendiwalla*s. Rohan's American friends were crowding around, getting the Indian traditional henna tattooed on their hands, while Deep was applying mehendi on a little girl's hand, who possibly couldn't catch the attention of the mehendiwalla as he was busy minting dollars. Another little princess with long, curly hair, sucking her thumb, was holding on to Deep's sleeves, waiting for her chance. Surrounded by cute, adorable girls, Deep looked so charming, so utterly irresistible. I stared harder at him absorbing every detail of his face and then closed my eyes to conjure up his Gorilla image that Dad had emailed to me a year ago. I couldn't and I knew why. Rather than the usual case of finding a guy attractive and hence falling in love, a reverse phenomenon had occurred. Deep had become attractive because of love. I knew now that there was no point in endlessly debating if Deep was the one for me. It was more important that I loved him enough today to commit to him forever.

If you are wondering how, in a short span of thirty minutes, it suddenly dawned on me that Deep was my powdered milk sachet, I will let you in on a big secret about women's psychology that I have uncovered. Women love limited time offers and flash sales not because it helps them save money. In fact, they always end up spending more in sales than otherwise. Women love the excitement and frenzy of flash sales because things become unavailable very quickly and women love to long for things they can't have. So, the realization that Deep would soon become unavailable if left unclaimed provided the missing impetus, adding fuel to my already smouldering fire. But what was I to do now? I couldn't possibly just walk up to him and tell him that I was in love with him. I had practically tried twice and even successfully rejecting him once. He would think I was a shopaholic who can't help buying a product from the shop only to return it the next day, or even worse, that I was like my mom who was pleading to a full-time maid she had chucked out last month to join back.

I couldn't seek Di's advice for she was nestled cosily in Champ's arms, ready to take off for her long overdue honeymoon immediately after the reception. I saw Neha was still busy on the international call with her beau. I rushed to the food stalls and was relieved to find Sanjeev and MD at the *jalebi-rabri* counter.

'*Jab kisi ko sachhe dil se chaho to saari kayenat tumhe usse milane mein lag jaati hai*,' reassured MD, addressing my quandary.

I gave her a sceptical 'real life is not the same as reel life' look.

'Kayenat is not some Bollywood bullshit. Its quantum physics,' she immediately retorted. 'Once we have made it clear what we strongly desire, then the conscious energies of the universe (quantum physics) line up actual events and encouragements to lead us to what we have asked for,' she elaborated. 'But God only helps who helps themselves,' she parroted the age-old saying.

My confidence bolstered, by the micro- and macro-elements of physics, I decided to take charge of the situation and start by asking Deep out for tea tomorrow in office. In the meanwhile, I requested Sanjeev to keep an eye on Deep who was now surrounded not only by cutesy caterpillars but also by giant, groom-hunting butterflies.

HOW DO I KNOW YOU ARE 'THE ONE'?

I adjusted the height of my chair and listened to the sound of keystrokes on Deep's keyboard. He was rapidly typing off a mail to someone. With my back facing his back, I breathlessly waited for the clickety-clack sound to stop so I could ask him for tea and send a deep-rooted kinship signal to the kayenat. To bide my time, I aimlessly searched on Google. 'Can the typing sound reveal the message being typed?' As always, I was amazed to learn that there actually was something called Acoustic Snooping and it had been well researched by UC-Berkeley students.

Suddenly I felt a drop in the background noise level. The sound from Deep's keyboard had stopped. His typical flight time, which is the time you take between key up and key down while typing on a keyboard, was one third of a second. I counted to two seconds and whirled around rapidly in my chair. I could see that Deep was about to get up from his seat and go for his morning cup.

'Tea?' I asked, trying to keep my nervousness at bay.

'Sure,' he smiled.

Now, that was easy. Why did I not do that earlier instead of waiting for him to ask? I followed him out of the cubicle like I had on many days in the past.

He poured my cup of premixed masala chai and handed it to

me. I silently watched him make his tea: 4/5th hot water, 1/5th milk, one teaspoon sugar and an Earl Grey teabag. He told me he was planning a musical evening at his place on Saturday. My heart thudded with excitement at the opportunity to spend time with him and listen to his sexy voice. I mean, life had been rather dull in the past few months. One could watch and read erotic stuff on the net, but that was nothing compared to a live titillating voice. I complimented him on his mehendi skills and he teasingly confided that it was another one of his palmistry-like excuses to hold a girl's hand. We talked about this and that and I felt like nothing had changed between us. It didn't matter that his purple plaid shirt didn't go well with his khaki trousers or that my hair had fuzzy ends due to a fading out perm. Everything seemed rosy. It was strange that a simple, routine chai with him was giving me such a high. I was enjoying the taste of to-get-him-ness when he was approached by a tall, large-framed, hugely overweight guy. The guy's face was covered with a weekend beard and his shirt was half tucked like he had come straight out of his bedroom. He obviously had a KS case. The guy said something in Deep's ears and expectantly awaited a solution to his 'super-sized' problem. Sipping my cup of tea, I happily observed the usual Monday morning ritual from a distance. 'I will tell Deep about my feelings once he has dispersed his pearls of sexdom to this horizontally challenged guy,' I thought to myself.

'It's important to build your stamina because it's not a spectator sport,' I heard Deep say after some time. Next minute, the burly guy strode out with a smug look on his face. I was all ready to bare my heart to Deep, but before I could open my mouth, he was whisked away from the cafeteria by the head of social media marketing.

Clearly kayenat hadn't yet received my 'I want Deep' message yet. Disappointed, I trudged back to my desk. I wanted to ask MD how long it takes for the universe before it starts aiding you in your pursuit, but she hadn't arrived. Both Sanjeev and Madhuri had opted for the 11 a.m. to 8 p.m. shift to deal with MD's morning sickness. I sat down on my seat and started browsing through FB updates.

I saw that Neetu had posted, 'Haven't packed my bags, but am ready to leave.' I clicked on 'Like' and commented that I was looking forward to recovering the cost of my designer lehenga that I had purchased for Di's reception, by wearing it for her wedding in Agra. Ashraf and Neetu had gotten legally married four months back in the US but their big fat Indian wedding was yet to happen. There was also a message for me from a lady who had bought one of my paintings asking if I could do a nude portrait of her and she was offering me an advance which was more than my monthly salary. I immediately responded with a yes. Heck! I never realized I could have charged Jay for his nude portrait.

Regaining some of my lost vigour, I absorbed myself in a hundred-page consumer dynamics book while I waited for Deep to reappear. The whole day passed by. Deep filed in and out of the cubicle many times but he didn't even so much as throw me a smile or say a friendly hi. He was back to behaving cold and indifferent like the morning chai never happened. Confident that my deep-ache message had been hacked and tampered with on its way to the quantum physics mail box, I checked out the latest spa deal in Gurgaon on Snapdeal.com and headed for a fish spa and nail therapy session. My FB status read, 'Man-agers, Man-datory, Man-ipulation or Man-s-laughter—I don't like these men. The only man I like is Manicure.'

Rejuvenated with fishyotherapy, I opened my purse to pay for the spa and saw the new message indicator on my phone. It was a message from Deep. Anxiously, I clicked to read the message. 'I enjoyed our little tête-à-tête today,' he had written.

Yes! I screamed in joy. Finally, the kayenat had received my intimation. Now that things were back on track, I didn't want my FB status to send out wrong signals and upset the quantum physics equation. I immediately changed it to, 'I must have had some Felix Felicis because I think I'm about to get lucky.'

I wanted to call up and talk to Deep asap, but deliberately decided to wait till morning. Some things were best done face to face.

Next morning, I didn't have to spy on Deep's keyboard sounds because he asked me out for tea himself. After yesterday's disappointment, I had figured that workday mornings were not a good time to discuss matters of the heart. So I asked Deep if he was free in the evening.

'Are you asking me out for a date, Suhaani?' Deep chuckled amusingly, his voice stirring up a mayhem of emotions in my heart.

Did he say 'date'? Does this mean he also wants to go on a date with me? Maybe, I should confess my love right away? Why wait till later? Love-struck and lost in my web of thoughts, I stared dumbly at his face.

If you have ever waited to propose to your love, you would know exactly how I felt. It was not easy to hold back the surge of temptation and yet I was enjoying how every passing day was strengthening my desire for him.

'How about tomorrow evening?' Deep suggested. 'Today, my chachaji is coming from the US and I need to pick him from the airport,' he explained.

'Sure,' I said gladly and kept gazing fixedly at his face. He could have asked me to do a striptease, lick him naked, or share my favourite cheese-flavoured corn chips, and I would have gladly agreed to do it all.

It was 7 p.m., Wednesday evening. Most of the crowd that availed of the office cab facility had left. I was springing with nervous energy when I heard Deep's humming from the corridor. It was the same song that had been playing in the car when I had first kissed him. I felt this sudden, uncontrollable urge to taste his lips. I looked around. Our floor was empty. I stood up and pushed myself towards him the moment I saw his frame materialize in our cubicle. And I halted on my tracks when I saw Kamini standing behind him.

'Aren't you late for the cab?' inquired Deep.

'I thought we were going to ... you said ... ,' I stuttered, but it was obvious from Deep's expression that he had forgotten.

'Oh! I completely forgot that I had promised to help Kamini with the use of the content moderation tool. Let me take you out for dinner tomorrow, my treat,' he offered.

Well, it was only a deferral till tomorrow. He wasn't saying a no, I assured myself. Feeling totally deep-somaniac, but somehow curbing the craving to smack Deep's lips, I mumbled a yes and rushed to the restroom.

Restrooms, I tell you, are mankind's most important creations. When you need to be on your own, totally unreachable, even by a mobile network, just lock yourself in the restroom and you will have your sanity back in no time.

Deep called me later in the night and sounded genuinely sorry for causing the confusion. He also said that his school gang was going out for dinner the next day, but since he had messed up badly today, he will just have a few drinks with them and then come over to pick me up from my home at eight in the evening. Somehow, although at one time it seemed to me like it would never happen, the earth completed one rotation around its axis in the stipulated twenty-four hours and Thursday evening arrived. It was half past seven. I hadn't told anything to my parents in case of a no show, but I was all ready. Dressed in a new, sleeveless dress, I stood in my balcony looking at the rapid speed with which the metro line was being constructed. It was scheduled to be operational by summer of 2010, in time for the Commonwealth Games. At exactly 8 p.m.,

I got a call from Deep. My heart skipped a beat as I pressed the talk button.

'Are you ready?' Deep asked in the most husky, seductive voice ever.

'I have been ready for the whole week,' I wanted to say. But getting a hold over my wet dreams, I simply said yes.

I could hear a lot of laughing and cheering in the background. It made me feel important that he was leaving all this fun to be with me.

'Great, I will be there in fifteen minutes,' he said. I was about to hang up when I heard a familiar female voice saying, 'Don't go, Deep. We have so much to catch up.'

What was she doing there? I wondered and it dawned on me that his school gang obviously also included his childhood romance, Meeta. She was there with him right now, perhaps holding his arms and flirtingly looking into his eyes. And then the line went dead. Deep had disconnected. I expected him to call up any time and tell me that he wasn't going to be able to make it. After all, he was already a couple of drinks down and his first love was pleading him to stay back. Why would he waste his time on me—a file he had closed long ago?

When my phone didn't buzz for the next five minutes, I picked it up and called Deep myself. I told him that we could talk another time and I was okay if he wanted to carry on with his party.

'I love you, Suhaani,' he said, in inebriated exaggeration and the line went dead.

'I love you too, Deep,' I said to the piece of metal in my hand.

Friday, 9 September 2009, was 09/09/09. It was the last set of repeating, single-digit date that we would see for almost a century before 1 January 2101. People were calling it a special day, and abundant discount offers of 99.99 were floating around on the web. FB was also full of status updates citing the lucky omen and its history.

I however didn't feel very lucky, especially after hearing Meeta's voice last night. I had updated MD with the latest in the morning, and she had suggested that I at least tell Deep sir how I felt, but I was undecided.

It was six in the evening. Deep was sitting in his chair. I hadn't asked Deep about a time today evening and he had not expressed any interest either. I stood up and peeked at his monitor. I saw his Facebook window open.

'Hi,' I sent him a Facebook chat message.

'Hi,' he replied promptly.

'Are you busy?' I asked absurdly.

'As busy as FB gets,' he wrote and added some smilies. 'Am waiting to have a word with Rohan. He is busy with the director right now.'

'I was thinking of leaving my job and pursuing painting full-time. What do you think?'

'What does your heart say?' he asked.

'My heart says that it loves you,' I typed and then quickly erased.

'Our heart never lies so do what it says,' typed Deep.

Was there a way he could know what I just typed and erased? Did he have an acoustic snooping tool? I wondered.

'Tell him you love him,' nudged my back office. I told my back office to shut down. We were sitting with our back towards each other, in the same cubicle. I was afraid Deep might hear the thumping of my heart or my back office's *bakwas*.

'What does your heart say? I mean you have been thinking about a start-up for some time as well,' I decided to toss the ball back.

'That is exactly what I want to discuss with Rohan.'

'You are serious about starting KSonline.com?'

':) :) Was thinking more on the lines of an *online condom store*.'

'Holy fuck! That would be a stupendous success.'

'Thanks. Your opinion counts. BTW do you think your mausi would still want to marry her daughters to me if I was the mastermind behind condomking.com?'

Embroiled in my Meeta maze, I had completely forgotten about this mausi trail. 'Dunno, but I thought you might have sorted things out with Meeta last night.' There I had said (typed) it and without sounding jealous.

There was a short pause.

'I told you she wasn't interested in me. We are great friends and will always stay that way,' he replied. I cursed the inability of text chats to communicate people's expressions. Yet, I didn't want to turn around and talk to him face to face. Not yet. I imagined a transient glimmer of hope on Deep's face as he thought about Meeta. He was still in love with her and it would always stay that way.

I remembered Dad's advice to marry the guy who loves you and not the guy whom you love. 'Deep doesn't love you. Forget him,' the back office whispered. I was amazed at my mind's ability to switch sides like a Gemini. Just minutes ago, it was telling me to confess my love. My heart, on the other hand, was still faithfully rooting for Deep.

'Are you seriously considering marrying one of my cousins?' I asked matter-of-factly.

'Is there a reason I shouldn't?'

Yes there was. The reason was that I loved him and I couldn't see him showering his affections on any other girl. Definitely not Pinki, Dinki or Chinki. If he was going to marry one of my cousins, he might as well marry me. Taking this as my clue to follow my heart, I wrote on the chat before I lost courage again. 'Do you think we are compatible?'

'Compatible? For what? Friendship?' he asked confused.

'Of course not, we are already friends,' I responded, moving my ring in and out of my finger with mounting excitement and anxiety. But I gave him no more hints.

'Did you have a change of mind?'

I wasn't sure what change he was talking about as my mind was shunting rapidly from one side to the other like a shuttlecock in Saina Nehwal's hand.

'Sort of,' I typed vaguely, drumming my artificial nails on the table in a nervous frenzy.

'Cool. So you want to be my business partner in condomking. com now?'

Fuck! I cursed a man's inability to get deeper into a woman's mind.

'How about life partner?' I asked, restless and running out of patience.

Just then Rohan stopped by our cubicle, gave me a warm smile and told Deep that he was free to talk.

'Umm . . . I have just discovered a bizarre bug in Suhaani's code,' spoke Deep with utmost seriousness. 'I want to get down to the bottom of the problem and try fixing it. Can I drop by your place later in the night?'

'Ah. I am a married man now Deep. I work elsewhere in the night shift,' said Rohan and winked. 'Come over tomorrow morning for breakfast and we can chat at my place. You can also come, Suhaani. Tanu makes awesome *besan cheela*s.'

'Sure, Jiju,' I smiled and saw him walk away from our cubicle.

'You think my marriage proposal is a bizarre bug?' I turned around to face Deep in shocked disbelief.

'Well, I asked you three months ago if you saw a future for us together and you said no. Today you are asking me to marry you. That's bizarre in a guy's world.'

I figured Deep's dilemma was justified. In any case, if we were to get married, he would have to know the whole truth. So I told him about my affair with Jay. How my parents were against it. How I thought Deep was terrible to look at in the beginning and then fell in love with him over time.

'So what do you say?' I prompted him for a response.

'I don't know,' he said blankly.

I gave him another weird look.

'Did you sleep with Jay?' he asked, looking concerned.

'Would it bother you if I did?'

'I guess.'

'Well, I did lie down naked with him; but we didn't make love.'

'So are you a virgin?'

'Yes. Are you?'

'Mentally no, but technically yes,' he answered.

I knew what he meant by that. He had advised and assisted so many people in consummating their marriages that the art of making love was like second nature to him. I looked at his lips and he looked at mine. I thought we were about to kiss, when he threw a googly. 'How do I know I love you?' he asked baffled.

'What do you mean? I thought you loved me and that is why you asked me in the first place.' I was obviously taken by surprise. Although obvious had long stopped being obvious when it came to Deep, so obviously I should have expected something unobvious.

'Well, I had feelings for you, but then you said no,' he stated.

'Hello! I am saying a yes now!' I almost shouted at the top of my voice.

'What if you change your mind again in a month's time?'

'It wouldn't matter …'

He gave me this most, kissable, quizzical, cute look.

'It doesn't matter what my mind says any more, coz my heart will always beat for you,' I continued. 'Besides we are soulmates.'

'What do you mean?'

'You love to cook and I can eat anything cooked by others. I read only fiction and you only non-fiction, so no conflicts there. You love to sing and I love to paint while listening to music. I also like to kiss you when you sing, but I think we can overlook such minor incongruities. You like sex and so do I. We both love our parents. My parents love you and I am sure yours will love me too.'

'My mom has two sons and she has always wanted a girl.'

'See, and I am a girl! So she will definitely love me.'

'And I like your raspberry lips,' he added.

'Yes,' I encouraged. He was sitting very close to me now and I could smell his spicy aftershave and feel the tension building between us. We melted into each other's arms and soon ours lips locked in a feverish kiss.

'I need to ask my friends,' he said, once we had disengaged our lips.

'Okay. Sure,' I said and grabbed his lips again.

'What does he mean he needs to ask his friends?' Neha screamed into the phone when I told her after reaching home what had transpired between Deep and me at the office.

'I don't know. Do you think he doesn't love me?'

'He loves you all right honey. He is just having pre-penetration jitters.'

I didn't even know such a thing existed, but I took Neha's word for it.

'What should I do?'

'Give him an ultimatum of twenty-four hours.'

'What if he says no?'

'He won't. Guys are not very different from girls. They also love flash sales.'

'Cool'.

I sent Deep a message saying he better let me know what his

friends think in a day's time. He immediately responded saying he was going to his friend's place in Noida and would let me know asap. There was no time to lose. I knew I had to be prepared to convince Deep to marry me. I opened a spreadsheet and went about doing what I was best at. Making a list. If you are judging me for being a listmaniac just look around yourself. From the 'Top Ten' lists sprawling across the web, to the playlists in your iTune, the contacts list in your mobile or the weekend shopping list, everything in our lives is nothing but a part of some list. Our very existence in this world is merely a tick in our parents' list of milestones. Haven't you heard the new, revised saying? 'Behind every successful man is a woman who manages his lists.'

I must have fallen asleep working on my list because it was dark when I opened my eyes. Cuddled in a starched, ironed cotton *dohar*, I noticed the keep-alive signal from my laptop, on the bedside table. Mom must have switched off the lights and put the sheet on me. The little gestures that I had come to value only after I had missed them when I was away from home. I unlocked my mobile to check the time. It was 2 a.m. There was no missed call or messages from Deep. Six hours had passed since I gave Deep the time limit. I had eighteen more to wait. I was sure that I was going to exceed the average of sixty-two minutes/day wait time that Kavita had mentioned during my first meeting with her.

I sighed, got up, and went to the loo. When I got back, I saw my mobile flashing for attention. I quickly checked. It was a message from Deep. My heart sank. My fingers trembling with trepidation, I read what I assumed to be another rejection by an IITian. 'Are you awake? Can I call?' it said.

Why did he not communicate his disinterest straight away with a message? Why call? 'He was just trying to ease the blow. Better to get it over with,' I thought and called him up myself. He picked up the phone even before I could hear it ring.

'Can you come on Skype?' Deep asked.

'Yes,' I replied.

He disconnected the phone. Tensed and jittery as the financial markets, I awakened my laptop from its sleep. Seconds later we were face to face. He was still wearing the same shirt and trousers he had worn to work, so he perhaps hadn't gone to bed yet. I looked crappy without any make-up, hair dishevelled, in my well-worn, baggy night suit. I waited for him to start.

'Bhawre ki gunjan hai mera dil, kabse sambhale rakha tha dil, tere liye, tere liye …'

As he confessed his love for me with the song, a tear of joy fell from my eye and then my face turned into a colon dash bracket :-)

ACKNOWLEDGEMENTS

I had never thought I would write a novel in my life, leave aside a second one. Thanks to all my readers and Facebook fans for their emails and FB posts inquiring about my next novel. Many of them wanted to know what happened to Tanu, my protagonist in *Heartbreaks and Dreams*, after she left IIT. I could have written a sequel but I wanted an FB gen, spunky, racy and humorous voice this time. So I chose to have bring Tanu di as the protagonist's cousin and run her story in parallel.

I would also like to thank Sujatha and Pwana Kumar, Shivani and Sanjeev Kapoor, Priyanka and Neeraj Aggarwal, Nisha and Bhupi Singh, Nidhi and Rajul Jain, Kamal and Amarinder Dhaliwal, Tanima and Umesh Gupta, Anu and Yash Jagdhari who related their own marriage experiences. When I asked them how did they know if this person was The One, they mostly failed miserably. So I have concluded Love is indescribable and cannot be put on FB timeline.

Shilpi Agarwal, Varsha Mittal, Aditi Saronwala and Pooja Goyal who helped me understand the current generation's views on sex, love and marriage.

My literary agent Kanishka Gupta of Writer's Side who said, 'It looks promising and fun. Better than last time.'

My first book's publisher Jayantakumar Bose for giving the clearance to publish this book with Penguin.

The entire Penguin team, Chiki Sarkar for reading my synopsis and liking it. Senior Commissioning Editor Vaishali Mathur, for having the confidence in my book and its youth appeal. My editor-in-charge, Paloma Dutta, for her careful edits and Diksha Wadhwa, my marketing manager, for her ongoing efforts to make this book a big success.

My friend Sonal Bansal, the only person with whom I shared my manuscript as I wrote it, for feedback and reassurance. No, my husband hasn't read it. He only glanced through a few printed pages once, was shocked at what he read and asked if I was writing an adult novel!

My in-laws for their constant support and encouragement.

My brother Mohit and my friend Punam who helped arrange my love and my parents for bringing Alok in my life.

My husband Alok for loving me unconditionally.

My daughters, Smiti and Muskaan, who had to bear the brunt of my bad writing days. I love you both and I hope you don't read this book until you are eighteen.